BEACH STONES

AND OTHER STORIES

J R MADORE

http://wwwamazon.com

D1519179

Copyright © 2023 J.R. Madore

All rights reserved

The characters and events portrayed in this book are fictitious. Any similarity to real persons, living or dead, is coincidental and not intended by the author.

No part of this book may be reproduced, or stored in a retrieval system, or transmitted in any form or by any means, electronic, mechanical, photocopying, recording, or otherwise, without express written permission of the publisher.

ISBN-13: 9798397842525

Cover design by: Onur Burconur
Library of Congress Control Number: 2018675309
Printed in the United States of America

Dedicated to Archie, Mary, Eliza Stewart and Evelyn Madore. May their journey be filled with wonder.

CONTENTS

Title Page

Copyright

Dedication

Introduction

The Cotton Mouth

1

2   1

3   6

4   11

5   19

6   24

7   29

8   33

A Small Love Story   36

1   37

2   40

3   45

4   49

5   51

6   55

The Carrot Field   57

1	58
2	61
3	66
4	72
5	77
6	84
7	90
8	98
9	103
Chico	107
1	108
2	112
3	116
4	118
5	122
6	124
7	127
CASH AND BOB	133
1	134
2	141
3	144
4	148
5	154
6	159
7	164
8	166
9	169
10	173

BEACH STONES   177

1   178

2   185

3   194

4   205

5   217

6   226

7   231

8   238

About The Author   243

Books By This Author   245

                                                    247

INTRODUCTION

Paul McCartney, the legendary English songwriter and member of the Beatles, was asked how he came up with the lyrics to his songs. He response, "… I just look around until an idea pops into my head and build the song from that." McCartney viewed writing his songs as a kind of black hole, and eventually that hole would be filled.

After completing, 'The Stick: A Family's Journey', an historical fiction novel; rising early remained part of my daily routine. To fill that void I continued the writing process, but in another direction and once again I reached into my large family and friend's experiences for inspiration. The result are six short stories.

A venemous snake takes over a home, my brother Michael's racing pigeon hobby, my first job working on a farm, a lap dog discovers a new life, my daughter Tara's end of college experience meeting her husband, and our family's habit of collecting bright stones while walking on a New Hampshire beach inspired these tales.

In the stillness before dawn, black holes would be filled.

J.R.M.

THE COTTON MOUTH

1

It was time to hunt. The hot day was over, and her body was energized from hours of basking in the sun. She had recently shed her outer skin in her annual molt and had not eaten in four days. At her full growth now, close to thirty-nine inches, hunger possessed her since emerging from her new den. Her ability to detect heat higher than the night air was her guide. Her two heat seekers located in front of her eyes knew exactly where the warm mammal was. There was no warning. In a millisecond, the snake had the palm rat in her jaws, biting down hard, releasing her venom and just as quickly releasing the doomed animal. The rat scurried off, but the snake knew it would not go too far. It would die from the venom. Her flickering tongue would locate the dead rat and swallow it whole, a meal that would satisfy her for a few days.

Her old den, in a hole at the edge of the pond, had been destroyed. She had no concept of why. All she knew was it was gone, and her normal path through the rotting plants and mud was no longer there. Her environment was now a forboding place of jagged stone and gravel. She was exposed and in a precarious situation. Basking in the sun for most of the day, was dangerous.

She had survived five seasons now, and her hunting area had changed drastically. In her second season, there was much turmoil around her as she felt the strange, powerful vibrations in the ground and in the air. The chaos lasted through her second year. An attempt at mating that spring was hampered. At the beginning of the third hot season, the vibrations lessened and eventually stopped, replaced by a variety of hard sounds in the air, and gradually they, too, ceased and quiet returned. She began to search for a new den, a new dark place to give birth to her babies.

The snake had survived this long by her instincts. There was no logical thinking going on, only what had to be done to survive and produce young. If danger lurked, her defense was to coil her bulky body under her, open her white-rimmed fanged jaws, and dare the threat to come closer. This was seldom used. In most cases, if an escape route was available she would quickly slither or swim away. If she did have to strike out at a larger enemy, she would strike hard but not release her venom, which she did to a nosy black bear a few nights before, sinking her teeth into the flesh but not releasing venom. She would save that for prey she could swallow. Releasing the venom meant she could not hunt until her body replenished it, which could take days.

Her search for a new den brought her to a different environment. The grass she slithered through was shorter, and she found a few nice spots to seek the sun. For the past few seasons, she had found and adapted to a place near the pond with its food source of frogs, rats, and any form of carrion. Her new den was protected, a place she could give birth to her babies and molt.

***

"I don't know, Sal; I was hoping we could find a place closer to Naples."

"I looked at it online last week and I really like the price. They have some nice options, and downtown Naples is only five miles from here up on forty-one," replied her husband.

Sal and May Lombard were on vacation in Naples, Florida, a place they had visited in the past, and Sal was on a mission to find a winter home. They owned a small printing business in

Poughkeepsie, New York, that their sons had taken over, and he was getting tired of the winters. He would be retiring next year.

He was an avid golfer, and she liked to read. Her enthusiasm for this venture was next to zero, and Sal knew it. They had five grandchildren that May did not want to leave, plus she hated heat, especially hot, muggy Florida heat. It was January now, and the tropical heat would not return till June. Sal had come down a few times to play golf, and if May went along, she stayed indoors. However, she did like the shops and restaurants in Naples. If it was up to Sal, he'd spend the whole day on a golf course, club house, or driving range. He was not a fan of shopping and dining in a fancy restaurant, but he knew this purchase depended a great deal on his wife's happiness. He would do what he had to do to please her.

They pulled into a construction site off the east trail, where Route 41, a major roadway in southwest Florida, takes a quick left and continues over the Everglades and terminates in Miami. They noted the sign. 'Opening Soon, The Eagles Nest Golf and Country Club.' Next to the sign was a large double-wide trailer, and next to the trailer was an equally large map of the future community. They parked their rental next to four other cars in the small parking lot and walked in. The double-wide had been transformed into a large show area featuring paintings of the future homes. They were greeted by a young man wearing khaki pants, shiny slip-on loafers, and wearing a white golf shirt with the marketing logo featuring a pair of adult bald eagles. There were two other agents in the trailer attending to other clients

"Welcome to the Eagles Nest," said the agent extending his hand, and introductions were made, bottled water was offered, and the proper questions were asked. Sal did most of the talking as May tagged along, holding back with a skeptical expression. This had been the third property they had visited, and she was wearing down.

Sal knew his wife's frame of mind and realized he didn't want to push too much. They had talked and came to an agreement. If they made a purchase, it would be a condo, not too big, two bedrooms, two baths, ground floor, and Sal insisted on a garage. The Eagles Nest offered carriage homes that would fit their needs.

In the middle of the trailer was a mock-up of the vast property. The young agent pointed out the buildings that consisted of the desired carriage home, named so because on large estates in previous centuries in England, the carriage and horse barn were a separate building, and the driver and his family lived above in the carriage house.

Today, the offerings featured five buildings, each containing ten carriage homes, first floor or second, and all had garages.

"This is building number one." The agent pointed with his pencil. "It will have a nice view of one of our lakes nestled in a preserve area," he stated and paused. "The interior ground-floor units are being offered at a nice pre-construction price, only this week, and construction will start next month. We estimate the move-in date will be in mid-September."

They talked more, but May had reached her limit and decided to wait in the car, frustrating Sal. "She's tired," he explained and turned to follow his wife.

"I can take ten percent off the pre-construction price," the agent slipped in quickly. Sal looked at the agent and said he would be back. They shook hands. "That offer will be good till Friday." Sal walked out.

"Sal, I don't care. If that's what you want, buy it." They had been out to eat and were back at the hotel on 5th Avenue in downtown Naples. His enthusiasm about the carriage home and the new price offer were too much for May. She realized this was his dream. She gave in. They went back the next day, completed the paperwork, and put down the deposit for condo unit 105, in building one at Eagles Nest in Naples, Florida.

* * *

Their building was completed in early September. They

contacted a local Naples furniture store, and despite the cost, had 'Bards on Fifth Furniture' decorate and furnish their new carriage home. The unit was move-in ready. They drove to Florida and would stay until Thanksgiving.

When Sal and May arrived, after four days of travel, May was ecstatic. She loved the look and feel of the well-appointed interior. They had dinner in the new clubhouse that night, and the next day Sal took her shopping in Naples, where she bought two outfits at Angela's, a high-end dress store. For the next few days, things were wonderful, and May could not have been happier. The golf cart Sal had ordered arrived, and they went for a ride around their new community. During the ride, May's enthusiasm began to diminish slightly. September in Poughkeepsie was the beginning of leaf-peeping season. Summer days would linger, and the nights were pleasant, if not a little cooler. The screens would still be in the windows as pleasant breezes flowed through homes.

"Sal, it's September, I thought it would be cooler." He had neglected to tell her that September in South Florida could be the hottest month of the year.

"As soon as October arrives, it will be a lot cooler. Besides, we're just down here now to check out the place. We won't be coming down most years till after the holidays and stay till May, I think."

"Hmm," was all she could come up with.

Sal looked over and pulled her in. "You're gonna love it, hon." And he gave her a peck on the cheek. May bought into Sal's explanation, but by the middle of the next week, there were other things to dislike. Their unit 105 had issues. Possibly in a rush to finish, bad planning, bad workmanship, or a combination of all, there were problems. Water leaks cropped up, there were cracks in the walls, sloppy paint work, and there was something May did not anticipate, the closeness of the preserve.

In Florida, when a property is cleared for new homes, a percentage of the land must be kept in its natural state. Their lanai faced a small pond surrounded by tall, unattractive scrub pines, Cypress trees with ghostly gray Spanish moss hanging in abundance, cabbage or Sabal palms, possibly the ugliest of all palm trees, surrounded by the ever-present palmetto plants, with their razor-sharp fronds, was not an inviting view. She was a city girl. The pond and strange-looking landscape unnerved her.

Sal, in the meantime, was playing golf three times a week. At first she was content to sit in the air conditioning and read. But then when the issues began to creep up, there would invariably be someone from the construction company intruding on her solitude. Today there was a worker dealing with a leaky kitchen faucet. Finding it hard to concentrate on her book, out of curiosity, she got up and walked into the kitchen.

"How are you doing, Miguel?" She was getting to know the workers by their first names.

"Shouldn't be long, Mrs. Lombard," she heard his muffled voice say. He was not a big man, and all she could see was the lower part of his body. He was well into the confines of the cabinet under the sink. She went back to her reading, but her quiet was once again interrupted by his humming and tools as they hit against the pipes.

And then it all changed. The humming turned into a piercing loud yell along with banging and scraping and more banging. She looked up with a start and paused for a moment. "WHAT'S THE PROBLEM!" she yelled and walked to the kitchen entrance.

"There's a snake in there." He pointed at the cabinet while looking at May and rubbing his elbow.

"But I think it's dead." He reached into his toolkit and took out a flashlight. "Ya, it's dead," he assured as he poked it with the flashlight. He reached in, grabbed the stiff creature by its tail; a foot-long snake. May backed away and stared. She got a chill. "Sorry about that." The worker walked through the house to deposit the snake in the plastic trash container in the garage.

May stood staring at the broken cabinet door thinking, what else?

Sal was getting to the point where he was leery of going home. If it wasn't the heat, May would complain about another problem from the contractor's 'punch list' and the most recently added, a new cabinet door.

A day later, May was shopping. Two painters would be arriving that morning, and Sal would be there to let them in. He looked out as the white panel truck pulled up. He clicked off the TV and met them at the door. Introductions were made, and he took them into the master bedroom. The original paintwork had been shoddy. "Listen, guys, I'm going up to the driving range for a bit. Could you move the truck?"

"No problem," said the painter who seemed to be in charge, as his assistant began to bring in the drop cloths and various paint brushes and rollers into the condo. Sal went through the laundry room to the inside entrance to the garage. A moment later, sitting in his golf cart, he waved and yelled thanks to the painter on his way to the driving range. They got busy preparing the room, first moving the king-size bed.

"Holy shit!

"What!"

"Look!" When they pulled the bed away from the wall, laying along the baseboard was a three-foot-long snakeskin. The two painters stared, looking at the thin, translucent remnant.

"Wow, that is creepy," said Franky, the teenage assistant. Al, the owner of the company, was a classic Florida Cracker and proud of it. He was raised to hunt and fish in the Everglades and didn't have a great deal of patience with how Florida and its wild habitat was disappearing. Although he was making a living of off it, he was still resentful of the people from 'up-north.'

"Franky, it's like paper. I'll get rid of it." He proceeded to gather it up and crumple it in his hands, mumbling to himself as he left the room. He deposited the scaly skin in the garage waste container. Al had no intention of stopping the job or notifying the owner or the property manager. The job was completed, and the painters left to do another project in another unit.

In the meantime, Sal had decided to go the clubhouse bar after practicing at the range. He called May, and they met for lunch. "I'm sorry, Sal, I know you think I'm a nag, but I'm not happy here."

This discussion would not be the last concerning her happiness and at times would be heated. But after a while, she made a few lady friends, and the temperature was gradually cooling down, and the humidity was dissipating. She was beginning to mellow, but the small things that cropped up in their unit were beginning to wear at both of them. They were at the clubhouse having dinner a few days before they would drive back to Poughkeepsie. "I guess I just have to be patient, Sal. I know how much you love golf. We'll be leaving Monday, giving the contractor time to fix the other problems. Things will be better." And she added, "At least it's cooler."

May was at Publix grocery shopping a day later. Sal was reading the paper on the lanai. He couldn't focus on what he was reading. He was distracted thinking he may have made a mistake. If May wasn't happy, he wasn't happy. During his musing, he looked up and caught a movement under the large sectional in the living room. He looked again.

"Oh, my God," he said quietly to himself. He froze, watching a large snake slither and disappear under the largest piece of the sectional. He immediately felt a chill go through his whole body. He heard the door from the garage entrance in the laundry room open.

"Hi, Sal, I'm back!" The sectional was a three-piece arrangement meant to seat up to eight or more people, with a large glass-topped coffee table in the middle. It would take three or four men to wrangle it into place. He stared at it as he walked by to greet his wife.

"It must be Thanksgiving. Publix was really crowded," said May. Sal's mind was conflicted. He couldn't tell her what he had just witnessed. "It's the start of the holiday season, but it doesn't seem like it down here," said May as she walked in holding three small bags and continued talking. "I didn't get much, just some milk, bread, and a few oranges." She opened the refrigerator and paused. "Damn, I hope this cabinet door gets fixed," she said as she looked at the doorless opening and looked up at her husband. "Are you okay?"

"Yeah, yeah, I was just thinking, why don't we go out to dinner?"

"No, I don't want to waste the food in the fridge. I have some chicken that I have to cook before it goes bad. Maybe tomorrow. It's our last day here."

"Okay."

"I'm gonna take a shower just to freshen up. I thought I'd make chicken cacciatore with pasta tonight."

"Oh... sounds great." replied Sal.

May turned and froze as the snake emerged from under the sectional inches from her feet and slithered through the open door to the guest bedroom.

2

"I like it," said Bill to the realtor. "What do you think, Doris?"

"It's nice," she responded, with not quite as much enthusiasm as Bill. "I thought it would be bigger."

"Well, I couldn't ignore the price."

Bill Kelly was 65, and Doris Andrews was 56. He had been married for thirty years to Sally, his only love. She died six years ago after a long battle with cancer. Bill and Doris were at the beginning stages of a relationship that was three weeks old. He had two daughters, Milly and Virginia. Milly was a teacher, like her dad, and taught chemistry at Immokalee High School. She was married to Jake, a financial adviser, who she met in college. They had a two-year-old son, William. Her sister, Virginia, was a senior at the University of South Florida.

During Sally's long battle with the dreaded disease, she and Bill had many conversations centered on hope. Then the day came when they were told all hope was gone. The talks now, in most cases through sobs and tears, were primarily about William, the girls, and their future.

"Bill, I think you should try and meet someone when I'm gone." When that topic arose, there was no enthusiasm from either one of them. On most occasions, Bill would say nothing and just take her hand.

And then the inevitable arrived.

Alex, the hospice nurse, came quietly into the room. "Bill,

she's asking for you and the girls."

"Thanks, Alex." They were on the lanai of their modest, but neat, three-bedroom home in Orange Grove Estates, a housing development three miles west of the community of Immokalee and twenty miles east of Naples. Sally was propped up in the hospital bed in her and Bill's bedroom. She wanted to die at home. When her family walked in, she patted both sides of the bed. They all got in. Milly sat, holding William, on Sally's right, and Virginia sat on her left, leaving space for Bill next to Sally.

"I don't think I'm going to make it through the night." She was heavily sedated and in pain and knew she had been given another heavy dose of morphine and was having a spurt of energy. She wanted to be as alert as possible for this moment.

"I just want see your faces, hold your hands, and tell you I love you one last time." She had her hands on her stomach. Nothing was said as they all reached over and held a portion of her hands and fingers. She looked to her grandson and her daughters' faces and finally to Bill. She had a contented smile as she closed her eyes. They all felt it. Her expression did not change, but her fingers relaxed as her life left her.

After Sally passed, Bill kept teaching his science and biology classes and coaching the golf team at Pine Ridge High School in Naples. A year later at 62, he retired. But he did not retire from his other job.

For many summers, he worked at The Naples Zoo and continued to work two or three days a week. He loved it. He was a busy man. Because of his experience at the zoo, he was entrusted to work in all the areas. He was regarded as a keeper. What he loved the most was giving the mini lectures to the guests while holding or standing near an animal. If he needed assistance, in many cases, it would be one of the young interns or Agatha.

Agatha lived next door to the zoo. She was 45, a single mother of two adult children Cordell 22, and Martha 21. They lived in an all-black neighborhood where she had grown up Her family had lived in the small close-knit community for years. The neighborhood was an incongruous phenomenon. The address was Fifth Avenue, well known to the upper crust visitors and snow-birds that visited the Naples area, except it was not 'that' Fifth Avenue. This was Fifth Avenue North, a decidedly different street address.

The swanky street with its boutique bars and high fashion clothing stores was Fifth Avenue North, the same street separated by Route 41 bisecting Naples, except property values on the south side could be in the hundreds of thousands to millions of dollars.

The Gordon River ran through Fifth Avenue North, as it flowed into the Gulf Of Mexico. The neighborhood was called River Park. The people that lived here knew the real value of the property and could not afford to move to a location with the same waterfront amenity. The tight community stayed together, hanging on to their piece of paradise. Developers drooled over it.

As a child, Agatha was always fascinated by the zoo creatures next door. One year she remembered looking out her bedroom window and seeing a spider monkey feasting on the ripe fruit of her dad's orange tree. It had escaped from the zoo. Years later the zoo solved the escaping problem when it created a large island as the monkey habitat with a moat. Most monkeys did not like to swim.

In high school, Agatha was a good student, a better than average athlete, playing basketball as well as volleyball. She went on to junior college with the intention of becoming a nurse. This was where she met Eric from California attending junior college on a baseball scholarship, that would eventually lead to The University of Florida and possibly professional baseball.

Midway through her second year, she became pregnant. They married and both dropped out of college. Eric's dream of a career in baseball was put on hold and he decided to pursue work in Orlando in the amusement hospitality industry and Agatha was soon pregnant again. Despite her new husband's pleading she would not terminate the pregnancy and Martha was born.

The young couple began to struggle. Day-care was not an option, she wanted to be home with her children. Eric's family had connections at Disneyland in California. His attempts to convince Agatha to move fell on deaf ears. Their marriage was being challenged by forces they could not imagine, her father died suddenly from heart failure and her mother passed a year later. The young family moved to Naples and lived in the house she had grown up in. This was a sound economic decision. Her mother had deeded the mortgage free house to her. The first thing they did was look for employment at the Zoo. The daily care of the children would be less of a struggle as her next door neighbors had been a friends of the family for many years and would care for Cordell and Martha, and Agatha was only minutes away if an emergency arose. She began work in the gift shop, but her experience in Orlando proved to be beneficial. She would soon become a guide.

Eric hated the zoo and Naples in general. His attempts at working various jobs in the popular venue failed, and told Agatha he would try to rekindle his baseball dream with a minor league team in Fort Myers. After three years the nemesis of many ball player, the curveball, forced him to realize the dream was truly over. He was a good fastball hitter, but not having the ability to hit the spinning curve consistently turned him from a prospect with potential to a substitute minor league player at best, plus he was getting older. His future in professional baseball was frustratingly limited. His quest was over after three years. He tried substitute teaching, construction, roofing and even thought about law enforcement. And as time went by, his unhappiness was a constant grind on the marriage. He and another former baseball player devised a plan to go into the bar restaurant business, this too failed and lost money for he and Agatha. This also proved to be the final chapter in their now rocky marriage. During this business venture he began a relationship with another woman. A year later he asked Agatha for a divorce, moved to California and was no longer a part of their lives as all communication ceased.

Agatha was devastated but she knew she was in a good place, she loved the animals, the neighborhood and eventually attained a new job title at the zoo as an assistant to the keepers, where she met Bill.

They were having a Coke in the Zoo's small restaurant and gift shop. "Has Gypsy gained weight?" asked Agatha. Gypsy was the Burmese python that had been part of the zoo for years and was the featured animal in Bill's presentation. Agatha had her draped over her shoulders as Bill controlled the snake's head.

"I think you're right. She may be pregnant."

"Well that should be interesting," replied Agatha.

They had been friends for years. Bill witnessed the ups and downs of her family situation, and was always there to help when needed. Marta and Cordell were both in his classes and were good students. Cordell was an excellent golfer and was now playing on the Florida Gulf Coast University golf team. Marta, a year younger than her brother, was also attending F.G.C.U. and hoped to become a nurse.

Agatha and Eric's divorce occurred at the beginning of her children's high school years. She was not a heavy drinker, but she turned to alcohol for solace and spiraled down quickly, hitting bottom when she passed out while watching one of Cordell's golf matches. To her son's dismay, as well as Bill's, they watched her being carried off the golf course and placed in an ambulance. It was then that Bill realized the seriousness of the situation.

He had always had a close relationship with Cordell and Marta. The two mature high-school-age children agreed with Bill that their mother needed help and convinced her to join AA. She went through the program and became a sponsor. She had been sober for four years.

3

On his way home from the zoo, Bill would occasionally stop at the Publix supermarket off of Immokalee road. He still lived in the home he and Sally had bought twenty years ago. She had been gone three years now. There were only three registers open, and all he had was quart of milk. The young man working the customer service counter noticed Bill and waved him over.

"I can take that."

"Hey, thanks."

"No prob, sir."

Bill handed him a five dollar bill, which resulted in change. He noticed the lottery tickets and bought one, something he had never done. That night, while watching the local news, to his amazement, he realized he had won five-hundred thousand dollars.

When Bill received his gift, he promptly went back to the Publix and gave the young man a thousand dollars. He gifted his daughters twenty thousand dollars apiece and paid off the mortgage on his home. He then sat down with Jake, his son-in-law, who reigned him in. Jake explained that most lottery winners lose their wealth a year after the windfall. He helped him strategize what to do with his money.

Bill's work at the zoo resulted in many other relationships. Two of the patrons at the zoo were Sam and Bridget Fordham. Sam owned three car dealerships in Ohio, but he and his wife spent most of their time in Florida. They had become close friends of Bill and Sally Kelly. Their mutual affection for the zoo and its animals, plus golf, had drawn them together. During Sally's fight with cancer, the Fordhams organized fundraisers at the zoo as well as other events at their country club. They lived at The Eagles Nest, a gated golf community, where Sam was on the board of directors and, like most people that lived there, played golf at least twice a week. He was a very good golfer.

Every Fourth of July, Sam's club sponsored a member-guest golf tournament, a two-day tournament. Bill was Sam's guest and partner this year and had just completed the first day of the event. After congratulating each other at the bar and toasting to their success, they heard, "Mind if I join you?"

Bill had no interest in dating. His daughter, Milly, encouraged him to meet other women, and when Virginia jumped onboard, he felt less guilty. This was also echoed by his golf buddies and friends.

Bill looked up, and there was a very pretty, blonde and curvy, middle-aged woman. She was dressed in a festive Fourth outfit, wearing a short blue skirt with large white stars. It stopped just above her knees. She wore a bright red sleeveless blouse a little too tight. The top two of the three buttons were undone.

"No," said Sam. "Please, join us, Doris."

Bill had kept his youthful looks. He still had a full head of salt and pepper hair that he kept in a crew cut and was only a few pounds overweight for a man his age. The only medication he was taking was for high cholesterol, a genetic issue he had under control.

"Hi, Doris, this is the guy I wanted you to meet. Bill, meet Doris."

"Nice to meet you," Doris said and extended her hand. "Boy, you guys are doing great," she commented as she put her empty glass on the bar.

"Can I get you another drink, Doris?"

"Yes, that'd be great, thanks."

Sam waved the bartender over. "Paul, get us two more beers and whatever Mrs. Andrews wants."

"I'll have the usual, Paul, a Tito's on the rocks." She handed him her empty glass.

"Sam, I'm good," said Bill. "I've got to drive home. Two beers are enough."

Nodding in agreement, Sam said, "Okay. I want my partner ready to go tomorrow."

Bill had a Coke.

"Yeah, we made a few putts when we needed them, but tomorrow's another day," said Sam, replying to Doris. They stayed at the bar for another hour. Bill discovered that Doris had been divorced twice. She was an avid golfer, lived at the club, and had a part-time job working in an upscale dress shop called Agatha's on Fifth Avenue. She asked Bill many probing questions, but he had a feeling Sam had already filled her in on most of the answers. Sam and Doris ordered two more drinks. Bill declined, had another Coke, drank half, and decided it was time to go.

"Well, partner, I've got to get going. Nice to meet you, Doris."

"Nice to meet you as well, Bill." She surprised him with a little too aggressive hug, leaning her chest into him and losing her balance.

"Oops, sorry about that." Reaching for the bar to gain her balance.

The next day, while playing the second round, Bill questioned Sam about Doris. He learned that she lived in one of the small condo units that were part of the housing options.

"Bridget is not very fond of Doris."

"Why?"

"I don't know, I think it's just a woman thing. She think she's a little too flirty. Could be the reason her second husband left her a year ago." He paused. "Jeez, listen to me. I'm sounding like my wife." And he added, "Anyway, I think she's a good egg, and we've seen enough divorces to know things get weird, for both parties."

They would win the four-ball. The post tournament cookout was fun, leaving Bill full and very intoxicated. He knew he could not drive. Sam and Bridget offered him a place to stay, and so did Doris. He accepted her offer. Bridget discreetly gave Sam the eye roll as Bill followed Doris out of the country club's bar. He would share a bed with another woman for the first time in his life.

The morning after the "sleepover," as Doris described it, was awkward more so for Bill. He was embarrassed at first but began to relax when she joked about saving his life by not having him drive home as she walked around the kitchen wearing a long T-shirt and nothing else. He had to admit, it had been a long time since he had sex; what he could remember through a pounding headache.

He agreed to go to "Happy Hour" the following Wednesday where he met some of her friends and had a good time. He drank too much again and stayed over Doris's. There were frequent phone and text conversations in the days to follow, and more than once the topic of his lottery win would enter their conversations. At first Bill was more than happy to tell her about the day he bought the ticket and how excited he was, but then some of the questions about his wealth became too probing, and she would catch herself and apologize for being too nosy.

He learned she had a son, Johnny, living in Arizona who had flunked out of the university. He was content to stay and work in Phoenix with his father, Tom Andrews, Doris's first husband. He had a successful tile business. She had no idea where her second husband was.

He invited her to the zoo the next Sunday. It would be her first and last visit. She did not like the smells, animal sounds, or crowds and found it annoying that she had to have lunch with an attractive Black woman so relaxed around Bill.

The relationship was moving along tentatively. On her initial visit to meet his daughters, son-in-law Jake, and baby William, a few cracks began to appear in the young relationship.

Milly and Jake lived in the same neighborhood, and younger daughter Virginia still lived with Bill. "You never knew this development was here?" questioned Bill.

"The only time I came out here was to go to the casino."

Immokalee was a rural farm community twenty-five miles east of Naples. The majority of its inhabitants worked the vegetable farms or sugarcane fields, and many were employed by the Seminole Casino Hotel. The average income for the area was less than thirty-five thousand dollars per year.

"Well this is a nice neighborhood. The girls had nice friends growing up. It's a safe place, and it was all Sally and I could afford. Housing costs in and around Naples are not geared to a teacher's income," was Bill's response. This was an ongoing issue he was not afraid to voice.

"Oh, I'm just saying I didn't know about the homes out here," Doris remarked, sensing that she was out of her social class comfort level. Driving back to Naples after visiting Bill's family, she knew she had crossed a line by his mood. "Sorry, Bill. I know you're a hard-working guy. You remind me of Tom. In many ways."

"Don't worry about it, I'm good." He would stay another night with Doris after having dinner with Sam and Bridget, but sleeping was all he was interested in.

During the meal, the subject of moving came up. Sam suggested he should look at the Eagles Nest. "We have a variety of homes here, including coach homes and apartments. I know there are a couple of coach homes for sale near the preserve by the 12th hole."

Bill had actually been thinking about moving to a gated golf community. Jake, his son-in-law had suggested a market price. Suddenly, Bill blurted out, "Doris, do you know a good realtor?" They would start the process the next day.

4

"I think it's a great unit," said Brad Hepworth, the young real estate agent. This was the final property he would show for the day. He had been working for Sunshine Tropical Realty for a week and was anxious to make his first sale.

"It's turn-key, just move in. You have a great view of the lake and the 12th fairway. I'm sure we can agree on a fair price." He knew the owner had already lowered the price. The property had been sitting for two and a half years. The other agents stayed away from the two bedroom, two bath, single car garage because of issues related to the inspection. For whatever reason, small imperfections kept cropping up; cracks in the wall and ceilings, pipes leaking, windows scratched, and a myriad of other irritants. If it was a car, it would be classified as a lemon.

Brad, Bill, and Doris were standing in the living room looking out the large sliding glass door. Brad slid it open to the lanai. Where he came from, New Hampshire, it would have been described as a screened-in porch. It took Brad a few sales appointments to remember to not call it a porch, and the lake, more like a small pond, was also suspect. But he learned these were the buzz words needed to sell golf property in Florida, and lake it was.

He stepped aside and let the woman lead him out to the outdoor room and the drastic change in temperature and humidity. "What do you think?"

But before Bill could answer, he heard, "The previous owner

certainly had great taste in furniture, both here on the lanai and in the rest of the unit. It's a shame they couldn't have enjoyed it more." It was Doris. "Patrick and Phillis Green, they're up north for the summer, have the unit above. They're friends of mine and my ex. We actually looked into buying here." She looked at Bill and continued. "I'm not sure if you know what happened." She turned to look at the agent with a serious face. "The previous owner bought the place, and soon after they moved in, for some unexpected reason, they moved out."

"No, I didn't know that," Brad lied.

There was a pause as Brad felt the momentum of his sales pitch slowing down, and then Bill announced, "I really like it."

"Great," replied Brad, recovering enthusiastically.

"Let me think about it," said Bill to the young realtor.

Later, in the car. "Bill, you can afford something bigger and with a better view." She was beginning to irritate Bill.

There were also comments from his daughters, particularly from 23-year-old Virginia who, unlike her sister, enjoyed an array of boyfriends and was not about to get married anytime soon. "Dad, you know they're fake," was blurted out one evening after she and her dad were sipping wine and watching TV, referring to Doris's enhanced breasts. There were other remarks about a possible face lift and other cosmetic work done to her body. Bill was okay with the extra work done on Doris, but it bothered him that his children could not warm up to her.

Sam pulled him aside the day after the meeting with the realtor. They were having a coffee after Sam had had his monthly meeting with other zoo patrons. "I feel a little guilty telling you this." He stopped to think a moment. "We were going over the financial reports the other day, checking on units that are in arrears. Doris hasn't paid her fees in the last three quarters. We sent her the final warning the other day."

The two men were having their coffee break in the maintenance shed. "I saw a snake again behind building one." He was slurping his coffee and smoking his cigarette.

"Yeah, I've seen it before," replied Alberto. "It could be a cottonmouth."

"That thing creeps me out."

"It's a big one, although I've seen them bigger down at Seahorse Key."

"Where?"

"It's a bird sanctuary that my brother works at down in the Thousand Islands. I've seen some almost five feet long, and fat."

"Sounds creepy and dangerous."

"Not according to him," said Alberto, looking at his co-worker. "My brother says the snakes just lay under the trees and collect anything that falls from the nests, mostly regurgitated food that the bird chicks drop."

"They still creep me out."

"Yeah, I know."

◆ ◆ ◆

Bill opened the door and took in the welcoming view as he looked through the room's space and observed a portion of the 12th fairway. He had done it. He had a home on a golf course. It was perfect. He had his own golf cart, which had come with the property, and one of the amenities he loved was the driving range. Hitting golf balls was very cathartic to him. He loved the course, with its narrow fairways and challenging greens. Accuracy was the key to success on this course. As he walked in, setting his few groceries on the marble-top counter, his cell phone buzzed. He looked at the name; it was Doris.

"Hi, what's up," said Bill. There was a pause. "Doris?" There was no answer. The phone went dead. He went to recent calls and punched in her number, but there was still no answer. This was not unusual. On some occasions, she denied making the call, and all Bill had to do was show her on his phone, and she would still deny she made the call. Doris was drinking a lot. The phone rang again. It was Agatha. "So how is your new place?"

"I love it, Aga." Over the years, that had become her nickname. "Hey, I have a great idea, are Cordell and Marta around?"

"Not at the moment, but I can text them."

"Why don't you come out here, and I'll treat you to dinner?"

"Okay, sounds wonderful."

"Yes, Mr. Kelly is expecting you," said the gate guard. He pressed the button to raise the candy-apple striped bar, and they drove in.

They looked through clumps of palm trees and flowering plants at a manicured fairway with its menacing sand traps on their right. On their left was the entrance to the address Bill had given Agatha. He opened the door on the first knock. "Welcome," he said enthusiastically, putting his left arm around Agatha's shoulder and pulling her in and at the same time shaking Cordell's hand. Marta was behind her mother, and she received the same hug as her mother.

"Wow, Mr. K, this is great," said Agatha's son, walking straight ahead and taking in the view of the preserve and golf course.

"That's the 12th fairway, and off to the left you can see a portion of the 11th green. I'll get you out here, Cordell, but you better be straight with that drive of yours."

"Yeah, I can see that."

"I have a reservation for dinner in an hour. So what do you think, Aga?"

"I think I'm not on the Gordon River listening to the monkeys and traffic."

"Yeah, it is quiet out here."

"No, just kidding, this is very nice, Bill." And Agatha noticed the furniture. "This all came with it you said?"

"Yep, anyone want a soda or water, coffee, Aga?"

Bill walked into the small kitchen area and opened the

fridge. "Marta, what can I get you?"

"Water's fine, Mr. K."

"Me too," piped in Cordial. "Mind if I go out in the lanai? I want to get a better look at the course."

"No, go right ahead."

"I can make the coffee, Bill." She could see a basket of Keurig pods and coffee cups in a rack next to the brewing machine.

"There's milk or cream in the fridge."

"Do you want one, Bill?"

"Sure."

Cordell and Marta were content to sit on the lanai and watch a foursome of men tee off, followed by two couples making up another foursome go by in their golf carts. Leaning against the counter, while Agatha sat on a barstool, they were talking quietly. "So how is your girlfriend doing these days?"

Agatha was very protective of her friend. He had told her as much as he thought he should share with her about Agatha. One of the topics was her drinking.

"Yes, just before you called, I got a call from her. I don't know, Aga. There are times when she's fun to be around, but lately, well…" And he just let the thought go away, shaking his head.

"If you think she needs help, you know I'm here."

"Yeah, thanks, but to be honest, I don't think she would listen to you, or anyone for that matter."

"MOM, MR. K. COME QUICK!"

The two adults instantly turned toward the yelling and looked out at the lanai. Cordell was waving one hand frantically and pointing and looking in the grass outside the lanai with the other. Marta was standing on one of the cushioned chairs with her hands to her mouth.

"Why are you yelling?" demanded Agatha.

"LOOK!" In the grass next to the lanai, they could see snakes, all about nine to ten inches in length, slithering through the grass and heading away from the building.

"Oh my," said Agatha and put her hand up to her mouth.

"Are we being invaded?" said Marta still standing on the furniture, but her hands were now on top of her head.

"I think there were at least ten of them," said Cordial as they dispersed, heading in the direction of the woods and pond and finally disappearing from view.

"Wow," was all Bill could say at the moment.

"I think we just had a birth, Bill," said Agatha. That's what it looked like when Gypsy had her litter, brood, gang of snakes, or whatever it's called. Remember? They were all over the place."

"Where did they come from?" asked Bill.

Still standing on the lounge, pointing in the direction of the corner, Marta said, "Right there in the corner where the floor of the lanai and the building come together, they just poured out of the ground."

"Hmmm, are you thinking what I'm thinking, Aga?"

"Mama could still be in there."

"Yep, and I think we are looking at a cottonmouth mama."

"You mean like the ones in that *Lonesome Dove* movie that you like, Cordell?"

"What?" questioned Agatha.

"There's a scene where a cowboy falls off his horse while crossing a river and lands in a cottonmouth nest, is attacked by about a hundred snakes, and dies."

"Yeah, I like Western movies too, but that was a stretch. That couldn't happen," said Bill, and was interrupted by Agatha.

"He couldn't fall off his horse?" Knowing where he was going with his explanation,

She laughed in her low-register voice, a part of her he really liked.

"What's so funny? Those things are scary, Mum." Agatha put her hand up to help her daughter down from her perch.

"Yes, you're right, honey. Bill and I are pretty comfortable around snakes, and I get the creepy part... I really do."

Bill continued. "Marta, like Mum says, and I get the creepy crawly thing too, but snakes are no different than any animal. All they want is to eat and have babies. They don't have snake

16

nests, and they're not like hornets or bees attacking things that threaten the hive or nest."

"Mr. K. and Mum, no offense, but we are not at the zoo explaining what snakes do. We are in Mr. K's backyard, and a whole bunch of snakes just came crawling out of his house," Marta said as she wrapped her arms around herself, looking at the pond. Bill smiled looking at Agatha's pretty daughter.

"Yeah, that's something you don't see every day, is it? But, if you don't mind, let me continue with my zoo lecture. It might help," he said with a grin.

"I doubt it," said Marta.

"So when they are about to have their babies, they look for a den, and it looks like she found a safe spot in that corner. My guess is there is a hole in the concrete foundation." Going over to investigate, he turned and looked at Marta. "So job one is done. Those little ones are on their own. Instinct was telling them to get out of Dodge and get out quickly before mama gets hungry."

"Can we stop with the cowboy stuff, please," said Marta, now sitting on the cushioned chair.

"She probably won't come out until dark to hunt," said Agatha.

"You can't live here, Mr. K.," said Marta. "There are going to be snakes everywhere."

"Marta, we have to understand, first of all, they were here way before we were, and nature has a way of making sure snakes won't be everywhere." He pointed in the direction of the pond. "If they are lucky, one of those little guys may live to be a year old." He walked over to look in the direction of the pond. "When they go in the water, a large-mouth bass, alligators, or other snakes will be lurking." He pointed toward the sky. "In the air, hawks, owls, eagles, or osprey will be waiting for them, and if Mother Nature doesn't intervene in their existence, they could be run over by a golf cart, car, or lawnmower. It's a tough life out there." And he added, "So, the lecture is over, but I have to add one more thing. There is a possibility that mama snake, and not a whole gang of snakes, is still in the ground next to the building."

"Great," said Marta as she sat looking at the spot where she first saw the snakes.

"Hey, we have reservations. Let's get something to eat." Just then Bill's cell phone rang. Once again looking at the screen, he saw it was Doris. He swiped the phone.

"Hello."

"Bill, can I come over? I have a problem."

"Are you okay?" he asked concerned.

"Yeah, I'm okay. I just have to see you about something and would like to do it in person.

"Aga and the kids are here. We have dinner reservations at the club in a few minutes, but you're welcome to join us."

"No, thanks." This was followed by an awkward pause. "What's she doing there?"

Once again, the probing inappropriate question. Bill could feel his temper rising. Agatha was sensitive to the tone of the conversation and walked back into the house, followed by Marta and Cordial.

The snake would rest until dark. She would stay in place, protected by the ragged cement hole until the next day, and then seek the sun.

5

"The new owner is a good guy; he still has a house out at Orange Grove Estates and will be in and out. I told him about the cabinet door under the sink," said Alberto.

"Did you tell him how it got broken?" asked Miguel.

"Shit no."

"There's no problem. It's fixed except the closing mechanism needs that little magnet thing to hold it shut. I have to go to ACE Hardware to pick up a few more. It closes okay. I told him about it. So, I think that takes care of the punch list for that unit once I pick up the stuff at ACE."

"Hope so," replied Miguel.

Doris was not cognizant of where she was. There was a bang on the car's window to her left and then another. All she knew at the moment was pain, pain behind her eyes, the kind of pain only a migraine headache could produce. The pounding on the window began again. It was harder and louder.

"Ma'am!" She slowly looked to her left. There was a young police officer.

"Ma'am, open the door."

The pounding in her head became worse. She leaned into

the steering wheel and felt nauseous. She grabbed the wheel with both hands and threw up. The pain in her head was excruciating as she passed out.

"She's not responding, Pete, and she just puked all over herself," said the Naples police officer.

"Open the door, Ray."

Bill was doing his rounds at the zoo and was about to meet Aga for coffee. He had been thinking about his new place and wanted to know her thoughts about the dinner they had last night as well as her thoughts about the snake-birthing incident. He really was not comfortable having a cottonmouth living in the wall of his unit. His phone went off. It was Doris. He swiped the phone. "Hello, are you still mad?"

"Bill, I'm in trouble."

"How?"

"I'm in jail."

Bill stopped and held the smart phone to his ear and stared at the monkey island, but he wasn't seeing it. He listened as Doris tried to explain. The Collier County Jail was only a few miles from the zoo. He would go and help her, but first he'd let Agatha know.

"I don't know, Aga. Yesterday when she called, she said she had something she had to talk to me about and got all mad when I told her you and the kids were with me. She stopped the call."

"I know," responded Agatha. "I figured something was wrong."

"I don't know, I was going to call her back, but I wasn't about to try and talk to her when she was in the condition she was in. She sounded drunk." He shook his head and looked down at the gravel walk. "I just met her a few weeks ago, and I'm not sure what to do."

"Bill, you helped me, remember," Agatha said and looked at him. "She needs help."

He drove to the Collier County Jail and spoke to the officer at the front desk, explaining who he was and why he was there. According to the report, she had blacked out. They found her in the parking garage on Fifth Avenue. She had crashed into the third-level cable fence, and the right front of the car was hanging over the edge. The cable prevented the car from landing on the street below. This had taken place at 3:30 a.m.

Doris was sitting off to the side of the room wearing a green jail-issued jumpsuit, talking to a man in a business suit. When Bill walked in, her first reaction was to put her hands up to her face and cry.

The man in the suit was a lawyer. Introductions were made, and the situation was explained to Bill. After two hours, she was released and would be under Bill's supervision.

He brought her back to her apartment and stayed with her while she showered. She took her time freshening up. When she appeared from her room, she wore a pair of jeans, a loose-fitting Arizona Wildcats basketball sweatshirt, and flip flops. She had shampooed her hair. There was no makeup in evidence. Bill was sitting in one of the overstuffed chairs looking off to his right.

He turned and looked at her. "I never realized what a nice view of the course you have."

She said nothing as she sat on the couch across from him, drawing her legs up under her.

"Doris, I have a feeling this thing that just happened may have begun when you called me last night." There was a long pause. No one spoke. She turned to look out the lanai and began.

"I called to tell you I had been fired from the dress store. I've lost the use of any amenities here at the club because I'm late in my payments, and I was hoping you might help me." She looked down at the expensive oriental rug. "Yes, I got mad, got in my car, and drove to Fifth Avenue. There's a bar across the street from Agatha's. That's the last I remember until I woke up in jail." She put her hands up to her face and began sobbing, then looked up at Bill and, through red eyes and tears, blurted out, "I have no license, no car, no job, no money. I don't know what to do!" And quietly she said, "Bill, you are the most stable guy I've met in a long time. I didn't know where to turn, and I've made it worse!" They both sat looking out the lanai. The weight of his responsibility finally hit him. She would need him.

"Look, why don't you stay at my place, and we can talk more about your future. You have to start a program tomorrow."

"Great, I can hardly wait." And she continued to vent. "Just what I want to do, hear a bunch of drunks spilling their guts."

Bill didn't respond to that but said, "C'mon, get some stuff together and we'll go over to my place."

He had set up the other bedroom for guests, mainly thinking of his daughters. It was bright with its western exposure, neat, with a closet, small dresser, and a TV mounted on the wall. There was a bathroom across a small hall next to the kitchen.

The next day, Bill called the zoo and explained that he had to take some time off. He and Doris went to Collier County Community Services. There they met the coordinator of special services who Doris would have her first AA meeting with. Bill waited and drove her back to his place. She hated the meeting and told Bill so, but the idea of him paying attention to her appealed to her immensely. She really liked the guy, plus he was loaded. The arrangement went on for a week. They did make love on the third night, but Bill still didn't feel right about it.

At the daily meetings, her attitude was still very defensive. She knew she was required to attend a minimum of ten meetings. She had decided she was not giving up alcohol, and on a couple of occasions, she walked back to her apartment if Bill wasn't around and would sneak a drink of vodka. She filled her mouthwash bottle with vodka, keeping it in the bathroom. She would fill small screw-top jars with vodka and hide them in other places. Most nights she would wait for Bill to retire to his room and she would fall asleep drunk. Getting her license back was another story. She had contacted a drunk driving attorney and was waiting for his return call. Possibly Bill could help with this expense.

They had been watching TV. "Doris, I have a couple of presentations I'd like to do at the zoo tomorrow. How you doing?"

"Hey, I'm fine."

"I was thinking, you have your meeting in the morning at nine. I'd like to spend the morning doing the presentations. I could drop you off, and after your meeting, you could get some exercise, walk to the zoo, and we can go home from there."

"Sounds like a plan," she said and gave him a peck on the cheek as she went to her bedroom. She was disappointed he didn't follow.

6

"I was a little suspicious a few times, but not sure. I don't have any alcohol in the condo, but I thought I smelled it on her once or twice." Agatha was curious about how he was doing as they finished up the last presentation, a lecture featuring a red-shouldered hawk, a native bird of prey found in Florida. The bird could not fly due to an encounter with a high-tension wire. They were bringing "Red" back to his habitat near the aviary.

"Bill, you cannot trust an alcoholic; they lie." And she thought quickly, "But not about some things." She looked at Bill who had a quizzical confused look and was staring at her. "I'm just saying, you're talking to one."

They would meet Doris in the small restaurant at the zoo, have lunch, and head back to Bill's condo. While waiting, he checked his text messages. There was usually one or two from his daughters, but the first one he noticed was from Doris sent two hours ago. "I got a text from Doris; she didn't feel like waiting and took an Uber home." Raising her eyebrows, Agatha cocked her head and looked across the small table and didn't say a thing.

Doris was having trouble getting the key in the slot. She began to panic when she dropped it and the small chain with the Saint Christopher medal. She fell forward at one point and hit her head on the door reaching for the key. She knew she had really screwed up and was feeling the guilt return. She had to get inside and have another drink from the pint bottle of vodka and hide it. She gained control of the key chain, stood, and finally had the key in the slot and turned it. She twisted the door handle and pushed the door in, then closed it quietly behind her.

During the AA meeting, she knew what she was going to do. As soon as it ended with the Lord's Prayer, she got up, texted Bill, walked to the liquor store a block away, and went behind the building and took two satisfying gulps from the pint bottle. She began walking, making stops along the way. Then she remembered the Uber app on her phone and thought her credit card was still good; it was.

She walked unsteadily into the kitchen, putting her bag on the counter. She would have one more pull on the bottle and then hide it under the sink with the screw-top jars.

The snake could feel the movement and began to go into her defensive mode. Her thirty-nine inches of black mass was coiled beneath her as she backed against the rear wall of the cabinet. Her neck and head were up, and her white-rimmed jaws were open wide, exposing the long fangs. Suddenly, the interior was awash in light, and just as quickly, the interior was black again. She retreated to the craggy cavern in the cement.

Consumed with guilt, Doris staggered into the guest bedroom and got on the bed, folding herself in a fetal position and passing out, achieving her goal.

When Bill arrived home, he was relieved when he saw her safe, but that was about all. Frustration was the predominant feeling, followed by disappointment. The room reeked of alcohol. He went out to the lanai and called Agatha.

"Bill, you can't force someone to stop drinking. They have to want to. They have to have a reason to stop. Alcohol is a powerful drug to some people. They have to reach rock bottom and recognize they have to stop, and sadly, many never find that purpose to quit." And she added, "When I was drinking, I always made sure I had a drink hidden in the house. If you think you smelled it on her, then you did. More than likely, she has vodka hidden away. That's what I did." She stopped. "I remember one day being so embarrassed and disappointed with myself. I had promised the kids I would quit, and Cordell found a bottle hidden in an old golf bag of his." And she added, "Bill, you and the kids saved my life."

"Thanks, Aga, but you were the one who did all the heavy lifting."

"You know I think the world of you, and so do the kids," said Agatha. They both paused, sensing they were going into a different level of their relationship. Bill broke the silence.

"I'll call you later, I'm going to the driving range to get rid of some frustration." And he added, "I sometimes do my best thinking hitting golf balls."

"That sounds like a good idea. I know Cordell would do that all the time a few years ago."

"Thanks again." And clicked the phone off. Bill checked on her one more time as the smell once again confirmed what she had done. She did not appear to be in any form of distress and was breathing normally.

The snake had discovered there was a very quiet place she could go to during the day to re-energize and, at times, molt. At the moment, she needed the sun. She left the craggy hole and went through the opening that moved when her nose touched it. She was now in light. Her forked tung flicked out, testing the air. Her senses told her she could proceed along the same route as before. The first surface was cool, but she knew that would change. Her tongue picked up the different smell of the surface and proceeded over it to the hot spot where the sun was always shining, and she extended her whole length in its warmth.

Bill had his pitching wedge out and was hitting lazy high-arching balls onto the practice green. While in the midst of one shot, he had an idea. Family.

That's what saved Aga. He went back to his golf cart and got out his phone and did a Google search.

"Aha, I wonder," he said to himself.

"Andrews Tiles, this is Johnny. How can I help you?"

"Hi Johnny. My name is Bill Kelly." He stopped briefly, thinking about his good fortune at contacting her son, but wasn't quite sure what to say next. He quickly figured he should just come out and say what had to be said.

"Johnny, I'm a friend of your mother, Doris... she's in trouble."

"Is this some kind of crank sympathy call, because if it is —" and he slammed the land line phone down. Bill looked at the phone and pushed the recent call button. After numerous rings and no response, he gave up. He sat in the cart, not sure what to do next, when his phone went off. The name of the caller was a business, Andrews Tile, Phoenix, Arizona.

"Hello."

"This better be the real deal, mister."

"Is this Tom?"

"And you are Bill?"

"This is the real deal," he answered and explained who he was, his background, and how he met Doris. He sat in his golf cart for an hour as the two men talked. As it turned out, Tom was a heavy drinker and a recovering alcoholic. He had been sober for four years. When Bill mentioned her blacking out and her obstructive attitude toward her program, Tom knew she was in a bad place.

Through the long conversation, Bill discovered the reason for the divorce. Tom stopped drinking and Doris would not.

"I think of her all the time, Bill. She was the love of my life." Outside of making contact with Doris's family, nothing was said that would indicate what the next step should be. They ended the conversation promising to keep in touch.

* * *

The headache was back. She needed a drink. She wasn't

sure what time it was, but the glare from the late afternoon sun was making the pounding in her head worse. She rolled herself over and put her feet on the soft bedroom carpet. She stood, steadying herself by leaning against the side of the bed.

All she could do was scream. Directly in front of Doris, in the middle of the sun-splashed carpet, was the snake coiled in her defensive posture, fangs out, daring Doris to come closer. On unsteady legs, Doris turned and ran to the open bedroom door. She was reeling in confusion and pain from her migraine. She staggered into the bathroom and slammed the door shut, turned, picked up the toilet cover, and threw up.

Moments later, she was now laying on the cold tile floor. When the retching subsided, she stood, took out the bottle of mouthwash, and drank its entirety. She then got in the bathtub, sat in the corner near the faucet, curled her legs up to her chest, and pulled them against her and passed out.

The danger was over. Energized once again from the sun, the snake retraced her route back to the craggy hole in the cement. She would wait until dark and begin her nightly hunt.

7

The first thing Bill noticed when he came into the kitchen after parking and plugging in the golf cart was the cabinet door under the sink was ajar and made a mental note to get in touch with Alberto. He closed it and went in to check on Doris. She was not in the bed, but the bathroom door was closed. He had a moment of dread as he knocked on the door.

"Doris." He turned the door handle, and the door opened. He pushed it open slowly. He could see her feet protruding from the open, flowered shower curtain his daughter had installed and noticed the vomit on the floor and in the toilet. He walked in. She was passed out again sitting in the tub. He called Agatha.

"I'll be right over."

Not knowing what else to do, he took the clean monogrammed towels from the rack on the bathroom wall and proceeded to clean up the vomit.

"I don't know what to do," he said in complete resignation when Agatha arrived.

"Let me take it from here." He and Agatha were standing in the bathroom.

"Now don't get any crazy ideas." She looked at him and pulled her Naples Zoo T-shirt, featuring a Bengal tiger on the back, over her head. She was wearing a white lacy bra and stepped out of her green FGCU gym shorts, revealing her thong-style pink panties. She looked at Bill, pointing to her underwear. "These were Marta's idea." And she continued, "Believe it or not, my kids did this to me."

She removed her flip flops and stepped in the tub. "Bill can you help me turn her so she's facing the shower?"

Bill removed his shoes and socks and stepped in, pushing the shower curtain aside. They maneuvered Doris to the opposite end of the tub where Agatha sat, holding Doris in her arms, and Bill stepped out.

"Turn on the cold water all the way, Bill."

He did as he was told. Doris began shaking her head, flailing her arms, and kicking.

"What are you doing to me!!"

"We are getting you sober, my friend." Agatha held on to her.

Doris gradually began to return to reality. The first thing she noticed beyond the cold was the person holding her was black. Agatha's long legs were wrapped around Doris's, and her arms were wrapped around her as well. She was speaking to her quietly in her right ear.

"Is that you, Agatha?"

"Yes it is, and I'm here to help you." Doris began to cry and could not stop.

"Doris, I'm only doing what my son and daughter did for me. Now you let me know when you are ready to get out of this tub." They stayed where they were for a long time. Bill retrieved some dry clothing from the bedroom dresser. He couldn't help but notice a small covered jar among her underwear and opened it. As he suspected, it was vodka. He opened the bathroom door wide enough to get his arm through and held out the dry clothes.

"Thanks, Bill," said Agatha.

"Bill, could you get some dry panties and a bra for Aga?" said Doris.

"That's okay. I'm good, Bill."

A moment later, she opened the bathroom door holding a bundle of towels and undergarments. She was wearing her T-shirt, gym shorts, and flip flops. "Let me put these in the laundry room."

"Okay if I make some coffee, Aga?"

"Great idea." They were sitting on the lanai, looking out at the small pond.

Doris joined them, still a little disoriented, holding a cup of black coffee with two shaking hands.

"I think I'm hallucinating," said Doris quietly and continued staring at the pond. "I saw a snake in the bedroom. It was big, black, and its mouth was wide open ready to bite me."

Bill looked at Agatha, raising his eyebrows as they made eye contact, both putting down their coffee cups. Doris continued. "I know in the meetings some of the people talked about hallucinations being a sign that you are in serious trouble. I think I may be at that point." Doris looked at the two people in front of her with a bewildered expression. There was more silence, then Bill spoke.

"Doris, I talked to Tom."

"Oh."

"I think you should call him."

"What did he say?"

"I think you should call him and Johnny."

"I can't."

Agatha interrupted. "Doris, you have to start. Do you realize what we just did? Is that normal? Is that what you want your life to be?" And she gathered her thoughts. "Doris, I know what you are going through. Like I told you in the tub a little while ago, I can help you, but you have to be the one who wants to be helped. I know how hard it will be for you."

Doris nodded her head.

"You have a wonderful friend in Bill, and if he says you should call Tom, I think you should do just that."

J R MADORE

8

"Bill, check this out." Agatha had been visiting quite frequently. She had the cabinet door open under the kitchen sink, putting trash in the waste basket, when she noticed off to the side a partially filled pint bottle of vodka.

"Yeah, I've been finding them all over. I found one in the garage next to the workbench yesterday." And he added, "I hope she's doing okay."

Doris did call Tom, and he and Johnny flew to Florida. She would have to stay in Florida to complete her DUI sentencing, and Tom paid all fines associated with her case as well as her condo fees. Later, she sold the small apartment and moved to Phoenix.

"The last text I got from her she said she had been six months sober. She, Tom and Johnny were all going to counseling."

Bill opened his 'junk' drawer next to the sink and took out a flashlight to search for more containers. He knelt on the floor removed the waste basket and pointed it in.

There she was, in full defensive mode. The sight startled Bill briefly. He clicked off the light and closed the door, stood, turned and looked at Agatha. "We have a visitor," and leaned against the counter. "Remember when the kids saw all those baby snakes?"

"Yes."

"I think mama is still here and is under my sink at the

moment."

Agatha put her hand to her mouth and stared wide eyed at Bill. There was a pause as they both tried to make sense of this.

"Maybe Doris wasn't hallucinating," said Agatha.

Pointing at the cabinet door, Bill came back from his initial reaction "You're right, yes. She has been living here, rent free I might add, for a few years." And he thought for a moment. "It makes sense. This condo was an extension of her den, no one lived in it. There has to be an opening in the foundation and the wall behind the cabinet."

"Yeah, but how could she get into the house?"

"That's another thing. When I bought the place, the previous owner had only lived in it a short time and sold it. The crack or hole or whatever it is must have caused all kinds of problems, not the least having a snake wandering around."

"Still, how did she get in the bedroom?"

It dawned on him. "The magnet."

"The what?"

Pointing to the cabinet again, he said, "The door would close, but could easily open because the magnet that held it closed was missing. I mentioned it to Alberto last week. The door would be open for no reason. He apologized and fixed it the other day."

"So, she's been wandering around your house for a while now, hasn't she?" said Agatha.

"It appears that way."

* * *

"Yes, she has her own entrance, and it's not the front door." Bill was talking to the two maintenance men. He explained that she would not be in her den during the day.

While Bill spent time visiting his daughters and grandson, Alberto and Miguel had another punch list to complete in unit 105. All the kitchen cabinets were torn out. The hole in the foundation was sealed, and with the influence of his friend

Sam, the community paid for the repairs with the best products available.

A few weeks later, while having coffee on the lanai, Bill and Agatha were watching the sunset as a red-shouldered hawk slowly raised itself from the edge of the pond and in its talons was a large snake.

"I wonder if that's my ex-tenant."

"Could be, that's probably where she hunted."

"If it is, I kind of feel sorry for her." He paused to think. "You know, Doris should have thanked that snake," he pointed his coffee cup in the direction of the spectacle. "She wasn't hallucinating. Doris witnessed what that cottonmouth snake does best." He paused to look at Agatha.

"And pray tell, what would that be?" she asked, gazing at him with a quizzical look.

"Get your attention." And he added, "In Doris's case, save her life."

"Yes, if you look at it that way, you're right, Mr. K." She looked at him and put her hand on his arm and said softly, "It's a tough world out there Bill, but it doesn't have to be if you have people to love... thank you."

A SMALL LOVE STORY

1

"Grampy, how do you think Patchy will do in the race?" said five-year-old Constance in her French-English patois.

"All we can do is wait and hope, Connie," replied the grandfather, "like always."

The grandfather and grand daughter lived on an old family farm by the Gulf of Saint Lawrence in Gaspe, Quebec they were sitting in the kitchen having breakfast after watched the truck leave with Patch.

He was unusual-looking for a rock dove or pigeon. His feathers were a bright white except for a splotch of black around his left eye. He and 100 other birds had been transported by a special truck to a large field in Quebec City, where they would take part in the annual Plains of Abraham Classic, a 400 mle race that was one of the more popular events in homing pigeon clubs that dotted Canada. Patch was the reigning champion. If all went well, he would be in his nesting box in the red barn with his mate of eight years, Genevieve, at suppertime.

The race planners knew there may be a weather issue. A cold front had stalled over Hudson Bay and was pulling warmer air up from the south, a normal occurrence in late November, but normal weather lately had changed into violent weather. At exactly 6 a.m. on a Saturday, the birds were released. When the flock gained altitude and Patch turned east at 3,000 feet, intent on following the mighty Saint Lawrence River, he encountered a 70-mile-an-hour headwind. In an instant, he and the flock disappeared, blown westerly with no ability to combat the powerful air current.

All Patch could do was keep flying. His instincts were telling him he was going in the wrong direction, but his instinct to survive was stronger. Throughout the long day and into the night, the gale force wind continued to push him further and further south and west. Gradually, the storm dissipated and stars appeared. He turned toward home, but exhaustion was beginning to take its toll. Eventually, gray and pink began to appear in the eastern sky. His instincts told him there was danger from predators at lower altitudes, but he had no choice; he had to rest.

With full daylight an hour away, he managed to find a perch in a large oak.

"I don't know, Constance. The storm was a bad one. The birds should have been back before dark yesterday. I had a bad feeling about this race. I should have paid more attention to the weather." It was Sunday morning. He had contacted other members of the club, and not one bird had returned.

"I hope Genevieve isn't worried," said five-year-old Constance.

"No more than me, honey," he replied in French.

Below the ancient oak was a brook. After a few hours' rest, he carefully glided down. He knew he was in danger. At the edge of the fast-moving water, he located a water-filled impression among the rotted leaves and put his beak in, sucking in a satisfying gulp. He raised up his head to swallow and then took another.

He quickly flew back and perched in the tree. All he could do was listen to his instincts.

Her keen eyes were on him the moment she spotted the

bright white blur rising up and slowly crept to the base of the tree. Bobcats were excellent climbers, and she had kittens to feed. She gathered herself, staring up at her prey.

Patch didn't notice her until she was under the branch. He had the advantage, and with a quick flick of his wings, he was able to lift up, but not before a paw caught his left wing, pulling out a few feathers and knocking him sideways. He continued flapping, avoiding branches, and flew to the top of the tree. The cat attempted to climb, but as the branches became thinner, she stopped. Both animals stayed in place for a long while. The bobcat eventually worked her way back to earth, and Patch flew off in the opposite direction. The missing feathers would hamper his flying effectiveness. His inner compass was still working, and he kept flying, but once again, exhaustion began to set in. He was still a long way from home.

2

The low, late afternoon sun penetrated through the leafless sugar maples and would disappear in an hour. She was washing the day's dishes and looking out the kitchen window, trying to get through her melancholy. She and her husband had not spoken a word all day, ever since she suggested he prop up the bird feeder. The suggestion resulted in another argument. That storm had left the yard a mess. The bird feeder was laying on the ground, but the birdbath survived.

She smiled at her friends, the nuthatches, cardinals, titmice, and the ever-aggressive blue jays, enjoying the banquet of seed that had spilled among what was left of the summer perennials. She had just put the last plate in the drying rack when she took a final glance out the window. Among the birds was a pigeon.

"That's odd," she said out loud to herself.

Her husband was at the kitchen table staring at his laptop screen. "What?" he asked but kept his focus. Everything irritated him, he had been drinking and watching football.

"A pigeon, there's a pigeon at the birdbath." They lived in a rural area between Augusta and Belfast, Maine, near Sheepscot Pond, one of the many lakes that dotted the area. Most of the pigeons they encountered were found in densely populated towns and cities. This was an anomaly. To appease his wife, Jack got up slowly and came to the window.

Jack Watkins, 27, and his wife, Mary, 25, had been married

for three years. He worked for an investment company in Portland, and she was an out-of-work waitress. They had been confined to the house they rented because of COVID, and like many, Jack worked remotely at home. The only family either one had near them was Mary's dad, Walter, a retired shipyard worker who still lived in nearby Belfast. His wife, Anna, had passed away five years ago from cancer.

The young couple had issues. Jack hated his job, and being confined to the house had made matters worse. She was pregnant. When he heard the news, Jack suggested terminating the pregnancy. She would have none of it. The loss of Mary's income grated at him, and the rent they were paying, in what was once a vacation home, he felt was exorbitant. That was the elephant in the room every day. After some spats, he would leave the house and drive off for hours. He would always return. If not arguing, the silence between them some days was stifling. She was concerned about her marriage and was two weeks away from her delivery date.

Just as Jack got to the window, the birds scattered. In a blink, the white pigeon disappeared. A larger bird had it pinned to the ground.

"Oh no," yelled Mary, putting a hand to her face and banging on the window with her other.

"Jack, do something!"

"What?"

"Do something!" And she pushed him aside hard, all her frustrations with him boiling to the surface as she ran to the mudroom that led to the backyard.

"Mary, no, don't run." He came up behind her and gently took both arms, steering her out of the way. Next to the back door, leaning against the wall, was a broom. He grabbed it and opened the door simultaneously.

The bird was a raven. At the moment, it did not have a firm grip on the smaller bird as white wings flapped in desperation.

Jack ran, waving the broom and yelling. The predator turned its head and body, staring menacingly at Jack, and launched himself at the human, but the broom waving was enough to deter the bird, causing an abrupt, wing-flapping stop in the air as the large bird quickly peeled back in the opposite direction and slowly gained altitude, heading for a perch at the top of a tall white pine a distance away. The pigeon flapped its wings and flew to the roof of their rented home.

"That's a racing pigeon," said Jack. One of the things that Jack and Mary had in common was birds. They both grew up with parents who were fascinated with birds.

"Look, he's banded. He must be lost and very tired to be on the ground." Mary joined him next to the birdbath. The incident, although emotional, seemed to help seal a fraction of the broken bond between them.

"I'm sorry I yelled and pushed you Jack. I just felt so bad for the pigeon."

Jack was taken aback by the sudden apology and didn't respond. The pigeon flew down to the flower bed and began pecking away at the seeds.

"He's used to people," said Jack as they slowly walked toward the bird.

Patch was content to pick away at his newfound food supply, and when the human put his hands around him, he resisted briefly but gave in. He was still fatigued.

"I'll take him into the garage."

As Jack held the bird, Mary opened the door to the back of the one-car garage where there was a workbench. Jack immediately noted blood on the top of the bird's head as well as a small droplet on the palm of his own hand. There was a wound under the left wing.

"He's hurt, but I don't think seriously. He did fly up to the roof. Why don't you get some bacitracin from the medicine cabinet, and we can dab it on these wounds," suggested Jack.

"Good idea, hon." And she left to go in the house. Jack paused to consider the affectionate salutation. It seemed out of place and had been missing for a long time.

When his wife returned, they carefully inspected the bird

for other wounds but found none. "Mary, let's see what the band says." While maintaining a gentle hold on the bird, he turned it so she could view the blue plastic band. He watched his wife's expression change to concentration and could smell the light fragrance from the soap she used. She leaned in inches away from his face and brushed strands of blonde hair from her lovely face, the face he fell in love with the day he met her at the restaurant.

"Looks like," and for lack of a better writing surface, Mary took a pencil from the nearby workbench, and said, "CU11/30/10-367," as she wrote the letters and numbers on the surface of the bench.

They found a cardboard box big enough to hold a cereal bowl for water and one for seed, cut holes in the sides, and placed the bird in it. Patch was content to stay put and stood quietly in the box. As Jack looked at this aerial wanderer that trusted him and Mary, he could not help but think. The pigeon had learned to trust humans. If the bird felt these basic concepts, why was it so difficult for Jack to accept the good things in his own life? They gently folded the box's top loosely over the wayward bird.

As they retreated back to the house and stepped into the kitchen, Mary doubled over, crossed her hands over her stomach, and let out an Oh! She had never experienced this kind of pain.

The bird was immediately forgotten.

"Mary! Are you okay?" He reached around her back to pull her to him and guided her to a chair.

"Oh, Jack, I don't know, but it hurts so bad. It may be time." She doubled over again and then looked up. "Jack I have a travel bag on the floor of my closet. Get it, we have to go to the hospital."

In rural Maine, getting to a hospital in an emergency was always a challenge. Hospitals were never close. Augusta General was thirty miles away, and none of the roads were straight or flat.

Jack helped Mary get in their 2003 Ford Bronco and then he

got in, pushed the remote to open the garage door, and backed out to the dark street. There was a fine line between driving fast and too fast. He did not want to scare his already scared wife.

The trip took 45 minutes. When they arrived at the portico with the brightly lit emergency sign, Jack noticed a wheelchair next to the heavy glass door, which had already slid open when the electric eye was sent into action. He stopped the car and went around to open her door. Two nurses appeared.

"We'll take her, sir," said one of them, as the other brought the wheelchair over to the Bronco.

They told him where to park and wheeled Mary into the hospital. After an anxious half hour of sitting in the prenatal waiting area, he was directed to her room.

"My water broke right after you left to park the car."

"Is that bad?"

"No, it means I'm going into labor."

3

"I'm scared, Jack."

Things were happening so fast. Not an hour ago they were having one of the first civil conversations they had had in a long time over a pigeon that happened to stop for a drink of water. And now the thought of a child entering their world was more than Jack could comprehend.

He reached over and took her hand. They held hands, but nothing was said. He didn't know what to say and eventually, "You'll be fine, hon," repeating what she had called him during the pigeon incident and feeling awkward. He had not called her that in a long time. "We're where we should to be." They stayed like that for a long time. At one point, the subject of the pigeon was brought up by Mary.

"Wasn't that interesting today? Oh, Jack, the poor bird is still in that box. Why don't you call Dad in the morning and ask him to check on him?"

"Good idea, and I might as well tell him what's going on with his daughter." He paused. "I'll do it now." Jack went out into the lobby and made the call on his cell phone. "Oh, and could you do us a favor," he said after letting Walter know where they were and added what had happened in their backyard. "Yes, a racing pigeon in a box on the workbench."

"Now let's focus on what we've made here," said Jack upon returning to the room.

"Ya, guess you're right." She took his hand in hers and rubbed her stomach.

"I love you, Mary." Jack stared into her eyes and kissed his wife.

It was 5:00 a.m. Mary had been in labor for over 14 hours. At one point, the staff asked him to leave the birthing area and wait in the common waiting room, where he called his father-in-law.

"I'm worried, Walt."

"I think she'll be okay," the older man said, trying to express confidence. "I stopped by the house and looked in the garage. You were in a big hurry; you left the garage door open."

"Did you check on the pigeon?"

"The box was on the workbench, but no pigeon."

"Really! We folded the top over."

"Well you must have folded it loosely, because it was wide open." Walt paused to gather his thoughts. He knew Jack and Mary were having issues and was compelled to share an interesting fact about pigeons. "You know, there's a reason those birds are called homing pigeons," he said and paused. "They have a strong need to be home, and in his case, the nest and, more importantly, his mate. Maybe his mate was the only thing on his mind."

"Well, I hope he makes it home, wherever it may be. Thanks for checking, Walt. I'll call you as soon as I know anything from this end." Jack knew he deserved that lecture from Walt and sat in one of the worn stuffed chairs staring at a magazine. He was alone in the waiting room. The minutes turned to hours. He would occasionally walk over to one of the large windows that looked over the parking lot where the Bronco was illuminated from a fluorescent light at the top of a light pole. It was raining and would continue through the arrival of dawn and into the morning.

It was now 11:30 am. The door to the waiting room opened, and a nurse was carrying a bundle of blankets. "Mr. Watkins, I'd like you to meet your daughter."

Jack got up and walked over. The nurse parted the blankets to reveal a fat, chubby red face that was made up mostly of cheeks. He was amazed at his incomprehension. His daughter, what does that mean? He reached in and gently touched a cheek with the knuckle of his right hand. His first indication of how soft and precious this life was.

"Would you like to hold her?" said the nurse. Jack had never held a baby before, and the nurse had to guide him through the process. He held her and stared at her scrunched-up face, at peace with the world, and suddenly it dawned on him; he was a dad.

"Mr. Watkins, there were some problems. The doctor will explain." Just then, the door opened, and Dr. Paterson appeared. "Why don't you let me take your daughter, Mr. Watkins," said the nurse.

"Mr. Watkins, Jack, is it? Let's take a seat." The doctor chose a far corner of the room, and they sat as the nurse disappeared with his daughter.

"Mary had a very long and exhausting labor. Your daughter is perfectly healthy. I have to be honest, Mary's blood pressure spiked at one point, and we were very worried we would lose her. She's okay now but needs a lot of rest. We're going to keep her for a few days and watch her. I'm afraid she's not out of the woods yet." The doctor waited for that to sink in. "You can go in and see her now, but she's asleep. She needs all she can get." Jack went in and could only stay a few minutes. He held her hand and kissed her on the cheek.

The hand-written sign in front of the small crib said Anna Jaqueline Watkins. She was with the other newborn babies. In all his turmoil from the past months, he had forgotten what their child would be named. He put his hand up to his mouth and smiled as tears fell through his fingers.

After calling Walt and his family, he decided to go home. He would let Mary get the rest she deserved and go to their bed for a few hours of sleep. He pulled into the driveway, hit the remote to open the garage door, and drove in. In front of him was the cardboard box. He sat and stared at it for a good long time and broke down again. He thought about what his father-in-law said and what Dr. Paterson had said. He realized he almost lost Mary.

4

Connie and her grandfather were sitting at the old farm's kitchen table having their lunch when they heard the unmistakable sound. It was a loud ping from a small speaker set on a sideboard under a cabinet. They both got up immediately, Connie much more agile than her grandfather, ran to the kitchen door, threw it open, and ran to the pigeon coop. Claude Dupre was right behind her but walking at a sensible pace with a hopeful grin on his weathered face.

Connie anxiously opened the side door and peered up at Genevieve and Patch's nesting box. Sure enough, there he was. As only pigeons could do, they were performing their dance. Patch was strutting with his tail feathers spread and loudly cooing, while Genevieve bobbed her neck, cooing a happy greeting.

Connie was jumping up and down clapping her hands in the middle of the coop, causing all the other pigeon couples to stand and stare from their cribs.

Patch had just arrived. As soon as he stepped through the one-way gate of hanging plastic rods, an electric eye recognized the chip in Patch's blue band, triggering the speaker in the kitchen and the clock that was still set for his return.

"Let's finish our lunch and let them have their reunion. We can see how he is after he has a good long drink of water and some food."

In the meantime, Claude contacted the racing club and

recorded Patch's arrival time. There was no way of knowing how far he traveled, and he was told that Patch was one of only twelve birds from the original one hundred that returned to their lofts. The grandfather relayed that information to his granddaughter.

"So our Patchy must have had himself quite an adventure." Like many Canadians, he added an "ie or y" on the end of a name as a sign of friendship and affection.

He examined his friend and discovered the missing wing feathers, a scab on the bird's head, and blood in the feathers on his side under a wing.

"Someone helped him along the way. See this, Connie? It looks like some kind of disinfectant around the cut on his head."

"What's that, Grampy?"

"A kind of medicine so a boo-boo will get better."

"Oh, that was nice of them to do that."

5

Because she was young, Mary recovered from her delivery quickly. Jack had a few days to contemplate his actions from the past year and realized what he almost let slip away. Anna came home with Mary after three days, and life seemed to begin anew for Jack.

Mary didn't ask any questions but knew her husband had changed. Little things didn't seem to bother him as he found himself appreciating the fact that he was home with his family and twenty-four seven with his daughter. The bird feeder was replaced and was busy everyday with an assortment of feathered friends, including squirrels and a few hardy chipmunks.

A year would pass, and the COVID restrictions were lifted. Jack found a position managing the Belfast First and Trust, and the restaurant that Mary had worked at as a waitress had reopened. Walter had been hinting that they could move in with him. The house had two floors with plenty of room. They accepted the offer. They would move in the fall.

The packing process had been going on for a while. Jack took a day off here and there, while Walter watched Anna, who was beginning to talk. Jack and Mary would take boxes and assorted pieces of furniture to her childhood home. She was delighted; it had many happy memories.

The moving company had just left with the large pieces of furniture, and Jack went with them. Mary stayed at the old rental to make sure they hadn't forgotten anything. Anna was with her. She had locked the house for the last time and was walking into the garage followed by her babbling daughter with another question.

"Yes, honey, we're getting in the car to go to our new house." Looking down at her daughter, she noticed one of Anna's shoes was untied.

"Oops, we have a problem here." Instead of bending down to tie the shoe, she picked her up and sat her on the edge of the workbench. As Mary began to tie the lace, Anna pointed to the surface of the bench and announced, "C."

"What, honey?"

"C." She repeated the word and simultaneously put her thumb in her mouth using the other hand. Mary looked down and cocked her head and stared at the series of letters and numbers.

"Oh my gosh!" She put Anna down and took out a pen from her purse and wrote down CU 11/30/10 367 on the back of her left hand.

"Did we leave anything behind?" asked Jack.

"No, but Anna noticed this on the workbench in the garage." And she showed him the back of her hand with the numbers and letters.

"Do you remember what they are?"

"The racing pigeon?"

"You know what else?" she asked, looking at her husband.

"I'm not sure," he answered, looking at Mary.

Pointing with the index finger of her right hand, she read, "Eleven slash thirty, that's Anna's birthday. She was born on the day after the pigeon stopped for a drink."

He thought for a moment. "I wonder if it ever made it home? You know what we should do?" suggested Jack as he unfolded his laptop on the kitchen table. "Look up lost racing pigeons."

Mary sat next to him as they looked through the menu of subjects about racing pigeons. When they put in the figures from the leg band, they discovered that CU stood for Canadian Racing Pigeon Union, and the next six numbers were the day the bird was hatched, and the final three were the zip code of the bird's loft.

"Okay, so what we know is he was from Canada, he was ten years old then, and he lives in zip code three sixty-seven, if he made it home."

"I didn't know pigeons could live that long," said Walter as he walked into the room.

"Okay, try racing pigeon clubs," suggested Mary.

"Hey," interrupted Walter. "Wasn't there a big storm the night before you found the pigeon? You thought he was lost. That racing club must have a list of the races."

"Okay, that's worth a try." Jack typed that in. He reasoned the bird had to start somewhere in Canada, possibly on the twenty-eighth of November last year. "Well, I'll be," he said sitting back in his chair.

"What?" responded Mary.

"His name was Patch. Check this out, guys."

And he read the caption under a picture of a white pigeon. "The Canadian Racing Pigeon Union wishes to apologize for using poor judgement in allowing The Plains of Abraham Classic to take place. Despite warnings of high winds, the race was allowed to go forward. Unfortunately, of the one hundred racers that started, only twelve returned to their respective lofts. One of the twelve was last year's winner, Patch, from The Leduc Farm loft in Gaspe, Quebec."

"Wow, so he made it," said Mary.

"Where is Gaspe, Quebec?" asked Walter.

Jack typed in Google Maps and did a quick search. He also calculated the distance from Belfast, Maine, to Gaspe.

"Walt, that's close to four hundred miles from here."

"My, my," said Mary, "and there is no telling how far south that wind took him before landing on our birdbath."

"I think he must have really been in love, Walt." He reached over to take Mary's hand as she patted her husband on the shoulder, smiling.

"Now I'm really curious," said Jack. And he took out his cell phone.

6

They were met by eight-year-old year old Connie and her grandfather Claude.

"There they are," said Claude, the birds had been let out for their daily flight before feeding time. "They don't go too far, maybe a mile or two from the loft and circle back, then go in another direction for about the same distance. They mostly follow Patch and Genevieve."

"I get worried sometimes when Patch takes some of them very high and I can't see them, but he always brings them back. Those are his babies," said Connie, adding her personal opinion.

What they discovered from the phone call to The Leduc Farm was that Patch was not only alive, but he and Genevieve had since had two more hatches. They decided they had to take a trip to celebrate Anna's birthday and headed for Gaspe, Quebec.

After a visit to the coop, when the birds all returned and a reunion with Patch. Claude invited them to have a lunch of beans and fresh caught haddock. He explained how he thought Patch had an advantage over other homing pigeons because he was a high flyer. "He comes from stock that prefer higher altitudes and avoids predator birds at lower levels." And added, "he's been at it for 16 years now, and always comes home to Genevieve."

"Yes, our Patchy and Genevieve are still in love and will be forever. Don't you think, Gramp?"

"*Oui, my Cherie.*"

A few weeks later, back in Belfast, Maine, Anna asked, "Instead of reading one of my books, could you tell me the story about Patchy the pigeon again?" Walter was laying in his four-year-old granddaughter's bed ready to read the nightly bedtime story. He closed the book, with its children's stories and rested his head on the pillow.

"Sure, honey."

"And don't forget to tell me the whole story. Sometimes you think I'm asleep and skip parts." He smiled at this beautiful blonde angel as she put her thumb in her mouth and cuddled a faded pinkish strand of what was once a blanket.

"I promise." And he began, "There once was this white pigeon called…"

THE CARROT FIELD

1

Under an elm near to the village, a young boy was watching his grandfather's scarred and gnarled fingers perform magic. The old man was the tribe's shaman, responsible for healing, prophesying, and keeping tribal traditions. The village members were part of the Wampanoag culture and lived in what was called 'great-hill-small-place,' which would later be called Massachusetts. Their small village was located near a bog land not considered suitable for farming by the colonial settlers in the area.

Big Hand was holding a bright piece of blackish-green stone that sparkled in the dappled shade. He had received the prized stone in a trade with an Algonquin traveler from the north. He was making an arrowhead. The process was called napping.

Sitting on the trunk of a fallen tree that had succumbed to a storm that past winter, he had draped a remnant of moose skin on his left knee. While holding the brittle stone against the thick skin, he would strike the edges with a piece of granite, a harder stone. Each strike would produce a chip, which he would brush away, and turn the stone, creating the triangular shape he was seeking.

"Watch where you're stepping, Little Turtle; these pieces are very sharp, and you don't want to step on one." The child drew his feet in closer to the log. "Your job will be to find the right shaft from the dogwood shoots in the bog. This arrow will have great accuracy."

Before the white man came with their guns, he was sought after among the many villages. His arrowheads brought many precious items to his lodge. The bloody King Philip's War had ended twenty years ago, resulting in many Wampanoag deaths. Big Hand still had nagging injuries from the battles. He walked with a noticeable limp from a rifle ball that had shattered his left foot. He had other scars as well and was blind in his left eye, not the result of a battle but the remnant of his body's fight with the pox.

Big Hand's village consisted of only four lodges now housing twelve people. Little Turtle was the youngest member. The number of deaths due to the 'rotting-face illness' was gradually killing the village. Last year ten members, including his mate, had died. Fall was approaching and there were signs that some would not make it through the winter. Big Hand had tried all he could to kill the disease. His all night and day vigils in the smoke house, self-flagellation, and jabbing himself with sharp sticks would not stem the death in his village. Why he had survived the illness was a mystery. The horrible scarring on his skin, including blindness in his left eye, were lasting lifelong effects. A handful of tribal members had survived, and like him, with lasting deformities. Little Turtle's mother, Red Sun, was still healthy, and so was his father, Moon Bird.

He had done all he could and hoped the great spirit would intervene on behalf of his village. To clear his mind, he would return to his flint napping. He was very good at this skill and was known as the Spiritual Arrowhead maker. The points he made always found their mark.

"It is a good one, Big Hand," said Moon Bird. He had carried the carcass of a young buck and laid it in front of the lodge he shared with Big Hand. "The hunts have been successful using that arrow. I managed to kill this rabbit from a great distance as well," he said, holding up the fat prize. "We can have it later today." He handed it to his mate, Red Sun, as she emerged from the lodge.

"Are you well, Red Sun?"

"There is an ache in my head that won't go away," she replied with a worried look. This was one of the first signs that the disease was lurking. Two days later, the spots began, and Moon Bird was also developing similar symptoms. A month later, Big Hand placed his only grandson next to his parents in the shallow grave near the bog. His family was gone. In an act of despair, he picked up the powerful bow that Moon Bird had used in his hunts and placed the precious arrow across its midpoint and looked at the giant fall moon.

He raised the bow and pulled the gut string back as far as he could and shot the arrow at the center of the blue orb. And with that, despite his painful limp and impaired vision, he left his doomed village. He would go east to the great ocean, away from the killer pox.

2

I t was a bright, blustery Saturday in May with a lingering winter chill. The Braves, Tim's Little League baseball team, was about to have a practice game. To Tim, baseball was just another thing to do. He had always played baseball with the other kids in his neighborhood, but organized baseball on a regular team was not in his makeup, but Tim's father, who loved the game, finally convinced him to go out for the Tipton Little League team. He was twelve, his last year of eligibility. Tim knew the fundamentals, basic rules, and strategies of the game. He knew he had a pretty strong throwing arm. He just didn't have the passion for the game his dad had. He loved riding his bike around the small town and exploring in the woods, and the sheer joy of running. He would challenge himself by running between the houses delivering his papers nd fantasize he was an Indian and run in the wooded areas down by the swamp, dodging tree limbs and jumping over logs. He and his friend Bobby LaChance were constantly dreaming up scenarios about the local Indian culture that they had learned in school. They were both in the sixth grade.

"Ouch, Tim," said his friend, quickly taking off his fielder's mitt and vigorously shaking his hand. "It's too cold for this." He was having a catch with Bobby.

"I know. My hands are still stinging from batting practice," said Tim.

Coach Catoia, who worked at the Oldsmobile dealership

that sponsored the team, had set up a preseason game against the Red Sox, another team from the league.

"Okay, guys, let's have it in," said the coach, leaning against the protective chain-link fencing outside the front of the concrete three-sided dugout. The twelve players trooped in, thankful to be out of the wind. Catoia announced the batting order. Tim was not in the starting lineup and would have to wait his turn to play, as would Bobby, and also Paul, the coach's son. The Braves were at bat first, and the first three batters struck out, not a good sign for the coach and his team.

It was now the Red Sox's turn at bat. The first batter hit a double to the left, and the next hit a single through the Braves' first baseman's legs. This would be an indicator. The Red Sox were a very strong team. They scored 5 runs before the Braves could get them out. The second and third innings were very similar; the Braves could not score, and the Red Sox added 3 more runs.

Before the fourth inning began, coach Catoia, while looking at his paperwork, announced, "Tim, you go to third; Bobby, you take right field; and, Paul, I want you to try pitching." They were finally getting a chance to play. Tim was a naturally athletic. He really didn't have one favorite sport. He just liked to be active and busy. The first thing Tim noticed when he took his place next to the third base bag was the wind; it was blowing hard, and it was cold. He could also hear a voice from the visitor's dugout. "Keep your eyes open, loser. You could be very busy." Tim looked over, which was his first mistake. The voice had achieved what he wanted and kept up a steady stream of chatter directed at Tim.

"Focus, Tim," he heard his father say from the four-tiered set of bleachers along the first baseline, which only made the situation worse when the voice heard Tim's dad. But he did focus.

Paul's first pitch was a ball, and so were the next eight. This drew the voice's attention away from Tim and brought Coach Catoia out of the dugout. He signaled for Bobby LaChance to come in and pitch. His friend proceeded to walk the next batter, but not until he threw a dozen pitches that were fouled off. The bases were full again. The next batter hit a ground ball to Tim. He ranged to his left, scooped up the ball, and threw it toward the catcher for the force out. The ball sailed over the catcher's head and hit the chain-link backstop as another run scored. Once more, Catoia came out and this time called for Tim to come in and pitch. Bobby would take his place at third base. After some warm-up pitches and a brief coaching tip from Catoia, "Just get the ball over the plate."

The batter was the voice, probably one of the twelve-year-old players, Tim's age. Using the wind-up his father had taught him, he threw his first pitch; a fastball. It went into the dirt in front of Larry Newman, the catcher, also a twelve-year-old. The ball bounced in the dirt and hit him in the chest protector. He picked up the ball and fired a fastball back to Tim with a look, sending a message. He was tired of this. Tim's glove hand felt like he had a handful of bees from the impact of the throw from his catcher. He looked at Larry and knew he better get the next pitch over the plate. And it was, right down the middle. The ball flew off the rangy kid's bat in an instant. Despite the wind blowing in, the ball went out and over the center field fence for a grand-slam home run.

"Nice pitch, loser," was the comment Tim heard as the kid was jogging down the third baseline about to step on home plate.

"That's enough, Zack," the Red Sox coach said to his player when he heard the comment. The game was out of hand. Coach Catoia signaled to the Red Sox coach to come over. They met at home plate briefly and shook hands. They decided to call it a day.

Coach Catoia had the team all gather in the dugout. "Look, we just need a little more practice. We'll get better." He had a few more things to say but knew it would be best to get out of the cold and head home. As the team was leaving the dugout, he pulled Bobby and Tim aside. "Bobby, you did a great job on your batters. They could have whiffed on any one of those balls fouled off. And, Tim, you did just what I asked you to do. That was a good pitch. Lowrey is one of the better hitters in the league."

Freeman was a smaller community and did not have Little League baseball. The Tipton league invited the boys from Freeman to join the league, which was good because of the expanded competition, but there was also the element of intra-town rivalry. Zack Lowrey was Bill Lowrey's son, the coach of the Red Sox. The majority of the players on the team lived in Freeman, and so did the Lowreys. He thought his son was doing what all good ball players did, try and get under your opponent's skin, but had to rein him in once in a while.

The schedule was set up so all eight teams played each other twice in the season, and the four teams with the best record would have a playoff to decide the league championship. Most games were on Tuesday or Thursday evenings during the week and on Saturday.

The school year ended the second week in June. The baseball season was sputtering along. The Braves were mired in last place at one win and three losses. Coach Catoia was still experimenting with players and positions. Every game would find Tim at a different spot on the field. He began to be part of the starting lineup when the coach realized how fast he was. He would use this asset to steal bases. The team's one win was due to Tim stealing four bases, including home plate. He would get an occasional hit, which helped.

It was now Monday morning, the beginning of summer vacation for some, and a new work week for others. Bobby LaChance's mother knew Harold Preston and his wife, Stella. They owned and operated Preston Farm and Vegetable Stand where Bobby would work occasionally. Tim had a good work ethic and was curious about what his friend was doing. The farm stand was the retail part of the business. All produce grown by the farm ended up at the stand along with other related items, such as homemade pies, preserves, and any other farm-related item. The stand, along with the farm, were well known in the area.

"Yeah, I get 25 cents an hour, and I do all kinds of stuff. I know when school is out they'll need help working the fields. Are you interested?"

The next thing Tim knew he had his first real job, working on a farm. He still had his paper route, but that didn't seem quite like a job.

"Did you make your lunch?" asked Doris, his mother.

"Yep, made it last night."

"Looks like this is going to be the first hot day of the summer, so make sure you drink lots of water and bring your hat," she reminded him as she was cleaning up the breakfast dishes. "You know the number of Mr. Lawrence's office?" She worked for an insurance agent in town, a short walk from their old Victorian home on Massasoit Street, the main street in town.

"I have it in my wallet, Mum. You always ask me that."

"I'm just making sure," she answered, concentrating on her task in the sink.

"Do you need a ride to the farm, Tim?" questioned his dad as he appeared in the kitchen. Frank Mathison was a guidance counselor at Freeman Regional High School.

"No, I'll take my bike. I told Bobby I'd meet him there."

"Okay, but you better get going. Didn't Mr. Preston say be there at eight sharp?"

"I know, see ya."

"Hey, give me a hug," said his mother.

"Mum, I have to go."

Drying her hands on a dishcloth, she walked over and hugged him. "Have a great day...farming?" She threw the dish towel over her shoulder and folded her arms, smiling at him.

Grabbing the paper lunch bag, his hat, and an old World War Two canteen full of water that he attached to his belt, he walked out the back door to get his bike from the one-car garage. Tim was the only son of Frank and Doris Mathison. It was the beginning of the summer of 1957; a summer to remember.

3

The farm was three miles away, an easy ride he had done many times. The smooth surface of Massasoit Street soon gave way to the gravel roads of farm country. He knew he was behind schedule and was pumping the bike pedals a little harder.

He had his head down when he hit the pothole. This jarred the paper bag which he was holding in his left hand and gripping the handle bar at the same time. The bag ripped and its contents fell on the packed gravel. He stood on the right pedal and came to a sliding stop and laid the bike down. He walked back to check on his lunch. Fortunately, the waxed paper that held the two peanut butter and jelly sandwiches stayed in place. The apple rolled into the weeds on the side of road, and the Oreo cookies just needed to be brushed off. He shoved the apple into his right pants pocket, put the two sandwiches down the front of his T-shirt, and ate the cookies as he continued his ride.

A few minutes later, he arrived at the farm with its two-story, hundred-year-old white house and red barn. He could see a group of people gathered around a flat farm wagon attached to a tractor. Two dogs began barking as Tim got off of his bike. The dogs trotted toward him, and he knew they were friendly by their dog body language; their tails were wagging and they showed a lot of interest in his T-shirt.

Bobby noticed Tim's arrival and yelled, "Come on, Tim," and waved him over.

"Put the bike over there, Tim," said the farmer, pointing to a spot near the barn. Tim recognized Bobby's bike and walked his over and leaned it against the barn and turned to join the group. There were two older men. He really couldn't judge older people's age, but both men were a lot older than his father.

"Hey, loser, do you have your lunch in your shirt?" It was Zack. The early part of the baseball season was not going well for the Braves. They had played the Red Sox, Zack's team, again the second week of the regular season and lost again. The score was a little closer, 9 to 3, and Zack was his usual obnoxious self, taunting from the dugout.

"Shut up, Zack. We're not playing baseball now, knock it off. The bag broke. It's the only way I could carry the sandwiches."

The outburst by Tim was the first reaction he had ever made toward Lowrey and was duly noted by Lowrey as they stared at each other. Tim was not a fighter by nature, and the reaction caused the hairs on his back to stand on end. Lowrey turned and took a step away from the farm wagon.

"Okay, guys, get on the wagon," said Harold Preston.

Tim walked toward the group, looked at Lowrey, and then looked away. Lowrey seemed satisfied with that reaction and turned to jump on the back end of the wagon. Tim walked to the other side where Bobby was standing, staring at his friend. Tim took his sandwiches out of his shirt and awkwardly climbed onto the wagon bed.

The Preston Farm was a fixture in the area, going back to the sixteen hundreds. At one time, it was a dairy farm. The large barn was now in disrepair, home to the green tractor, barn swallows, and pigeons. The farmer got on the metal seat and started the tractor. Smoke belched skyward from the rusted exhaust pipe. He put the tractor in gear with a loud clank, and they were on their way. Tim sat next to Bobby near the back of the wagon where a movable gate was in place. A wooden box used for collecting vegetables was next to Bobby. It was now used to hold lunches. Bobby reached in the box and took out a metal lunch box.

"Put your lunch in here, Tim."

"Thanks." He put the sandwiches and apple in the metal lunch box and then put it in the collecting box. Tim took off his canteen and put that in the box as well.

"That used to be my father's lunch box," said Bobby. His father had died in the Battle of the Imjin River in Korea. They bumped along the path leading to the distant field with the two mutts leading the way. The older men smoked and chatted, and Lowrey and the other boy talked quietly and on occasion would look back at Tim and Bobby, who tried to avoid eye contact. When they arrived at the field, Preston parked the tractor and wagon next to a stone wall under the shade of a stately old elm. They all jumped off.

"I don't know what's going on between you two, but we have work to do. So whatever it is, knock it off," said Harold, raising his voice slightly, and added, "You got it?"

Lowrey was the first to say, "Yep."

Preston looked at Tim. "You got it?"

"Yes, sir."

"Good, now let's get to work."

Tim jumped off the wagon and stood facing the field. He wasn't quite sure what an acre of land was, but in front of him were neat, straight green lines that stretched far into the distance. These lines seemed to overwhelm his sense of depth and space as he looked at the tree line at the far end of the field.

"Holy crap," he said quietly to himself.

Bobby sidled up to him and gave him a little poke in the ribs. "I should have warned you about Zack. He's still a jerk away from baseball. I just try to avoid him when he's around the farm." Bobby was a little shorter than Tim and quite skinny. Tim was starting to fill out, but Lowrey was an early bloomer and seemed older than his age.

"It's not as bad as you think, once you get going," said Bobby, getting back to the reason they were there. The job today was an essential and labor-intensive part of vegetable farming; thinning. There was no way around the techniques used to perform this task: bend at the waist to get close to the seedlings or crawl on your hands and knees.

This would be the first of two thinnings. The plants were now two inches tall. When the remaining plants were at four inches, there would be another thinning. The concept was to create more space between the plants for a larger carrot. In nature, it was called natural selection. In this case, the farmer and his helpers were Mother Nature and selected the ones that would ultimately find their way into someone's salad.

"Make sure you have at least an inch and a half space between them, no more," said Preston as he began his row.

Following the farmer's lead, Tim and Bobby began their rows.

"How do you know which ones to keep?" asked Tim as he stared at the hundreds of plants under him.

"Tim, inch and a half, about the length of your thumb. That's all you have to know."

Heeding the instructions from his friend, Tim began, slowly making hundreds of decisions about the fate of the young carrot seedlings. He was the slowest of the group of six workers. After a while, he tried crawling, but the ground was hot and uncomfortable. He alternated between standing and crawling, but in the end, it was all very hot and uncomfortable.

He eventually made it to the end of his row. Dirt mingled with sweat was now caked on his hands, arms, and pants, and to make things a little more uncomfortable, he had a hole in the left knee of his dungarees. Through the tear, he could see his knee was the color of the ground. His back ached and as very thirsty. He should have taken his canteen with him. He began a new row, focusing on his seedlings, and was making good progress, thinking only of water. His concentrating was interrupted with, "Inch and a half, loser." It was Zack, walking back from the wagon. "Wait till Preston sees this row, he's gonna be pissed," he said and kept walking.

Buoyed by his earlier response toward Lowrey, Tim said, "The name is Tim."

"Oh, sorry, loser… I mean Timmy." And he kept walking.

Tim looked up at Lowrey and then stood. Lowrey kept walking, stopped, and turned. "I'm just telling you," he said and continued back to the row he was working on.

He did not expect this would be part of his new job. He took a couple of deep breaths as his father had taught him and calmed himself down. He looked at his recent work. Maybe in his haste, the distance between the thinned seedlings was a little more than an inch and a half. He started to worry. If this was what real work was all about, he was in trouble. He finally finished the row and was not too far from the wagon when he heard a voice. "Bobby, you and Tim take a break, get a drink of water."

It was Harold Preston. He had been at this a long time and realized he could not push the kids too hard, especially if he wanted to keep them for the summer. He had already decided it would be an early lunch, and then they'd quit at one o'clock. They should have a good portion of the field done and could pick up where they left off tomorrow.

Tim walked to the farm wagon joined by Bobby, who had been in the middle of his third row. "Man, am I thirsty. I should have taken my canteen with me."

Bobby had a thermos full of iced lemonade his mother had prepared in the cover of the old lunch box. When they looked into the wooden box, Bobby noticed the latch to the lunch box was undone.

"What the heck?" He picked up the metal container and opened it. "Tim, one of your sandwiches is gone." He pulled out the thermos that had been in the cover and realized it was very light.

"That bastard."

This was huge. Bobby never swore. Tim looked at his friend and picked up his canteen. It, too, was surprisingly light. He also noticed his apple was missing. He stood up in the wagon looking out in the field. Looking up from his kneeling position was Lowrey, waving and smiling.

He and his cousin Warren had worked for the Prestons

for the last two summers. They were the same age. Lowrey was tall and rangy. Warren was slight and shorter with a bad complexion. Harol was aware of the shenanigans of the cousins but also knew they were hard and dependable workers.

Tim and Bobby returned to the rows they were working on, not quite sure what to do. They were worldly enough to know what a bully was. They weren't in their neighborhood or at school; they were working. They didn't want to go to Harold Preston. That could make matters worse

4

Tim fell into a routine working at the farm and looked forward to each day. He did as Bobby had done, as far as Lowrey and Warren were concerned. He avoided them when possible, and Lowrey was content to let things go in that direction as well. On Friday of the first week, when they returned to the farmhouse, Stella Preston, Harold's wife, was waiting for them and handed each a three-by-five-inch manila envelope with their name printed neatly on the flap. Inside was seven dollars and fifty cents. It was their wages for the week. Tim made it a point to ride by the insurance company office to show his mother.

The team won another game and then another. Work on the farm was pretty much crawling in the dirt. If they weren't thinning, they were weeding. He also was getting to know the two older men, Pauly and Red. What made the repetitive work pleasurable was talking or listening to them. Tim did not ask how old they were, but Pauly had said he and Red had both fought in World War One. They both lived together in a boarding house in Tipton and would walk to the farm early every day. During the winter, Henry would keep them busy doing things around the farm stand. At Christmas, they cut and sold Christmas trees. Red was especially adept at making Christmas wreaths and flint napping, making arrowheads. Red was Native American.

"Red and me didn't know each other then, but we were in

France at the same time in 1917. I was assigned to a supply unit behind the lines, but Red was in the front lines as a sniper. He doesn't talk about those times. He would rather smoke his cigarettes and read about the Boston Braves. We didn't meet till ten years ago."

This was a typical conversation while working together, and Tim was feeling more and more comfortable with the two old men. Two weeks after working at the farm, on a Sunday afternoon, he rode his bike over to the farm stand to see Bobby and get a Coke.

In the dusty wood-framed stand there was a Coke machine. Henry kept the temperature in the machine as cold as possible. As long as you returned the six-ounce bottle, you could by a Coke for a nickel. The more he worked at the farm, the more he liked it, and the Cokes tasted so good at the end of the day. Bobby was tending to a customer, and Tim was drinking his Coke when he noticed Red in the back room sitting and working at something.

"Hi, Red."

Red looked up waved and gestured that he come over. "Have a seat, Tim." He pointed to a spot on the bench next to him. Before Tim could ask, Red said, "This is called flint napping. I'm making an arrowhead."

"Oh, how'd you learn to do that?"

"My father taught me, and his father him."

He paused to hold the gray stone up to examine it and continued. "If I find a good enough piece if flint, that's what this is, I'll try to make an arrow or spearhead. People like to buy them here at the stand." He put the stone back on his knee and continued lightly hitting its edges. "I have some I've made in a case out front, and we also have some we've found in the fields from the Wampanoag, my ancestors. They used to live in the area. We keep those in a separate glass-covered case. They're not for sale."

Red proceeded to add more information about the Native Americans that once lived in Tipton and Freeman. "Do you know that Wampanoag means first light?" He was feeling comfortable with Tim's attention and added other personal pieces of information. He believed his nickname was a name used in his family in the past, and the carrot field was a special place on the farm. "I think there is something about that spot that I'm drawn too. I keep telling Pauly that, and he looks at me funny and says stuff like, 'That's old Indian hocus pocus,' but I can feel it when we are working there."

Tim was fascinated as Red kept working and talking. "How are the Braves doing?" asked the old man.

"Well we need to win a couple more games to make the playoffs. We've really improved though." He had finished his Coke, and Bobby was busy helping Stella with another customer looking through the canned preserves.

"Red, can I buy you a Coke?"

The napping stopped as Red looked at him. This simple gesture was the bond. "Why, that would be very nice of you Tim, thanks." Tim stayed for an hour.

On another occasion when he and Bobby were talking to Red, they discovered he had grown up on the south shore of Massachusetts near a town called Mashpee in a small Indian community. His parents worked on the local farms and crewed on some of the fishing boats. School and education came up, and they were surprised to hear that he went to a boarding school in Pennsylvania called the Carlisle Indian School.

"But you said you lived in Massachusetts?" said Tim.

"Yes, when I was little." And he explained, "The government wanted to change all Indians, so I was sent away so the government could take the Indian out of me." He talked about how strict the school was, but one of the good things was he got to play baseball on a team. "We were pretty good. We played some local white kids' schools and always beat them. They weren't too happy." Smiling, he paused. "Then everything changed. War broke out in France while I was at the school, and they let us quit and join the Army." And he added, "This was a good deal."

"Why?" asked Tim.

"If you joined the Army, you would become a citizen."

"Really?" questioned Bobby.

"I know to you it seems like a hundred years ago, but back when I was your age, many of my people weren't considered citizens. We were just Indians. So after the war, I was a free citizen. I came back to Massachusetts. I met my wife when we were both working in the shoe factories in Fall River. She was a Mi'kmaq Indian from Maine. We hated the work and decided to travel out west. We were invited to live on a Comanche Indian reservation."

They learned Red and his wife had two boys. "When they were young, my wife became ill. She died in 1935. I tried to raise my boys, but the government came in and made them go to an Indian school. It was their only way to become citizens. They are grown now and live in Oklahoma City. One is a school teacher and the other works for the government." He also told them that during the Second World War, they were code talkers.

"What's a code talker?" asked Bobby.

Red was very proud of his sons' involvement in helping the United States win the war in the Pacific. "The Indian language has never been written down. In our case, the language was Comanche. If a secret message had to be sent, it was sent using Comanche words. We had code talkers in World War One." He paused to think about what he was going to say next. "I wish I could have had that job, but because I was an Indian, I was a hunter and should be a sniper."

Bobby looked at Red and interrupted him before he could continue. "I heard my uncles tell Mom that's how my dad was killed... by a sniper."

Red had a pained look as he took in what he had just heard and looked away. "I'm sorry to hear that Bobby." There was now an uncomfortable moment, and then he said, "War is a terrible thing," and reached over to tap Bobby on his shoulder. Despite his youth, Bobby recognized he had sent the conversation into an awkward stall, and Red stopped talking for a long moment. There were enough of these sad conversations in his house;

maybe this was not the place for another one.

"Red, I'm sorry, you were talking about your sons and stuff."

This was another reason to like these two young men, and he smiled at Bobby. "Anyway, my boys are married and have children. The Carlisle Indian School didn't quite change me. The old ways were and still are part of my spirit. After the war ended in 1945, with their understanding, I told them I had to wander and left them. They knew my belief in the Indian ways was strong. I was drawn back to Massachusetts and this farm."

They were interrupted with, "Pauly, you and Red take the boys over to the west cornfield. I have to spend the day at the farm stand."

"Okay," replied Pauly to Harold's order.

Tim and Bobby were still processing what they had just heard from Red that day as the wagon made its slow trek to the far-off field. Tim marveled at the man's story and wanted to know more.

5

Weeding had become second nature to the group. They all tended to work at the same pace. Tim decided he was actually more comfortable crawling with the plants between his knees.

The tension was back among the boys on this day due to the game they had against the Red Sox the previous evening. The Braves lost once again. Zack hit two home runs; one was against Bobby. The final score was six to four. Tim had two hits and stole two bases.

Tim was focusing on the task at hand when out of the blue, while bent at the waist pulling weeds, Zack said, "Let's face it, you guys are just plain losers." And he added, "Next time, Bobby, I'd like that pitch a little higher, that one I hit off of you barely cleared the fence."

"F...k you, Zack!" was all that could be heard. Work stopped as all eyes focused on Bobby. Everyone stood except Warren. Zack started walking across the rows. Bobby stood his ground staring at him as he approached.

After the initial shock of his friend's outburst, Tim's protective instincts kicked in, and he quickly stepped over three rows of baby corn plants and stood between Zack and Bobby.

"What are you, his big protector now?"

"Hey, knock it off, you two," yelled Pauly.

Tim stared at Lowrey, once again feeling the hairs on his back raise. Bobby was standing next to Tim now. The stand-off continued until another voice was heard; it was Red. Looking at the three boys, he said, "Everyone back to work. We told Harold we would have this done today, and it will be done."

They finished the field in an atmosphere thick with silence. The only conversations were short-clipped sentences between Pauly and Red. When they were done, Pauly got on the tractor and started it up. Red climbed on the flat wagon bed and sat facing the front talking to Pauly. The four boys were all sitting on the back edge of the platform with their legs dangling. Nothing was said as they reached the back of the farm stand.

When the wagon stopped, they all jumped off. Suddenly, Warren turned and shoved Bobby from behind, sending him sprawling. And just as suddenly, Zack saw an opening and pounced on Tim's back. Bobby ran over, reached around Lowrey's waist, and tried to pull him off. That's when Warren sucker punched Bobby on the side of his face, knocking him down into the thick grass. Lowrey was now sitting on Tim's back and pushing his shoulders down. Tim tried to push up, but there was too much weight. Lowrey then felt two strong hands reach under his arms, pulling him up.

It was Red. "Okay, that's enough."

This caused everything to stop. Lowrey was smiling. He stood up, trying to shake away from Red's hold, but Red would have none of it and hung on to the teenager, pulling him in close.

"Let go, you crazy Indian! What do you think you're doing?" Zack shouted as Red released him from his grip. He spun around and stared at the old man.

"Okay, Zack, that's enough. It's time to go home and call it a day," said Pauly, coming up behind his friend Red.

Red kept staring at Lowrey and pointed his gnarled index finger at the boy. "You be careful," he said and turned to walk away.

"Ah, go back to the reservation," responded Lowrey. Red turned and took a step toward him and pointed once again without saying a word.

"What are you going to do, scalp me?" snarled Zack, keeping

the smirk on his face.

"That's enough, Zack," said Pauly. "You and Warren get going."

"I don't have to go anywhere," responded the now defiant Lowrey.

Warren hadn't moved after hitting Bobby, who was now standing with a red welt on the side of his face. He was crying. Warren was smiling. Tim stood up. He wasn't sure what to do as Bobby came up beside him. Just then, Harold came out of the back of the farm stand and looked around. "Everything okay back here?"

"Ya," said Pauly. "We're done for the day. The boys are going home." He looked at Lowrey with menace.

Pauly told Preston what happened, and the next day, there was a meeting in the middle of the west cornfield. Harold had the boys sit and explained in an expletive laden rant that, that was it. Keep what happened in baseball on the baseball field. Any more arguing or fighting would be money out of their pay envelopes. He made them all shake hands. Preston considered the matter closed, and for the most part, it was. But this was entirely against Lowrey's nature, and after a few days, he would refer to Tim as Timmy whenever he had to talk to him. The day after the meeting, Warren asked Bobby how his face was. "I'm really sorry about that," he said and turned to Zack with raised eyebrows and a smile.

The baseball season was approaching its conclusion, and the Red Sox were solidly in first place with only one loss. Zack and his father had gone on a fishing trip and missed that game. The incident behind the farm stand was not forgotten, but Harold's talk set the tone; they were there to work. The carrot greens were four inches tall now and ready for their second thinning. The atmosphere around work details became more relaxed.

"Okay, guys, same as the first time, except about two inches, and if you get hungry, you can eat the ones you take out and have a snack," said Pauly, grinning with his brown-stained gapped teeth.

Tim started on the same row he had worked the first day and was amazed at how much the carrots had grown. His thinning had worked, and the plants were filling in the spaces. He was crawling along nearing where the wagon and tractor were parked under the elm when he knelt on a rock, a common occurrence. He stood and reached down. It wasn't an ordinary stone. It was flat with a triangular shape. He had found an arrowhead. He turned it over in his hand and rubbed it against his pants. It was black, about an inch long, and a little more than an inch wide.

He walked over to the wagon to get a drink from his canteen, noting that it still had plenty of water. He unscrewed the top and took a swig. He poured some water into his hand holding the arrowhead. Green began to appear among the cut marks. When he polished it with his T-shirt, it reflected tiny bright spots at the crest of each mark. He looked around and spotted Bobby.

"Bobby," he shouted, waving him over. And then he shouted, "Red," waving him over.

Bobby knew by Tim's voice that this was important, careful not to step on any carrots he stood and began running, Red was a ways away and would not have stopped what he was doing, especially if a kid was calling him, but Tim was different. He liked Tim. Pauly looked up briefly but kept working. Zack and Warren had also stopped and were about to go investigate when they heard, "I don't believe he called you guys."

"But…" said Zack.

"Keep doing what you're doing, it's none of your business." Pauly was well aware of the bullying that was still going on and wanted to remind them that he was in charge and not Zack Lowrey.

"Bobby, check this out." As his friend approached, he held the prize in his right hand. "It's an arrowhead." And he handed it to his friend.

"Man, are you lucky or what?" said Bobby, just as excited as he was.

"What's going on, guys?" said Red as he approached the two boys.

"Look what Tim found." Bobby held out the artifact.

"Or it found me," Tim said, checking the spot of blood where it had pierced through his worn dungarees. Red looked at the stone and then at Tim.

"Oh my," Red said and carefully took it from Bobby's hand. "I haven't seen one of these for a long time." He turned it over in his hand a few more times.

"Tim, this is very special. It is made from a stone called dupi, and whoever made it was very good. My father would tell me about the different stones that were used. He wore a piece of rawhide around his neck with an arrowhead just like this in a pouch, only this one has more depth to it. See how the green shines through the black? He said that was the light of day replacing the dark of night." And he paused again, this time a little longer, looking up at the sky. "My father gave that rawhide necklace to me when I went to war. It served me well in many ways, but war changed me. I gave it back to him when I came home, and when he passed over to the other side, he took the arrowhead with him." He carefully placed the stone in Tim's hand and at the same time folded Tim's fingers over it and looked at him intently.

"Hey, Red, we've got work to do," yelled Pauly.

"Yeah, let me grab a drink of water," he answered and walked past Tim, tapping him on his shoulder.

Tim tore a piece of his lunch bag and wrapped the prize in it and put it deep in his dungaree pocket. He would occasionally check to make sure it was still there.

"Pauly says that's just more of Red's Indian hocus pokes," said Lowrey when he found out what the interruption was. I see those things all the time. It's no big deal, Timmy."

But to Tim it was. At the end of the day when they were at the farm stand he showed the arrowhead to Stella Preston, who considered herself the local expert on arrowheads. The Preston farmers' wives before her had started the arrowhead collection and over the years had placed them in a glass-topped wooden box with their dates of discovery. "Tim, this is a special one, and it's yours to keep. But if you'd like to add it to the collection, it would look good in the glass case."

"That's what Red said. He called the stone dupi."

"He's right," answered Stella. "That's the Indian name, and it was prized by the Wampanoag because the stone it was made from is rare around Massachusetts. The English name, or I guess the common name for the stone is obsidian. It may have been part of a trade and, by the looks of it, was carefully made." She turned it over in her gloved hand. "If you want, we can put it in the box for safekeeping, but like I said, it is yours to do what you want with. But be careful. You don't want to lose it," she warned and thought some more. "What else did Red say about it?"

"He said what you said, except for the name of the rock it came from."

"Oh," Stella said, and added, "I'm sure you'd like to show this to your parents." She thought a moment. "Tell you what, let me fix it up a little before you take it home." Tim had no problem with that. The next day, Friday, when Stella was handing out the pay envelopes, Tim noticed his had more than the bills and coins in it. Squeezing the edges, he looked inside and noticed a thin rawhide strip. He pulled it out. There was a small leather pouch attached. Tim opened the pouch and pulled out the now glistening arrowhead.

"Red suggested the necklace," said Stella.

Tim wore his new prize while riding his bike home. When he got there, no one was home. His newspaper bundle was on the front porch. He sat and quickly sorted them and began his delivery. When he was through, not knowing why, he had an urge to run. Despite working in the fields that morning, he had a quick drink of water and ran the mile through the woods to the junior high school and the baseball field. When he got there, he sat in the third base dugout staring at the field. He reached up and could feel the pouch inside his wet T-shirt. Tomorrow was

Saturday, and the Braves had a game.

6

In between innings during a baseball game, the pitcher is allowed eight warm-up pitches, and while this was happening, the infielders are warmed up by the first baseman. Bobby was playing first and throwing ground balls to his other infielders and they would throw them back to him. He noticed something different about Tim's throws from third base. They were perfect. Usually he had to work to catch them, and some would go over his head. He didn't say anything; he just thought it was interesting.

The Braves had two more regular season games to play. Paul Catoia was pitching this game and was struggling to get the ball over the plate. When he did, it usually meant a hit. The first and second innings were scoreless. When play resumed in the third, he walked the first batter. The next hit a line drive directly at Tim. The runner on first base had anticipated a hit and started running. Bobby yelled, "first," meaning throw it to him. He had his glove stretched out and his right foot reaching back touching the base. He didn't have to move the glove as the ball smacked into the pocket for a double play. Bobby then threw the ball back to Tim for the ritual infield throw-around after a first or second out when the bases are empty. Paul got the next batter to hit a ground ball to Tim, and he repeated what he had just done to end the inning. When they returned to the dugout, Coach Catoia and the rest of the team surrounded the two friends, slapping them on the back congratulating them, all knowing that what they had just witnessed was what baseball was all about when done right. They won the game handily, scoring eight runs and shutting out the other team. After the game, the coach reminded them that if they won the next game on Thursday, they would make the playoffs.

In a mistake-filled sloppy game, they won 11 to 10. An unexpected loss by the team above them in the standings had the Braves ending the regular season in third place, which meant they would play the second-place team in the playoffs. The Braves had just finished practice the next day when Coach Catoia had them all meet in the first-base dugout.

"Guys, remember when we sat here after our first practice game?"

"All I remember is how cold it was," said his son Paul, which was followed by head nods and comments agreeing with him.

"Well I remember what a pain in the ass Zack Lowrey was," said Larry Newman who was the catcher that day. Catoia looked at the twelve-year-old and paused as the whole dugout exploded in laughter.

"Yep, I agree, Larry," said the smiling coach. He paused and raised his hand, looking for attention once more. "We've come a long way since then and have jelled as a team. We have two more games." And he paused again. "Yes, we will win the next game, RIGHT!"

The team exploded with, RIGHT! and a cheer.

On Saturday afternoon, on a perfect summer day in central Massachusetts, the Braves would play in the first round of the playoffs. Lowrey's Red Sox would play the second.

Paul Catoia was the starting pitcher for the game and was not doing well. The team was losing two to four after three innings, and the bases were full with no outs. The infielders were gathered at the mound. "I don't know, Dad. I just can't get the ball over the plate," explained Paul to his father.

"Bobby, are you ready?"

"Coach, let's give Tim a shot," said Bobby.

Tim was playing center field for this game and had been for

the others. His speed on the base paths was an asset. Running down a fly ball in the outfield was also a part of the team's success. The coach had also noted his throws lately were very accurate. "Paul, take Tim's spot in center," he said and waved to Tim.

Tim jogged in. "Okay, Tim, just get the ball over the plate," and handed him the ball.

"Larry, show me where you want the ball."

"You got it, Tim," Larry assured him as he turned to go to his position behind home plate.

When Larry was ready, he held the catcher's mitt directly over the plate, squarely in front of him. Tim went into his wind-up. The catcher's mitt never moved as the ball hit the pocket with a loud 'smack.' Tim and Larry kept that strategy, and the batter was out in three pitches; he never swung. Tim would throw six more pitches to the next two batters. They struck out as well. This seemed to inspire the team. In the next inning, they scored three runs and gained the lead. Catoia was thinking he had found the winning formula when, in the bottom of the next inning, the first batter, the team's leading hitter, hit Tim's first pitch over the centerfield fence, and the next batter, also a strong hitter, hit a line drive directly at Tim's head. Always a sure fielder, he caught it. Catoia called a time-out and jogged to the mound.

"You okay, Tim?"

"Ya, why?"

Larry joined them on the mound. "That kid was lucky hitting that one out," said the catcher, and added, "Tim's doing great. I don't have to move the mitt an inch. Every pitch is right there." He pointed at the pocket of the mitt.

"Yes, I've noticed," said Catoia, just as the other team's coach erupted with, "Hey, are we gonna talk or play ball?!" Catoia looked over as the umpire was coming to the mound. "Listen, ya gotta move the target around, Larry. The next hitter is pretty good. I know I said just get it over the plate, but maybe not down the middle every time."

"HEY, let's go!" yelled the other coach.

Larry went back behind the plate. Being a catcher, his idea of the umpire's strike zone was important. When he squatted down this time, he held the mitt high in the strike zone. The batter swung and missed. The next pitch had the mitt low in the zone. Tim hit the target, another swing and miss. The next target was inside for a called strike and the second out. Using the new strategy, the next batter never swung on three pitches, each placed in a different part of the zone. Once again, the team was buoyed by Tim's success and put five runs together for a commanding lead and a win. They were in the championship game. They stayed and watched the next game. The Red Sox won easily as Zack connected for another home run and two doubles. He also pitched. The Braves and the Red Sox would play each other for the championship next Tuesday.

On Monday, Tim waited for Bobby to come by his house, and they would both ride their bikes to the farm stand. Tim couldn't wait to tell Red about the game.

When they got there, they propped their bikes up against the back wall next to the back entrance and walked in. Pauly was having a coffee and smoking his ever-present cigarette.

"Hi, Pauly," said Bobby. The old man looked up and then back at the cigarette, flicking an ash on the dirt floor.

"He's gone, boys."

"What, who?" said Tim in confusion.

Pauly looked up again as Stella and Henry Preston walked in from the front of the building.

"Did Pauly tell you?" asked Stella. Both boys looked at each other. "Red came by the farmhouse Saturday to tell us he was leaving. We gave him a ride to the Greyhound bus station in Framingham yesterday."

"Why?" asked Tim.

"He said it was time to go. He apologized for leaving so suddenly, but he said he needed to see his sons and their families in Oklahoma. He wanted you to have any of the arrowheads he made." Tim unconsciously reached up and felt the stone in the pouch under his T-shirt.

All Tim could say was, "Oh."

"So it looks like we'll be short-handed, unless," said Harold and looked at the two boys.

After a few moments, "Hey is anybody here?" was heard from the front of the stand. It was Zack.

Preston turned. "Back here, Zack." When they walked into the back, Warren appeared first and noted the atmosphere.

"What's going on?"

"Red won't be working for us anymore. He's gone back to Oklahoma."

"Oh," Warren replied, not knowing what else to say.

"Back to the reservation?" added Lowrey.

"He has two sons that have families in Oklahoma City, he told us, and hasn't seen them for quite some time. I don't know, but I think that arrowhead," he pointed at the bulge in Tim's shirt, "may have had something to do with his decision. Red said, 'That was a good find by Tim.'"

"Is that worth a lot of money?" asked Warren.

"We don't know," said Harod. "I asked him that, and he said no. You could sell it and make a few dollars, but it's worth more."

"You see, Red still believed in the old ways. When he came to our front door looking for work, he said he was drawn to our farm, and more than once, he told me there was something special about that field where we planted the carrots this year," explained Stella.

"I still think it's all Indian hocus pocus," interrupted Pauly. "But, I'm gonna miss him. He was a great friend." And he dropped his cigarette on the ground and stepped on it. "Are you boys ready? We've got some work to do," he said, looking at Harold.

The anticipation of telling Red about the game faded quickly and was replaced with annoyance when Lowrey said, "I still think he went back to the reservation," and started chirping about taking candy from a baby on Tuesday's championship game.

But before it got out of hand, Preston said, "Okay, let's get to work. Pauly, you and Zack go out to the carrot field and do some picking. We should have some ready to harvest by now. Warren, you and Bobby and Tim stay here and help Stella."

7

They had just stopped under the elm and were walking between the rows of carrots looking for the right size for picking when Paully asked "Have you ever heard of sportsmanship?

"Yeah, that's for losers. The idea is to win. I hate losing."

"We'll let me tell you something about winning and losing." He stopped to light a cigarette.

"Come on, Pauly, what do you know about anything?"

Pauly looked at Zack, shook out the match, inhaled the smoke, and blew it up toward the clouds and said, "You are a cocky little shit, ain't you?"and continued," Is Bill Lowrey your dad?"

Zack looked at him. "Yes, he is."

"Have you ever heard of the Golden Gloves?"

"No, not really. Where are we going with this, Pauly?"

"If you'll stop interrupting me, I'll tell you," he said and paused to look Zack in the eyes.

"Yeah, okay, I'm listening."

"Your dad used to be a fighter, an amateur fighter up in Lowell when he was a little older than you. I'd go watch the matches, sit right there at ringside. There were some good fighters around then. He used to fight in the welterweight class and was making his way through his division with a pretty good record with seven or eight wins and no losses. You didn't know this about your dad?"

"No, he never told me this."

"Hmm, I wonder why."

"So why are you telling me this?"

"Well, boxing is a different kinda sport. I did a little when I was kid and some in the Army, so I know a little about it, and one thing I learned was you can't hide in the ring. Well, like I said, your dad had a good-looking record back then, but we all knew he was ducking this one guy. When he was supposed to fight him, he would have an excuse not to." He bent down to pull out two good-sized carrots, and Zack did the same.

"You see, he was never tested. He was constantly being warned about low blows." He looked at Zack. "You know what that is, don't you?" Zack nodded. "And when he would win, he'd strut around the ring, not showing respect for his opponent." Zack was quiet now, listening to him as they continued to slowly work down the row. Pauly continued, "He was never hit really hard, and this guy that he was avoiding hit very hard. His name was Randel Shaman and was a Wampanoag Indian."

"Like Red."

"Yes, like Red. His ancestors lived around here as well." He stopped to gather his thoughts while he pulled out a few more carrots.

"So this is where the sportsmanship I asked you about comes in. The fight was finally scheduled to take place in a YMCA in Framingham. There was a good crowd. The rules were three two-minute rounds. Your dad's fight was scheduled to go next to last. There were ten fights scheduled." They had worked their way back to the flatbed wagon and had two full boxes of carrots. While leaning against the wagon facing Zack, Pauly continued.

"When the fight started, your dad stayed away from Randel, just circling. The crowd started to boo, and I heard some people say things like 'kill the Indian' and 'don't be a chicken.'

Randel was moving in, trying to box, but your dad kept backing away. With ten seconds left in the round, he swung at the Indian, which Randel blocked and counter-punched; and missed, a complete whiff." Pauly paused to emphasize the next point. "Your father went down as if he had been hit with this box of carrots." He pointed at the nearby box on the wagon. "The bell went off to end the round. People were booing. They knew what was going on."

"Then what happened?" asked Zack.

"Well the bell sounded to begin the second round. Your dad started doing the same thing, but Shaman cut the ring off and got close to your dad, not letting him move from side to side. He had your father in a corner, and your dad had his gloves up in front of his face for protection. We all expected Randel to start pounding on him, but he did a strange thing. He put his gloves down and started talking to your dad quietly for maybe ten seconds. He then put his gloves out in front of him, like boxers do before and after a bout, and backed away." Pauly stopped and said, "You'll have to ask your dad what he said to him and what happened after."

"That's it?!"

"Yep, now let's get these carrots back to the stand."

The game drew a good crowd. The small set of bleacher seats along the first-base line was full, and there were many parents and friends standing along the four-foot chain-link fence that encircled the field. Some parents elected to stay in their cars and watch. Because the Red Sox had the best record, they were the home team. They would have the last at-bat. Tim would be the starting pitcher, and Larry was behind home plate. Bobby was at third base.

"PLAY BALL," yelled the umpire.

The pitcher-catcher communication was working beautifully between Tim and Larry. Tim was hitting the targets Larry was putting up. But, this was baseball. Larry's idea of the strike zone and the umpire's interpretation were two different things, and a few comments by Larry directed at the umpire about what a ball and strike was began to grate on the veteran umpire.

In the meantime, Zack Lowrey was showing his stuff. He was good, but with one out in the third-inning game, Bobby got to him with a stinging double between the right and center fielders. Tim was up next. The first pitch was high and close to the visor of his hat. This elicited many oohs from the crowd. The next pitch was low and away; ball three was similar to the first pitch. Lowrey had to throw the next pitch over the plate. Tim made solid contact. He had never hit a ball that far... foul. The batter and the pitcher both could hear the ball hit the roof of a distant car, as kids ran to retrieve the wayward ball.

With a new ball, the next pitch by Lowrey was right down the middle, and Tim, once again, hit it solidly right at the first baseman, who stepped on the bag and tagged Bobby, who had taken a lead; a double play.

Meanwhile, frustration was setting in with Larry. With one out in the beginning of the next inning, Tim walked his first batter. On ball four, Larry Newman turned to the umpire and said, "You have got to be kidding me, are you blind?" With that, the umpire called a time-out and walked to the Braves' dugout. With his mask in hand, he gestured for Catoia to come out and meet him.

"Coach, I just want you to know, one more comment by your catcher and I'm throwing him out of the game."

"Got it, thanks, Tom." Tom and Coach Catoia both worked at the same car dealership.

The umpire went back behind home plate and slowly began to sweep off the plate. As play continued, the next batter struck out, but the runner stole second when Larry misjudged a low ball and let it get by him. There was no further damage in the inning when Bobby caught a pop-up near the third base dugout, despite the taunting and yelling of the Red Sox players, led by Zack.

Zack was still on the mound for the Red Sox. He, too, was getting frustrated with the umpire's wandering strike zone and walked the first two batters. Larry was the next batter and struck out on a called third strike. He turned and looked at the umpire. "LARRY," he heard from the dugout. The umpire had his mask off and was ready. "GET OVER HERE NOW!" was the next command from Catoia. This brought Larry's temper down a notch, and he responded by running back to the dugout. The umpire swept home plate and yelled for the next batter. Lowrey struck him out on 5 pitches. Tim was up next.

The first pitch was in the dirt in front of the plate. The catcher made a nice stop. The next one was inside and nearly hit him. Bill Lowrey called time and came out to check on his son.

"Are you okay?"

"I'm okay, Dad. I can get this loser. I've been getting him all season."

"Okay," said his father as he raised his eyebrows looking at his son.

And then it all unraveled. As Zack was making his wind-up and was about to release the ball, Tim turned his body toward Lowrey with the bat out in front horizontally. He bunted the ball.

The ball trickled down the first-base line. The catcher ran the ball down and was about to pick up the ball when he was knocked over by Lowrey, who picked it up and threw wildly in the direction of first base, hitting Tim in the back as he was running to the base. The ball bounced off of Tim's shoulder and rolled into foul territory, coming to rest against the chain-link fence in front of the bleacher seats.

Catoia and the entire dugout were yelling at the base runners to go. The Red Sox right fielder, who was backing up the play, ran to the fence, picked up the ball, and threw across the baseball diamond to third base. The ball was too high. The first runner stepped on third and kept running home, and so did the runner behind him. Tim was rounding second and hoping to make it to third. The Red Sox shortstop was covering third, anticipating Tim would be trying to reach third base. The third baseman had retrieved the ball from where it had stopped against the fence and threw to his teammate. Tim slid on his stomach, touching the base before he was tagged.

"SAFE," yelled the umpire.

Tim stood on the base brushing the dirt from his uniform as the umpire checked the ball, declaring it playable, and tossed it to Lowrey. Zack stood and stared at Tim, and Tim stared back with his hands on his hips.

The next Brave's batter Zack had struck out every time he faced him this season. Meanwhile, Bill Lowrey was thinking this was a crucial point in the game. If he went out to the mound again, he knew he had to replace Zack with another player; it was the rule. He decided to let things play out, crossed his arms, and sat back on the bench.

Zack confidently went into a full windup. With a runner on third base and two outs, his focus was on the batter, and as he had done in the past, would strike him out on three pitches. The first pitch was called a strike.

Tim's decision to bunt had changed things. Any troublesome situations this summer were the result of Lowrey being the intimidator. Tim decided at that moment that he now was in charge and had done that with his bunt and aggressive base running. He would use his speed again. His teammate at bat was a left-handed hitter and was standing in the first-base side batter's box, opening up an opportunity.

Tim's plan was to beat the pitch to the plate and steal home.

Lowrey focused on the batter, not paying attention to Tim. He started his windup and lifted his leg to throw, but in his peripheral vision, he saw Tim halfway down the third baseline. It was too late. By the time Zack's arm and hands were about to release the ball, Tim was starting his slide.

"SAFE," yelled the just as surprised umpire. Tim got up quickly and ran to the dugout as he was mobbed by his teammates. Bill Lowrey looked at his son.

"Forget it, Zack, just throw strikes," he said and clapped his hands to get his son and his team back on focus. Lowrey did strike out the batter on the next two pitches.

This was it, the bottom of the seventh inning, the last inning and the Lowrey's Red Sox were up last. The score was three to nothing in favor of the Braves. Catoia knew his catcher had a temper and decided to put him at third base and put dependable Bobby LaChance at catcher. He did not want to lose Larry because of his short fuse. They just needed three outs and the championship was theirs. When Tim got to the mound his adrenaline was still pumping, his focus was not as sharp and was missing his targets. Coach Catoia tried his best to calm everyone down.

But things were starting badly. The umpire's strike zone was once again moving. The result was a first batter walk, but the next batter struck out on pitches Bobby thought were balls, which was good at that moment, but he, too, was confused by the umpire's strike zone, so he just put the glove target in areas that he thought would result in strikes; which produced another walk. There were now two men on base. The next batter to face Tim hit a low pitch down the third baseline that took a hop and went by Larry Newman. The left fielder tracked down the ball and ran it into the infield, not risking a bad throw or missed catch. The bases were loaded. Larry, out of frustration, began to pick up stones from the dirt in front of him and tossing them aside. He picked up one item, but instead of throwing it aside, put it in the back pocket of his uniform and quickly focused back on the game. The next batter in the Red Sox lineup was looking for a walk. Not a bad strategy, considering the unpredictable strike zone. The umpire must have sensed this and called anything close a strike. Tim hit Bobby's targets easily for a strike out; two outs, one more to go.

Zack was up next.

Bobby gave Tim a low target and got a strike call. Lowrey turned and looked at the umpire who calmly registered the strike on his hand-held counter. The next pitch was also a low target, the same pitch, but the ump chose to call it a ball and clicked that one in.

Bobby changed the target to down the middle. Lowrey

fouled it off. The target was now inside and low, a ball. Bobby then gave Tim an outside target, another ball. The count was full, three balls and two strikes. Lowrey stepped out of the batter's box and asked for time and proceeded to take a couple of practice swings and looked at Bobby.

This simple gesture made Bobby think of Zack's comment when he hit a homer off of Bobby early in the season. Bobby called timeout, and looked over at Coach Catoia, who was about to come out of the dugout, but the young catcher put up his index finger as if to say, don't come out, I got this. He calmly walked to the mound as Tim walked toward him.

"What's up?" said Tim.

"Hey, do you remember what he said the day I told him to f...k off?"

"Ya, make that pitch a little higher."

"What do you think, let's give him a nice high one."

The umpire was walking out. "C'mon, guys."

"All set, Ump." And Bobby put the mask back on and walked to his position.

"Play ball," said the umpire as Zack got in the batter's box.

Without looking up, Bobby said, "Hey, Zack, here comes the pitch you wanted me to throw a few games ago, so get ready."

Bobby still wasn't quite sure of the upper limits of the umpire's strike zone and knew Lowrey was a good enough batter to not chase a pitch too high, so he guessed, and guessed right. Lowrey swung and hit the bottom half of the ball. It went straight up in the air. Bobby threw the mask off and looked up. The ball was directly over his head, a hard ball to catch. He settled under it, but the ball was drifting back toward the backstop. He reached up with his blunt-tipped mitt. It hit the top of the mitt and bounced sidewards. There was collision. It was Tim. Bobby watched the ball fall, just as Tim reached down. The ball settled in the pocket of Tim's glove for out number three.

8

Zack and his father were sitting in the dugout. The game had ended an hour ago. His reaction to the final out was still an on-going confused thought in his mind.

"C'mon, Zack, we've got to go home. It's over. We had a good season."

"Dad, we lost!" he yelled in frustration.

"Yep, we did and that's the way it is." And he leaned against the cinderblock wall and looked out over the baseball field. "And you know what? We played pretty well all season and just came up short in the end."

"Dad, I hate to lose."

"So do I, but that's part of life, Zack. Sometimes losing is the best thing that can happen to you if you look at it the right way."

"What do you mean?"

"Well, it can make you stronger," and he left it at that. "Come on. mom's waiting for us." Bill put his hand on his son's shoulder as he picked up the large equipment bag, and they left the dugout.

Coach Catoia took the whole team to a local ice cream stand and treated all the players. At one point, he yelled over to Tim and Bobby.

"Hey, what did you and Tim talk about when you called timeout, Bobby?" asked the coach.

"Well, Coach, it was just a little strategy," said Bobby and added, "We learned it on the farm."

"Oh, I don't think I want to know," responded the coach.

"Hey guys, check this out." Tim, Bobby, and Larry were sitting at one of the picnic-style wooden tables talking about the game, when Larry felt something in his back pocket. He stood up and reached back and pulled it out. "I found this in the dirt at third base."

It was the leather pouch.

Tim reached inside his uniform and pulled out the leather lanyard. The pouch was missing. "That's Tim's lucky arrowhead," said Bobby.

"Let me see that," said Tim and examined it. He could feel the stone inside.

"It must have come off when I slid on my stomach into third."

"You never had it on at the end of the game, Tim," said Bobby.

"Dad," Zack was watching TV with his father and having some after-dinner ice cream. "Do you know Pauly?"

"Who?"

"You know, the old guy at the farm."

"I've seen him there when I've gone to pick you up or when Mom and I get fresh vegetables. Why?"

"Were you in the Golden Gloves?"

Bill looked at his son. "Yes, when I was about your age or a little older."

"Well, Pauly remembers you. He said you were pretty good."

"That was a long time ago, Zack."

"How come you never told me about it?"

Bill looked at his son. "It's something I don't like to talk about."

"Why?"

"I don't know, I guess I was kind of a jerk then."

"What did that guy say to you?"

Zack knew he had to ask. The day's experience had put him in another place in his mind, and his conversation with Pauly was the trigger to dive deeper into that place and continue. "Pauly and I were talking the other day. He was mad at me about something and started talking about how he remembered you when you were fighting. He would be at ringside at all the big matches. He told me about your championship fight in Framingham. He was there that night when you and the guy you were fighting stopped in the middle of a round and talked."

Bill was staring at his son. And he finally said, "His name was Randel Shaman, and I was afraid of him. I actually faked getting hit and went down to the canvas. If I had done it earlier, they would have counted me out." He got up to shut off the TV and came back to sit next to his son. "You can't fake boxing, Zack… and I tried."

He gathered his thoughts. "In the second round, he had me tied up in a corner, and I thought, oh, here it comes." Bill stood up and demonstrated his position from that night. "I had my hands up in front of my face, expecting the worst. Randel backed away and said, and I'll never forget, 'You do not want to do this. You are a boxer; and you want to be known as a fighter. What label do you want to carry the rest of your life, quitter or fighter?' He backed away, I put my hands down, we touched gloves."

"What happened?"

"We boxed. He was better than me, with a stronger punch, but I boxed well, getting in my share of good blows. I lost the championship in my weight class, but at the end of the bout when we were in the dressing room, he came over to me and said, 'You are a warrior and a fighter.' And then thanked me for honoring him with a good fight. I'll never forget that, Zack."

It was Monday morning at the farm stand. Zack and Warren had arrived first and were talking to Henry and Stella when Tim and Bobby walked in. Zack put his hands in the air and bowed to his two competitors. "And here they are, the new world champs of the Tipton Little League." Tim and Bobby looked at each other, expecting the same obnoxious Zack. But Zack surprised them, walked over, and put out his hand, first to Bobby and then to Tim. Warren was behind him and did the same. He had been at the game. Zack backed away and said, "I want to apologize for the way I've treated you guys," and nudged his cousin.

"Me too. Sorry for hitting you, Bobby."

"I had a long talk with my dad last night. The thing is, the game could have gone either way." He continued after a pause. "That was a great pitch you threw me, Tim, and a great play to end the game. I still hate to lose, but as Dad said, that's life, learn and move on."

"Okay, we have some corn to pick. Everyone on the wagon," said Harod with a grin.

Later when Pauly and Zack were pulling the corn from the stalks near each other, Pauly asked Zack quietly, "So what did they talk about?"

"Who?"

"Your dad and the Shaman kid."

Zack winked at him. "Family secret."

Pauly smiled, nodded his head, and said, "Okay."

9

The farm routine moved along as it had for years. Harvesting the final crops of the year and getting the farm stand ready for the fall with its assortment of pumpkins and the final ears of corn was priority. Zack and Tim became friends, and on occasion, although underage, Pauly would let them drive the old tractor out on a task in a distant field.

The next summer would find Tim and Bobby back at the farm. Zack and Warren found work at a new place called a shopping center located in Framingham. Tim would see Zack occasionally and noticed he had not grown any taller. He had reached his full height that summer on the farm.

Babe Ruth baseball for ages 13 thru 18 was the next level of league baseball. The diamond was now regulation dimensions. This was to accomodate the natural growth of the players. The distance between the bases was longer, the outfield fence was further back but the distance from the pitches mound and home plate was the a major rule change, it was now over 60 feet. The little league length was 45 feet. Because of these changes Zack was no longer a dominant player. He lost interest and only played one season.

Tim and Zack lost contact and eventually went their seperate ways. Buoyed by his little league baseball experience Tim continued playing untill he reached high school and his sports interest changed. His friend Bobby, loved the game, and would play for the Tilton Regional High School.

Tim was drawn to the track team where his specialty would be the sprints, high hurdles, and jumping events. He would compete at a high level his four years at Tilton.

Despite his mother's disapproval, he kept wearing the rawhide necklace during and after competition. That all changed at the end of the spring track season in 1962 his senior year.

"Mom, it's my lucky charm," would be his reply. The stone's luster remained, but the rawhide began to show the grime from too many races and sweat-saturated shirts. Doris began to wonder about her son's hygiene.

"Tim, you've always been fast," she would say, and resumed what she was doing, having been down this family rabbit hole before.

Lessons learned on the farm and in baseball that summer of 57 would stay with him and be part of his life's foundation. The arrowhead had a permanent place in his possession. He would think of Red once in awhile.while working with Bobby. This would be their sixth year together on the farm.

They were working along with Stella putting up the early summer crops of cabbage, kale, and broccoli for display

"How's track going, Tim?" asked Stella.

"Okay. We have the district championships this weekend. Any problem with me missing work Saturday?"

"No, we should be fine. What events are you in?"

"The 110-meter-high hurdles and the triple jump."

"Do you think your ready?" asked Stella as she arranged the fresh-picked cauliflower. She and Harold had been following Tim and Bobby's athletic exploits over the years and were always interested.

"I'm ready. I'm running the highs against a kid I've raced before. He's pretty good. My hurdle technique, coach says, is as good as it can be. But the kid is really fast in between the hurdles. So, it's my technique against his speed. We've raced a couple of times, and he's beaten me, and I've beaten him. It's gonna be close."

"Sounds like it," said Stella as she went over to help a customer.

"Tim, this just came in the mail. It's addressed to you,"

Harold said as he walked in. Tim took the letter from him and looked at the return address. It was from Oklahoma. He went out back where Pauly smoked his cigarettes and sat on the old bench.

Tim,

My son is writing this letter for me. I hope this letter finds you and your family well. Since I left the farm, my health has not been good. I have diabetes, which has caused me to be blind, but there is something I have to tell you. I've been thinking quite a bit lately. You were a shining light to me when I met you on the farm. I have wanted to tell you that, and thank you. The day you found the arrowhead, I knew it was time for me to go, and here is why. I remember what you said, that it found you, and that was correct. Despite what my friend Pauly would say, I believe in many of the old ways, up to a point.

You see, my people believed that an arrowhead made of dupi would give the person who possessed it better focus. The person would come out of the dark and into the light. Remember I talked to you and Bobby about World War One, and I believe it helped me in the war. I had a gift. I killed many men as a sniper. But, there was another side that haunted me. I would have terrible dreams every night about those poor warrior soldiers I killed. When the war ended, I received a medal for what I did. I gave that to my father along with the arrowhead necklace. They are now both with him on the other side. I still have some dreams, but not as much. I think you may be the reason.

I have been thinking my whole life about those men, and I have come to this understanding. You see, we are still only human, and there are limits to what we can do and bear. My skill at aiming and killing was causing me to have too many sleepless nights and doubts. Your arrowhead helped me see the light. It was time for me to go home to my family.

I was at the game when you pitched for the first time. The arrowhead may have helped you. But, you must know this, and you can believe your old Indian friend and his ways or not, but what is inside your heart is the most important thing. Believe in yourself.

The truth, sometimes it will disappoint you, but the truth is the truth. Always do your best.
   Red

Tim sat for a long time and reading the letter over twice. Bobby was curious and approached the bench.

"What's up?"

Tim handed Bobby the letter and he began to read. When he finished he handed the letter back to his friend and thought for a moment.

"Tim, I think we were very lucky to have known that man."

Tim folded the letter and put it in his jeans pocket and paused as Stella came in the back room.

"Stella, let's put this in the glass case," as he took off the rawhide necklace with the arrowhead made of dupi.

CHICO

1

The dog was approaching four years old, was overweight, and a mental wreck. His instincts told him he should be moving, exploring, seeking, hunting, and his waste should be deposited away from his shelter; not in it. His existence was stupidly simple. He laid in a human's lap and was carried by a human wherever the human went. The places were always the same, and rarely was he carried to a place with interesting smells and sunshine. He liked sunshine and he slept a lot.

"Can that dog walk?" Joe asked sarcastically.

"Of course he can."

"Eliza, I haven't seen him on the floor or ground. Is there something wrong with him?"

Joe Flaherty and Eliza Pratt were seniors at Northeastern University in Boston and would be graduating in a few weeks. They were visiting Eliza's Aunt Florence, who lived on Beacon Hill, a very posh section of Boston. She lived on the first floor of a three-story Greek Revival style building, built in the seventeen hundreds, and was wealthy enough to have a full-time maid.

Joe was getting to know some of Eliza's family. Aunt Florence was the sister of her grandmother who had died ten years ago and was the last member of her generation. She was 89, and memory issues were beginning to creep in. This was the second time Joe had been to Aunt Florence's.

"You'll have to excuse me," said Aunt Florence. "Chico has to do potty." The miniature dog was in Florence's lap the entire dinner, eating the partially chewed food that the old woman was feeding him. Mabel, the maid, who had worked for Aunt Florence for many years, came around to help move the chair as the elderly woman left the dining room carrying the dog.

The question about the dog's mobility entered Joe's mind at that moment.

"Yep, he can," said Mabel, answering the question. And she continued with, "He is very wobbly and confused. I feel sorry for him," as he expanded on the thought. "Florence thinks she's doing the right thing and wants to be very helpful to Chico, but she isn't." She stopped to look in the direction of the backyard. "Right now she's put the dog down and the dog will just stand there." Mabel shook her head and changed the subject. "How did you like the pot roast?"

"That was really good, Mabel," said Eliza.

"Yeah, that's Fred's favorite too." Fred was Mabel's boyfriend who lived in Southey, a section of Boston. Until a few years ago they were living together. When Aunt Florence fell on ice-covered steps, Mabel moved in with Florence and didn't mind Fred staying over a few days once in a while.

"I'm curious, I don't know much about fancy dogs, but isn't that dog some kind of terrier, with curly fur? Where did the name Chico come from?"

Mabel looked at Eliza. They both had conspiratorial looks. "You tell him, Eliza," Mabel urged, looking in the direction of the back door.

"Well his real name is Charlie, but Aunt Florence couldn't stop calling him Chico." She continued quietly. "You see, the original Chico, a miniature Chihuahua, lived to be fifteen years old. And now that I think about it, I don't remember him running or walking much. She always carried him, and dinners were always the same. She fed Chico people food from the table. And when Chico began to lose his teeth, she would chew the food for him." And she paused. "Chico was a not a friendly dog and was afraid of everything. When I was ten, he bit me right here when Aunty was holding him." She paused to point out a mark on the side of her cheek. "But Aunt Florence loved that dog and always had him in her lap or was holding him in her arms. This is sad, and I know Fred still feels bad." And she paused to think. "One day, Aunty went in for a nap, and Chico would nap with her on the bed. We think she just forgot to carry him in with her. Her judgment had become more and more scrambled. It was just a bad set of circumstances. Chico was on the big couch asleep, kind of tucked in the cushions."

"Fred sat on him," said Mabel.

There was a long pause as Joe looked up at the maid, and she continued. "I was in the kitchen cleaning up, and Fred sat down to watch the Sox. He's a big guy and a little deaf and had the volume up." She shook her head and closed her eyes. "We think the poor little thing may have suffocated. I had just looked in on Florence and noticed the dog wasn't with her and started looking around. Fred got up to help me. I happened to see Chico's tail sticking out from the cushions, and that's when I knew. I called Eliza at school and she came right over."

"When Aunty woke up, she was a little confused about where Chico was. We couldn't tell her what really happened, but she accepted our excuse that he died in his sleep." Eliza paused and looked at Joe. "It was the truth, Joe. We didn't know how else to tell her." And she further explained how Chico was buried in a pet cemetery in Newton.

"This wasn't my idea," said Mabel jumping back quickly into the hushed conversation. "Last Christmas, Fred had had too much Christmas cheer, and he bought Charlie, or Chico Two… whatever," she said, shaking her head. "He felt so guilty because Florence was always asking about Chico and telling Chico stories. He thought she needed another dog." She looked out back hastily. "Do you think he would have asked my opinion?" she asked, pausing again and shaking her head.

Joe was beginning to feel like part of the family listening to this secret information when the back door opened.

"What a good Chico you are," said Florence as she went into the small bathroom by the back entrance and took out a sheet of toilet paper to wipe the dog's rear end. She returned to her chair at the dining room table. "Mabel, could you pick up Chico's poop in the yard? I don't want the neighbors to be mad at me."

"Will do, Florence." She looked at Joe, shrugging her

shoulders and mouthing, "Where do I look?" and walked out to make an attempt to find the prize.

"So how are you two doing?" asked Florence as the dog sat in her lap staring at a plate of half-eaten pot roast. "Are you still hungry? You little brat you." And she pulled him up for a hug and a kiss on his nose.

The dog didn't seem to mind this act of attention but was clearly more interested in the beef that was on the plate in front of him as he tried to stand on her lap and look toward the food. "Okay, Chico, let me get you one more bite, but that's it." She reached over, picked up a beef chunk, and as the dog stared at it going over its head, Florence put it in her mouth and chewed. She took it out and placed it in the dog's open mouth.

2

"I'm sorry, but that's not normal," said Joe as they were on the T, the public transportation for the city.

"What's not normal?" answered Eliza. She was staring out the window at the graffiti-tagged buildings from the rattling subway car.

"The way your aunt treats that dog."

"Yeah, it's a little weird, but after so many years, my mom and dad accept it, and I don't even think about it."

"Eliza, I grew up around dogs. They have personalities, they have instincts, they live to run, to explore, to hunt and play."

"Is she mistreating Chico?"

"Well no and yes—"

She cut him off. "Did you enjoy your meal?"

"Of course." He stopped to think a moment but continued. He was beginning to tread into the touchy area of family criticism. "I'm just saying."

"Joe, drop it, okay?"

Joe had grown up in West Newbury, Massachusetts, a rural community near the Merrimack River on the North Shore. His father, Don, was an OB/GYN doctor working out of Anna Jacques Hospital in Newburyport. His mother, Janet, was a stay-at-home mom who had raised four children. Joe was the youngest. They lived in a large empty nest Colonial-style home. When her husband wasn't home, she had two rescue dogs of questionable lineage as her companions. Wilma and Beatrice. The home was on four acres of what was once a large farm. A fieldstone wall was now part of their property line, a reminder of the early New England settlers. Gnarled apple trees on the property were well over two hundred years old. What was once cultivated land was now a hay field with rows of balsam firs, some of which would be harvested in December for Christmas trees.

Eliza was a city girl. She grew up in Brookline, Massachusetts, a town unto itself, but nestled into the expanded reaches of metropolitan Boston. She was an only child. Her father ran the family real estate business and her mother was a teacher in nearby Newton. Eliza and Joe met at a bar next to Fenway Park after a Red Sox game the spring of their sophomore years. The relationship blossomed. She was in the school of art media and design, and Joe was in the business school. At times, the relationship resembled and old married couple, but the simple fact was they enjoyed each other's company.

The next visit to Aunt Florence's, he met Mabel's boyfriend, Fred O'Callaghan. He owned and operated a very successful bar called 'The Well' in Charlestown, a neighborhood in Boston.

"Mabel said she told you what happened to the first Chico."

They were sitting on the large couch watching the Boston Bruins and drinking Sam Adams beer. When Mabel said Fred was a big guy, she underestimated. Fred was approaching three hundred pounds and was a little taller than Joe.

"I felt so bad," said Fred and looked at Joe. "It happened right where you're sitting…" He pointed with his bottle. Joe turned and looked down at the thick cushion and the space where the poor creature died. His only reaction was a grimace and had a swig of beer, just as…"SCORE!" yelled Fred. "Ah, ya missed it, what a great goal."

"What the devil is all the noise in there? You scared Chico and I half to death." Aunt Florence had just entered the room holding the dog.

"Brad Marchand just scored, Flo. He's a magician with that puck."

"He's a magician?"

"Well, no. He's just really good and tricky at what he does is all I mean."

"Oh, looks like hockey to me. Are those the Bruins?"

"Yes, you know that."

"And how are you doing, young man? Do you know Chico?"

"Yes, I do, Aunt Florence."

Conversations like this were becoming the norm. Eliza and Joe graduated that spring. Tom Pratt had known Joe Flaherty through his daughter for three years now. Joe had worked at Pratt Real Estate for his co-op work experience while at Northeastern.

"Mom and Dad were talking about Aunt Florence last night. They think it's time she moved to an extended care facility." They were at The Well when Fred came by.

"Hi, kids. How's it hanging, Joe?"

"Hi, Fred, how're you doing?" asked Joe, letting the vulgar guy-talk go. This was Fred's world, and Eliza was used to it. Fred did clean things up a bit when he was around Aunt Florence.

The big man slid into the booth and sat next to Eliza. "What is all the serious talk going on here?"

"I was just telling Joe that Mom and Dad have been talking about putting Aunt Florence into an extended care facility."

"Like a nursing home?"

"Actually, some are really nice, and she'd be very safe," said Joe.

"Yeah, all Mabel needs is for Flo to fall again." And he added, "Do they take dogs?"

"I think that would be a little tricky, particularly with the way she is with Chico. She couldn't have him sleep in bed with her, or feed him, not the way she's getting to be," said Eliza.

"You know there's more to it, don't ya?" said Fred. "For the last year or so, he's been pooping and peeing more in the house. Mabel said it's getting worse." He waved the waitress over. "Two more for Liz and Joe. Get me a scotch please, Blanche."

"You got it, Fred," Blanche answered and stopped and leaned against the table. "When are you two getting married?" asked the friendly middle-aged waitress.

Blanche was Mabel's sister. This question had become a standard part of her greeting. She always liked to guilt them since they moved in together. After graduation, Joe had found a reasonably priced rental in Newton, and with the assurance that they would be getting married soon, Eliza had moved in with him.

"Hi, Blanche. Pretty soon, we don't want to rush things."

"Yeah, kind of like my sister and this one," she said, taking a pencil from behind her ear and pointing it at Fred.

"I'd appreciate it if you would move along and get these customers their beverages," said Fred, also used to the guilt Blanche would direct his way. Blanche had been married thirty years to a local cop and had five kids.

3

The decision was made. Aunt Florence would move into an extended care facility called Beacon Place. She would have round-the-clock service and many amenities all meant to fit her lifestyle and comfort level, except, no pets. They could visit, but not stay.

What do we do with Chico? This was the big question. Florence's property would be put up for sale or rented as a long-term lease. Eliza and Joe weren't in their apartment for extended periods of time, so caring for the dog was not possible. They had discussed it from many angles, but as bad as Eliza felt, it just wouldn't be fair to Chico.

Eliza's mom and dad just said no. Mabel had moved in with Fred again, and he could not convince her to take in the dog. After too many times picking up Chico poop and cleaning pee spots, she said emphatically, "NO." Fred, on the other hand, felt a connection to the dog. He had grown attached to the dog, but from a distance. He felt good about replacing the original Chico with Charlie, who was much friendlier than the Chihuahua. He tried repeatedly to convince Mabel that they should take him in, but this only led to more arguments.

He put up a sign in the bar. If any patron was interested, he had a nice dog that needed a home. His friend Hugh Walsh said he would try to convince his wife, but after two days, Hugh said, "Sorry, Fred, the dog isn't house trained. If I can't leave him alone in the house without messing on the floor, this isn't going to work."

Blanche, who was in the bar when Fred decided the first time to give Aunt Florence Charlie as a replacement, thought her

116

youngest kids might like a dog. Once again, after a few days, she brought the dog back to the bar. "All he did was shake and pee when the kids tried to pet him."

As a last and desperate alternative, he called the guy he bought Charlie from in the first place. He had moved to Arizona. They would have to turn the dog in to a pet adoption center.

"I hate to do it," said Fred.

"The dog is cute. They'll find him a good home," said Mabel, as they were leaving the adoption center in Brookline. A week later they received a call from the center. Because of his issues, there had been no interest in adopting him. He may have to be put down.

The news hit Eliza hard. She was conflicted. The dog had done nothing wrong. Her aunt had always treated her little dogs the same way, and as long as they lived with her, they were safe and protected. The dog just happened to arrive in her aunt's life at a bad time. Because of circumstances beyond the little dog's control, he would be put down. He wasn't mean or dangerous. She and Joe decided they would step in. There was one last option.

4

It was not unusual for them to show up in West Newbury on a Saturday. The five-year-old Jeep pulled into the gravel driveway and was greeted by two very excited dogs. With her droopy sad eyes and hopelessly long ears, Wilma, a four-year-old rescue whose ancestry suggested a mix of greyhound, great dane, and bloodhound, was barking her deep southern bark. Behind her with just as much enthusiasm was Beatrice, also a mutt rescue. She was three years old. Her lineage was a mix of bull as in bulldog, bull terrier, and French bulldog. She was small in stature, but that didn't deter her.

Both dogs were people dogs, and despite the present moment, they were generally calm, but their job right now was to greet two of their favorite people; Joe and his girlfriend, who always smelled so nice and gave good ear scratches and at times would kiss them like humans.

Janet had been in the dining room of the large home dusting when she heard the greeting of the two dogs. She was in her fifties. Her light brown hair, with some help, was leaning toward blonde with a few gray streaks, but she maintained her youthful figure and appearance by being physically active. She loved her home and the grounds. She and Don maintained the large property with the help of a small tractor and other machines needed to plow the snow in the circular driveway, keep the grass in check, and tend to the apple and Christmas trees.

When she looked out and saw her youngest, who had grown into a handsome young man, she could only smile. She stepped out onto the porch and waved. When the car came to a stop, Joe opened the door and stepped out.

"Hey, what a nice surprise," she said as she walked toward the car and gave her son a hug and at the same time looked in and waved at Eliza, who was still sitting.

Joe bent to give Wilma a good ear scratch as her tail went into propellor mode. He then knelt on the ground to give Beatrice just as much attention and in the process got a wet ear lick from Wilma. The excitement was building.

In the meantime, the other door opened, and Eliza stepped out. Janet had already walked around the front of the car to greet her future daughter-in-law.

"What have you got there?"

Tucked in the crook of Eliza's left arm was Chico. Noting that Joe's girlfriend had gotten out of the car, Wilma and Beatrice came around for their scratches and possible kiss. Wilma noticed him first and immediately had her long nose in Chico's face. Never having this ever happen to him, the miniature dog barked, and instincts told him to snarl and snap at the intruder. To her credit, Wilma pulled back.

Beatrice would have none of this and stood on her hind legs. She was good at this. In many cases, this produced a treat, but this was different.

"Hi, Janet. This is Chico."

But before she could go any further, Janet said, "Boy, he is really scared. Is he all right?" Chico began to shake uncontrollably, and Eliza could feel pee running down her arm and elbow.

"The poor thing," said Janet and turned her attention to the two other dogs, who were now whimpering with curiosity and an occasional bark.

Janet walked to the edge of the driveway and into the grass. "Wilma, come." The big dog responded immediately as Janet tapped her left leg. Wilma walked to her master's left side and sat. Janet then said 'stay.' Wilma lowered herself down to the ground. Beatrice noticed what was happening to her friend and quickly followed when all Janet had to do was say, "You too, come on," as Beatrice sat next to Wilma. There was a pause. "All the way, Beatrice," said Janet. "Sometimes she cheats."

After a 'good job' scratch for both dogs, Janet turned her attention to her company. Eliza stood open-mouthed in amazement. She knew the dogs were well behaved, but this, to her, was a miracle.

"Will Chico let me hold him?"

"I think so."

Janet came over and took the wide-eyed dog from Eliza and held him in the same way, in the crook of her left arm, and gently stroked him.

"Joe, can I use your handkerchief? I got a little problem I have to clean up." Joe walked over. Eliza was wearing a sleeveless, light summer dress. He could see the wetness on her forearm and elbow and wiped it with a few quick strokes.

"I don't know," Joe said shaking his head.

Chico began to shake once again. "Has this dog ever been around other dogs?" Janet gave Chico a few gentle strokes to calm him down. "Has he ever socialized with other dogs?" asked Janet.

"Mabel's boyfriend said he got Chico from a kennel. He's a Norfolk Terrier and has a pedigree. He said he paid two hundred and fifty dollars for him because he was the runt of the litter."

"Oh," responded Janet.

While leaning against the Jeep holding Chico, and with Wilma and Beatrice staring with their heads between their paws, Eliza described Chico's history, including the story of Chico-One and his sad demise. All Janet could do was roll her eyes and keep stroking the scared dog.

"So we really don't know what to do, Mom. Any suggestions?"

"Well, maybe these two can help us." She nodded her head at the two observers patiently waiting, and when Janet focused her eyes on them, they both raised their heads in anticipation. "The first thing a dog wants to do when meeting a strange dog is check each other's identification, and when that's done, they are no longer strangers."

"Check their identification?" said Eliza with a screwed-up face.

"They have to sniff each other," said Joe, and added, "Dogs have great memories for smells. One sniff and they'll remember that scent for the rest of their lives."

Janet walked over and knelt down in the grass while still holding Chico. She extended her palm toward the two dogs and said quietly,"Stay." She set Chico down between them. The frightened dog continued to shake uncontrollably while standing and staring up at Janet as she backed away.

Wilma, with her long neck and snout, was able to stretch out within inches of the quaking animal's rear end covered by his tail between his legs. The tip of Wilma's nose was twitching as it took in every nuance and molecule of air that would be stored in her K-9 olfactory memory. Beatrice, always having to adjust to gain leverage and understanding what 'stay' meant, also knew her master was tolerant when she cheated a little, scooched forward in the grass to get her stubby nose close enough for her inspection.

Chico looked up. He didn't know it, but from that moment on, he would be viewing the world from ground level and was joining another world filled with adventure and a peculiar scent from Beatrice.

5

"I've been hesitant to call, but how is he doing?" Joe was at his office. It was Wednesday. Janet had agreed to take in the dog on a trial basis.

"I have to say, I almost called you Sunday morning. I never realized how needy this animal was."

"That bad, Mom?"

"He pooped on the kitchen floor and peed in the dining room, and Saturday night, it's a good thing Dad stayed at the hospital with some late night, early morning deliveries, Chico acted like a puppy and cried most of the night." She continued with her mini vent and paused. "But, I started to realize, he couldn't be in a better place." She paused. "I had this thought; this dog is going to be reborn." She explained. "I figured it was time to sink or swim, so I put Beatrice's extra collar on him and set him outside to fend for himself, hoping the electric fence doesn't scare him to death."

"How'd he do? I'm guessing he's still swimming," said Joe.

"Well, he is and it may be beyond a dog paddle," she said, smiling into the phone.

"You mean he's actually walking and running?"

"Ah, there may be a little more to it. He could be the luckiest dog in the world." And she giggled.

"What's going on, Mom?" It was now Joe's turn to smile into the phone.

"You know when we rescued Wilma, she had been spayed. Beatrice has never been fixed. I had this idea about her having at least one litter of puppies, and here is the lucky part for Chico." She paused again. "Actually, two things. Beatrice is in her heat cycle." She stopped. "You know Chico has never been fixed."

"How'd you know?"

"Ah, I checked."

"Oh."

"The bottom line is he has probably never walked as much in his life as he did Sunday. He followed Beatrice everywhere." And she continued. "You explained how he ate. Well he followed her to her feeding bowl, and I'm not sure if he's ever had to do this. Beatrice just moved over and shared her kibbles."

"How about… you know, pooping in the house?"

"So far so good, he's been outside pretty much all day every day. I think he's figured that part out by watching and sniffing." And she stopped again. "But here is the best part." And she warmed up to her next revelation. "I thought we were going to be in for a long night Sunday night, but he was quiet and asleep." And she giggled again.

"What happened?"

"He and Beatrice were sharing her kennel, both sound asleep."

"Mom, I think Chico's turned into a dog."

6

"Hey, Eliza, check this out." It was raining. They had gone for their jog and decided this afternoon they would do nothing and have a lazy Saturday to relax. "Isn't that the type of dog that Chico is?" Joe had been channel surfing and came across a re-run of the Westminster Dog Show held every year in Madison Square Garden. The announcer was introducing the Miniature Terrier group. "I wonder how he's doing. Why don't we drive up to West Newbury tomorrow?" It had been two weeks since they dropped Chico off.

The first things they noticed when they pulled into the driveway were Wilma's ears flapping up and down as she was running through the tall grass. When she reached the corner of the house and was in full view, Chico was right behind her, followed by Beatrice.

With a cacophony of barks in all octaves, they approached the car from Eliza's side. All she could do was put her hand to her mouth and stare wide-eyed at the sight of Chico. Joe had come around the front of the car, and the first thing he did was greet Wilma. With a final bark, close to a howl, she let herself be scratched and petted by Joe and Eliza, but during the whole greeting process, they could not keep their eyes off of Chico. Through the commotion came a voice from the front door. It was Joe's dad, Don Flaherty. "Hey, what's all the noise out here?" he said and walked down the stairs to greet them.

"Hi, Dad." Joe looked up as he was giving out ear scratches.

Meanwhile, Eliza was down on one knee attending to Chico. The barking had stopped and Wilma was content to stand next to Don as he gently ran his fingers along the bridge of her nose.

Beatrice joined Wilma sitting next to the doctor.

"I can't believe this is the same dog," said Eliza. Joe knelt next to Eliza and put his hands out to the terrier. Chico recognized these smells.

"He never wagged his tail," said Joe and paused. "He never did any of this stuff," he said, waving his arm indicating the yard and the large property.

All Chico could do was move frantically between the two humans, getting his ears and butt scratched. He jumped up on Eliza's bent knee. She bent down and gently held his head and kissed his snout as he reciprocated with a lick.

"Hi, everyone." It was Janet. "What happened to all my help?" She was riding the small tractor that was pulling a wagon. In the bed of the wagon was a bushel basket with some apples. After greeting the two young adults with her customary hug, she looked down at Chico.

"He is doing great." And she continued. "I had to meet some friends in Newburyport the other day. I took Chico and Beatrice to Maudsley State Park. I wanted to see how he is on a leash, and he was fine." And Janet bent down to reassure him and scratch his back. "Yes, we're talking about you."

Chico went over to check on Beatrice with a paw swipe and a quick run to nowhere and an abrupt stop with his butt and tail in the air like a beacon of dog happiness.

He had never played before.

"Come in, let's have some lunch." The dogs were allowed in the house, and everyone trooped in together.

"And another thing."

Eliza and Joe couldn't wait to tell Fred and Mabel about the weekend visit. They were at The Well after work on Tuesday.

"We were sitting on a couch talking to my parents, and he jumped up and sat between us." He paused. "Can you ever think of a time when he ever jumped? And he is so friendly and happy."

"What happened to change him so much?" asked Mabel.

"He met other dogs," explained Joe. "My mom is good at many things, but especially training dogs." And he continued proudly. "She figured he never socialized with other dogs, and fortunately she has two of the friendliest, smartest, and fun dogs you could ever meet." He went on to explain how she taught them basic dog behavior commands that are essential. He also added that the dogs are lucky to have a large space to run and explore. He concluded with, "Chico just had to have a pack and a reason to be, according to Mom."

"A pack?" questioned Fred.

"Ya, dogs are very social. You've heard of wolf packs. It's the same with Chico. He never had a pack." And he thought for a moment. "Humans can be part of the pack as well."

"I'd like to see him," said Fred.

The next Saturday, Fred and Mabel rode with Joe and Eliza to visit Chico. They had called ahead. Janet was anticipating their arrival, so when she heard the customary greeting begin, she whistled for the dogs. Just as the car came to a stop and after a final howl, Wilma ran to Janet and followed the signal to heel. Next came Beatrice settling in with Chico. She had them all lay and stay with a final, "Good job."

Fred and Mabel could not believe what they had witnessed, and once again Eliza marveled at what Janet had accomplished with Chico. Joe just looked at his mother and smiled.

7

It was the beginning of many things. Beatrice had her one litter of puppies, and to no one's surprise, of the six, two had a remarkable resemblance to Chico. All the pups found their forever homes on the North Shore, except for one called Chico-Three, who found his home in Charlestown.

Joe felt bad for Chico when they made the decision to have him 'fixed.' Janet explained, "Unless you want him being shocked by the electric fence now and again trying to wander, this is the best for everyone concerned. After all, becoming a dog comes with all the dog instincts."

Joe and Eliza got married and moved to Newburyport, where Eliza worked in an art gallery, and Joe started his own real estate business. They lived a few miles from West Newbury, but Chico would spend as much time with them as he did with Wilma and Beatrice.

Janet's tree farm had been in operation for ten years now. It took seven to eight years for a tree to be ready. The trees had to be fed. The old hay field they grew the trees in had to be cut back periodically, but the most labor-intensive part of their care was trimming and shaping. At times, Joe and Eliza would help Janet tend to her trees.

It was early June. Chico was enjoying his second year of being reborn and was in the tree field. Eliza was helping Janet plant some seedlings, while Joe was doing some trimming. The three dogs decided it was playtime among the saplings, the two-year-old trees. They were playing a canine version of tag, as far as Joe and his mother could figure out. Wilma and Beatrice were 'it,' and their prey was Chico. "He is very fast and agile," said

Janet as work stopped, and they watched the dogs play.

A week later. "What are you doing?" asked Joe. He and Eliza were visiting Janet.

"Watch this."

"Wow, he's very good at that," exclaimed Eliza.

"I got the idea from watching him run between all the saplings playing with Wilma and Beatrice.

"Yes, these are called the weave poles. I'm sending away for some more obstacles. He loves this."

"Yes, I've seen that on TV," said Joe.

Janet had thought his energy level was exceptionally high, something that was stifled and taken away from him, through no fault of his own. She knew many people who would rather have a smaller dog for a pet were caught up in the cute part and not the internal engine part of these dogs. Chico's breed was bred to be ratters. The vermin were the scourge of cities and towns in the past centuries, and once again, man's close relationship with dogs resulted in developing a fierce, quick, dependable friend that would help with a problem, just like the herding and hunting dogs.

Chico was high functioning, and Janet had a feeling he would be very good at this. After all, he was bred to seek out rats in a rat's environment, which could be anywhere underground, in walls, and in sewers and could be fearless.

As the summer went along, with the help of Joe, Eliza, and husband Don, they had Chico training. They put together an agility course consisting of jumps, tunnels, hoops, hurdles, and weave poles. Chico took to the challenges quickly.

His life was about to change once again.

◆ ◆ ◆

"Is he ready?" asked Janet as she walked into the simple ranch-style house of her son and his now very pregnant wife. Chico came running to the front door. Janet sat on the floor and let him smother her with dog licks. "Okay, okay, I love you too." And she stood and looked at Eliza. "How are you feeling? Do you want me to be the handler today?"

It was now October, and Chico had found his reason to be. He was now a formidable force in the local dog agility competition. They were going to the Essex County Fair, in Topsfield. This was the big one, the oldest in the country, with its beginnings in 1818, and today was race day.

Eliza had a special bond with Chico and his sport, having known him since the beginning and sharing this miraculous transition. So when they moved to their new home, Chico sleepovers were a common occurrence. She even let him sleep in the same bed as her and Joe.

"I'll be okay," she said as she patted her ever-growing stomach. She was wearing bib overalls. "These are the most comfortable pants I own." And she added, "Joe's gonna meet us down there. He had an appointment in Topsfield this morning."

The Topsfield Fair was considered one of the go-to events of the fall on the North Shore of Massachusetts, besides the small carnival with its midway, featuring rides designed to test your ability to hold down food, and booths with their stuffed animal prizes. There were the greyhound races for the gaming public, best in show contests from giant pumpkins, to pies, to rabbits, pigs, and even fancy pigeons.

And while the Miss Topsfield Fair pageant was going on off to the side in an arena that had been used the previous day for judging the giant bulls, it was now set up for the dogs and their agility dog competition. Today it would have 18 obstacles. The smaller dogs were the first group, and Chico was one of 10 competing.

They were next up. Eliza removed his collar and lead. Chico knew this meant it was time. He looked up at her. She had her hand up and palm open. He was ready.

He had been having trouble with the hurdle obstacle during training. It would be the first obstacle and a key to his success today. If he could clear the 11-inch height without a touch, he would be in good shape. Chico was six inches tall at his withers.

Her hand went down, and he took off. Eliza held her breath. He did it, a clean jump over the intimidating first obstacle. She yelled and he knew she was happy. That was all he needed. Eliza's job was to guide Chico, through quick voice commands and hand gestures, but he knew the course with its yellow tunnel, weave stakes, seesaw, doughnut hole, and thirteen others. He was flawless.

The race had ended a half hour ago, and he and Eliza were basking in the post-race congratulations.

"Are you okay, hon? I should have been his handler today," said Joe.

"I'm fine now. He knew where he was going. I think he felt sorry for me and just went on ahead of me. Man, he was fast today."

Chico knew he won. He had been competing all summer long. His instincts and the sound of Eliza's encouraging voice was all he needed to push him to his competitive limits, plus he knew at the end he got to jump up in her arms and be smothered with human kisses.

"Excuse me, how old is Charlie?" asked the local newspaper reporter as he approached the couple and the dog.

"Not sure. Six or seven, we think," said Eliza as she was holding the Norfolk Terrier in the crook of her left arm and gently stroking the side of his whiskered face.

"How long has he been competing?"

"A year," she replied, still a little red in the face.

"He broke the course record for his category and one category above him," said the reporter. "Where does he get his speed?"

"I guess he's been saving it up," she said, giving the reporter a goofy look and shrugging her shoulders, adding, "Right, Chico?" and kissed the top of the dog's head.

"I thought his name was Charlie?"

"That's his racing name. At home we call him Chico," said

the young and very pregnant woman looking at her husband.

They were walking down a corridor they had walked before. It was an environment familiar to Chico. He did not have to be on a leash, but it was the rules. He was with members of his pack. They stopped at an open door and all walked in.

"Hi, Aunty."

"Oh hi, dear, nice to see you." She had a questioning look on her face. "How do I know you?"

"I'm Eliza, you remember my husband Joe, and this is James."

"Oh, how nice."

"We brought a special friend of yours." And she reached down to unclasp Chico's leach. "Go ahead, Chico." He was familiar with the weekly routine as he jumped up on the couch in the large sunlit room of the retirement home and, without hesitating, curled up in Aunt Florence's lap.

"Oh, what a nice dog," she said as she gently stroked his back. "What's his name?"

"Chico," said Eliza, smiling as she held her son.

CASH AND BOB

1

Knees bent, head up, punching the pocket of his well-worn glove, Paul was focused. The pitcher delivered the ball, and the batter hit a high majestic fly in Paul's direction in left field. It was drifting toward foul territory and the five-foot-high chain-link fence that separated the baseball field from the pasture. It was the top of the ninth and two outs. UNH was leading by one run.

Paul looked quickly. Next to the fence was a horse and a person standing in a riding helmet, both looking down at the grass under the fence. Paul looked up again. The ball was out of play as it hit the horse in its rear, causing the big animal to raise its head quickly and dance momentarily. The girl in the helmet calmed the animal by stroking its neck and nose. Paul stared at her as the ump yelled, "FOUL BALL."

He returned to his position, but before the next pitch, he glanced over at the horse and the dismounted rider. Her attention was on Paul now. Paul refocused and got back to the game. The next pitch resulted in a ground ball to the shortstop and a routine throw to first base for the final out. As he ran to the infield to congratulate the pitcher, he looked over to the fence. She was in the same spot. He wasn't sure why, but he waved at her. She smiled and waved back.

After the game, Paul was talking to his parents, who would be heading back to Logan Airport in Boston for their flight back to Fort Myers. "What was that all about with the horse?" asked his mother Francine.

"That's my school," said Paul.

He grew up in Fort Myers, Florida, where he played high school football but excelled in baseball and loved ROTC. He was a senior at the University of New Hampshire, The Wildcats, but his journey to the school was different. He had been an Army Ranger deployed in Afghanistan, barely 18 when he joined. He would fulfill a dream by playing college baseball and receive a degree in business in three years. This was his last game.

Later that evening, Paul and members of the baseball team were at the Tug Boat, a local bar in nearby Portsmouth Harbor. The bartender was Tom, the day's winning pitcher and captain of the team. When it came time for fun, he was in the middle of it.

"Paul, I expected you to dive over that fence. Instead you let the horse take one for the team."

"Sorry, me and horses don't like each other."

Tom would always set up the banter around the bar. The friends were having a good time. "And speaking of horses," yelled Jackson looking up. "Hey, Liz, here's the guy that let that ball bounce off your horse's ass." Laughter erupted.

A group of coeds had just walked in. "Hi, Tom," one said and waved. She was petite, wearing tight jeans tucked into brown leather riding boots, a UNH varsity jacket, and a Red Sox baseball hat with a long, silky black ponytail protruding from the plastic adjuster in the back of the cap. "Elizabeth O'Brien, this is Paul Davis. I just told him, with a little more effort, he could have saved your horse."

"Hi, nice to meet you. How's your horse?" asked Paul.

"He's fine, don't worry. He's a big boy. He was more interested in the grass," she replied as Paul noted her extra-strong grip.

"Would you like a beer, Elizabeth?"

"My friends call me Liz. Thanks, I'll have what you're having." Tom was watching the conversation and had the beer in front of his friends a moment later. "Yeah, I had a moment there today when I looked up and saw your horse." He paused to think. "It's one of those things where, you know horses are not supposed to be right there, they should be running around over by the barns." And he became tongue tied. "It just surprised me, that's all." And he paused to take a sip of beer. This gave her an opportunity to help him.

"We shouldn't have been so close to the fence. I had just finished working out Bob. He needs the exercise."

"Bob is the name of the horse?"

"Yes."

"So, I've always wondered, what do the horses do? Do you study them? Do you have horse competitions? What does Bob do?" He took another sip of beer, watching her expression change, and she folded her arms across her chest.

"Okay, so you've been going to this school, playing baseball, and your position is left field, the closest part of the field to the barns, and it never occurred to you to look into what is going on down at the barns?"

"Pretty much."

"Okay, well Bob, in his younger days, was a very successful barrel racer."

"A what?"

"A barrel racer."

She had his complete attention now, but unfortunately, his focus was on her eyes and mouth. The best he could retain from her explanation was barrels, racing, quarter horse, and retired.

"You've never been to a rodeo, have you?"

"No."

"Well, Bob was pretty good. He's too old to be doing that now and has some arthritis but still needs his exercise. He came along in the deal when we got Cash."

"Cash?"

"His racing name is Johnny Cash Black Esquire. He's our other horse. He used to race at Rockingham Park over in Salem. His record wasn't that great. He came in second once and had a third and two fourths. But my mom saw something in him, and she bought him after a claiming race. Bob came with him. They're really sweet horses. We keep them stabled here at the school while I complete my program."

"I don't know why, but horses spook me," said Paul.

"Tell you what, why don't you come by the horse barn? That's the one you can see from left field, painted white."

"Okay, and why am I going by the horse barn?"

"To meet Cash. I heard you're from Florida," said Liz.

"Yes, Fort Myers," he sputtered after an awkward stare. The more she talked, looking him in his eyes, the more he felt drawn to her. Paul learned that Liz and her horse did compete.

The sport was called dressage, a riding competition that originated with European aristocracy. It took her a while, but she explained how the competition was all about communication between rider and mount. Using leg pressure, no verbal communication, no artificial aids such as crops, spurs or reins, the rider must direct the horse to perform a prescribed routine in the ring. Cash was an important part of the family's dressage team.

He explained how he arrived at UNH a little later than most. He deflected questions about his service by saying it was something he had to do. They stayed together till the 1 a.m. closing and agreed to meet the next morning at the horse barn.

Liz was in the stall with a shovel. "Just hold the carrot by the greens. He has very good table manners." Cash had his large, all black head and neck extended out from the opening of the half door entrance to the stall. Paul was transfixed by the size of the horse's head and neck and stood just far enough away with his hand extended holding the carrot. He inched closer as the big horse used his lips to grab the carrot and chomped away. Paul then bravely ran his hand down the horse's nose. Cash raised his head and snorted. "He can see the other carrot," he heard Liz say. She had her back to them as she continued to shovel. He gave the horse the other carrot from his left hand just as another large head appeared. It was Bob, the horse that had the baseball bounce off his rump.

"You better get a couple more carrots. I brought some extras this morning," Liz said and pointed across the barn to the carrot greens that were protruding from a wooden box. "Bob is going to want a treat too. Let me get rid of this." She walked by him with a bucket full of manure. "I'll be right back." Despite his nervous stomach and need to back away from the powerful animals, Paul did as he was instructed and retrieved two more carrots. He walked back to the two horses. Their ears were up and alert, and both horses were staring at what was in his hands. Cash was close to seventeen hands at his shoulders. He was big. Bob was fifteen hands, and his coloring was starkly different. He was a Paint, with a hodgepodge of black, brown, and white markings.

As Paul got closer, he extended both hands. Cash gently took the carrot from his left hand, and Bob did the same from his right and chewed away. The horses kept looking for more treats, sniffing at his hands and the pocket of his untucked plaid shirt. Paul then had a spurt of courage as he stroked the side of each horse's neck.

Liz returned. She took off her leather riding gloves, put them in her back pocket, and leaned against the side of the stall with her arms folded in front of her. "I had a good time last night."

There was an awkward pause.

"So did I," replied Paul, getting a little dry in his throat.

"Let me get these guys some water," said Liz and turned to pat the side of Cash's neck. "You were very smart today, my handsome boy." The horse responded with a loud snort and nodded his head. She looked at Paul. "He knows he did a good job."

Paul stared at her briefly, trying to take this all in. All he could come out with was, "What time did you get here?"

"Six, usual time." She patted Paul's chest as well and walked across the barn to retrieve a large, galvanized bucket.

"Hey, I can get that," said Paul walking behind her.

"They'll love that," she said without looking back at Paul, and added, "You deserve a treat, have a carrot."

"No thanks, I'd feel guilty. They'd be watching me."

Paul filled the bucket and brought it over to a water station next to the stall and filled it, put the bucket down, and gave each horse another scratch on his neck. "That is the most I have ever touched a horse."

Liz smiled and extended her right hand. "Congratulations, young man." Paul held onto her hand. They looked into each other's eyes. She let go of his hand and they kissed.

Paul and Liz would be together as much as possible the last two weeks of their senior year. As graduation loomed, the relationship become serious on many levels. He began to appreciate what dressage was all about and the discipline involved. The two horses opened up a whole new world to him. Liz explained that they had been together ever since Cash's racing days. She also explained how horses have to be around other horses. Many racing horses had a stablemate to help them cope with the anxiety and pressure of racing. In Cash's case, his talent would be discovered in another sport, but having his friend around made him better. Paul also learned that horses have a long memory. "If you treat them right, they will remember you the rest of their lives. Horses never forget." She also added that the opposite was true. "If they are treated badly, they will remember that as well." Paul and the two horses bonded over mucking the stall and treats.

A few weeks later, while sitting on one of the bleacher-style wooden seats in the cavernous, open-sided, roofed riding ring, he heard a voice giving Liz some instructions. It was her mother. Liz had introduced her to Paul a few days after they had first met. The meeting was cordial. She was built similar to Liz and appeared to be in her late fifties.

She had walked in from a side entrance unnoticed and had her back turned to Paul. Liz and Cash had just completed a routine. "That looked good, Liz. I hope he doesn't forget while we're away. I just received a letter from Hans Otto in Frankfurt. He would like us to start next week." Liz dismounted and led Cash in the direction of her mother. Despite having her back turned to where Paul was sitting, he could tell by the body language this was a serious moment for mother and daughter.

"Liz, what do you think this is all about?" She waited for a reply as her daughter looked up at the bleacher seats. And she continued. "I've spent a lot of money on this, and this is our big opportunity. You knew this could happen."

Her mother turned and walked away shaking her head, pausing at the barn's open end and turned to look at her daughter. "We'll talk when you're through with Cash," she said and walked stiffly away from the barn.

"That was serious, wasn't it?" said Paul. Liz had taken Cash's saddle off and was leading him outside next to the barn for his reward of grazing in uncut green grass. "We had talked about it, but I didn't think it would happen this soon." She went on to explain that dressage was a large part of her and her mother's life. "I've been riding horses ever since I can remember, and I do love them, and Mom has this dream." She paused to pet Cash as he was nibbling away.

"She wants us to go to Germany to learn some of their training methods. She also wants me to become a better rider with better horses." She stopped to scratch Cash's ear. "He's pretty good, but I guess the European horses are at another level." And she added, "She already has a place picked out in Ocala, Florida, to begin a riding school. I guess I should have mentioned this earlier."

They got together a few more times before graduation, but once the ceremony was over, they said their goodbye's. Paul would return to Fort Myers and join his father's business. As it turned out, Liz would be in Europe longer than a year. The separation cooled the relationship, and Paul resigned himself to remember the college encounter with Liz and her horses as a pleasant memory. Life would go on.

2

Old Oaks Ranch, with its double circle brand, was ten miles east of Clewiston, Florida. It was a working cattle ranch and had been since the 1800s, owned and operated by the Lofton family, Todd, his sister Sarah, and brother James.

Todd was the businessman in the family. His brother James was more intent on gambling and spending the ranch's wealth on fast cars. Sarah had her own ideas about the property and her attachment to its use. She was an independent woman. Her love was horses and wanted to have her own business, a place where people could board their horses, as well as a riding school, not attached to her brother's enterprises. They arrived at an agreement. She could have forty acres dedicated to her horses.

But after a while, both men realized they were a little too generous. The portion of land they gave her had a valuable asset, water. Todd coveted the pond and tried to persuade his sister that it would be of more use on his ranch. She wouldn't budge. "A deal is a deal, Todd. There are six other ponds on the ranch. This one is for my stock. If I let the cattle in, they'll be shitting and contaminating the water." This was a continuous argument.

James's life would be different. After graduating from high school, he went to Florida State University, met a co-ed from New Jersey, got her pregnant, and discovered the casinos. His son would be called Andrew and would be raised by the girl's family. James was content to let his siblings argue over the water issue and at one point told them he wanted out of the ranch. Todd bought him out. James left Florida for Vegas and severed all ties with his brother, sister, and his son, Andrew, in New Jersey.

Sarah's forty-acre riding school was showing signs of success. Her barn was full of boarders, and the school had a continuous clientele from nearby Clewiston. Four years would go by when they received the news that James died. It was a head-on collision in Arizona. Speed and drugs were the major factors in the crash. There was no will. The death of his father had little effect on James's son, Andrew. He was 22 at the time and still living in New Jersey.

Andrew, who would go by Andy, was different from his father. He liked to work and discovered his niche in used furniture. He became very proficient at bidding at estate sales, and when it came to selling, he was not above misrepresenting a piece with a little touch-up paint or fibbing about the make or age or type of wood. He made a living, although at times his products may have been tainted.

Andy met his wife, Stella, one weekend in Atlantic City. The courtship led to a quick wedding. She was pregnant, and her German family insisted she get married if Andy knew what was good for him. They would name their son Gunther, after his mother's grandfather, who ran the family restaurant business. The grandfather spoiled him to the point where he became willful and unruly. By the time he was ten, he had been suspended from elementary school numerous times. 'Incorrigibly undisciplined' was the term used by the public schools. It was the same when they enrolled him into private schools.

All this time, the marriage was falling apart. Andy contacted his uncle Todd and asked if he could move into the guest cottage on the ranch and build a used furniture business in Clewiston. Todd reluctantly gave the okay. He was hopeful Andy would make the business grow.

Andy's business did grow. There was also an unforeseen benefit, at least in Andy's mind, when he moved to Florida. The state's relaxed gun ownership policies fed into his gun obsession.

Two years after he moved to Florida, he was joined by his son Gunther. At 16-years of age he got on a Greyhound bus and headed to Clewiston. He walked into his father's store, now called 'High End Resales' and announced he was staying. He explained to his father he could not take the constant nagging by his mother. He hated working in his grandfather's restaurant where he was expected to be nice to all the customers, even the assholes.

Andy was okay having his son around, as long as he behaved, but Gunther's idea of behaving had been set at a young age. What the word meant was; don't get caught, or if you do get caught, make sure it's for a good reason. The restrictions he hated in New Jersey would be lifted, and as far as school, he knew exactly what he had to do to get thrown out. His formula was simple, and had been doing it for a while, pick a fight or swear at the teacher.

3

"Your father said you could use it?"

"He doesn't give a shit, as long as I don't shoot anybody." The two boys were sharing a joint and looking at the new AR-15 rifle. Gunther Lofton, now seventeen, and his friend, eighteen-year-old Donald Spencer, were sitting on their cam-o-painted four wheelers outside of the guest house located on the ranch. Gunther had just brought out his father's latest addition to his gun collection.

"Where'd he get it?"

"Well, he had to go through all kinds of f...k'n bullshit, paperwork and background checks and whatever, but he got what he needed and picked it up at Larry's Pawn Shop, the place where he gets all his guns." And he added, "But this is what's really f...k'n cool." He sucked on the joint. "Check these out," he said and opened a box containing bullets. The box said 'Winchester Super Magnum.' He took a shiny copper-cased round and gave it to his friend. "These f...krs could probably go through a house."

"How many will the mag hold?" Donald asked after handing back the bullet.

"Thirty. Yeah, and they ain't cheap." He took another pull on the joint and added, "That kinda sucks. He told me I pay for what I use, and shit, knowing me, I'd shoot the whole magazine in two minutes, probably shoot my whole paycheck. I don't get paid till next Friday. I don't want to be tempted; besides, he'll beat the shit out of me if I use all his ammo. He is going on a pig hunt tomorrow."

"You still working for your dad?"

"Have to since I f…k'n quit school."

"I thought you were thrown out?"

"Well yeah, I was tired of that f…k'n shit, and my father signed the papers saying it was okay with him. But my uncle told him I had to work or I was going back to Jersey, and that ain't gonna happen. I don't mind working. It's not that hard. I just move furniture around and put the price tags on shit. My dad and me run the place, and when my father isn't around, it's just me and my stash. I'll put this bad boy back and grab my thirty-two," he said as he got off the four-wheeler and headed back into the cottage. Gunther's name soon evolved into Gunner. When not working at the store, his other activities involved guns. Just like his dad, he loved guns.

He and Spence had discovered what may have been target shooting ranges way out on the western edges of the property. This was confirmed by his uncle. They had been used years ago during World War Two. "Go ahead and use them," his uncle said, "but keep your shots below the backstop. I don't want you shooting any of the cattle, or the men." His uncle wasn't particularly keen on Gunner's obsession with guns, but he convinced himself that because of the large land expanse and the controlled target shooting area, nothing of consequence could happen. His attitude was, out of sight, out of mind.

"Grab a couple of rods, and I'll get the beer," said Spence. His family owned a restaurant called the Pig House. The restaurant specialized in barbecued ribs. At times, the daily special would be wild pigs that had been hunted and killed by the locals, a favorite dish. He grew up in the business, and every once in a while, a few bottles of beer would go missing.

They were under one of the oaks next to the pond. A small group of Angus steer were grazing, keeping their distance from the noisy four-wheel cycles that had arrived. A few of the closest steer had moved and just as quickly settled back to grazing, all except for one, the Brahma bull, who slowly looked up and stared at the two humans. The Brahma were owned by Five Star Entertainment, a company that specialized in raising them for rodeos. Bred for their meanness and unpredictability, their sires were bulls with high testosterone levels. They were on the ranch to graze and grow to their 1800 pound weight.

"That's Bernie, he won't bother you," Gunner explained. "We got two more around, but they kinda stay away from each other," he continued as both boys watched the bull intently. "My uncle says they breed those f…krs to be mean, and the meanness really doesn't kick in until about three years old. Bernie is about a year and a half." The young bull lowered his head, turned, and wandered over to the shade of a large oak, grazing on the other side of the tree's thick trunk.

"That guy gives me the creeps," said Spence.

"Ya, his aggressive stuff hasn't kicked in yet. The cowboys told me to never turn your back on them."

Once the bull wandered off and got busy with the scraggly grass offerings, they both relaxed. Gunner was standing and casting his line and lure. The ranch had five hundred Black Angus and three Brahma bulls. The Angus were raised for their beef.

"I know you're in there, you big f…ker." Gunner had caught a 15-inch large-mouth bass the week before and was savvy enough to know that in a small pond there were not too many of them. Despite his selfishness, he threw the fish back.

"I'll get him this time," bragged Spence as he cast his lure.

"If you do…" Gunner pulled out the thirty-two pistol from the back of his belt and aimed it at his friend. Spence looked over.

"What the f…k! Are you crazy?"

"Just messing with you… Scared ya, didn't I," he taunted as he raised and pointed the gun in the direction of the young Brahma bull, firing three rounds into the trunk of the tree between him and the bull. The cattle in the vicinity scattered once again, the sharp retort of the thirty-two had a few running. The Brahma also reacted picking up his large head stared momentarily and moved along with the other cattle. "Don't mess with me, you dumb cows."

"Put that f…k'n thing away and get me a beer," said Spencer.

"Man, you are one crazy bastard, Gunner."

4

Supreme Roofing was the name of Paul's father's company. He joined the business after graduation and after two years became the general manager. With the help of two hurricanes, the workload tripled and so did the profit. The company purchased PTK-31 Cranes, essential for lifting damaged roofing material off of a two- to three-story roof and replacing it with the new material. The cranes made them a serious roofing company in Florida.

Paul was in the central part of the state to bid on a job. He was in horse country with its rolling meadows, white fencing, and live oak trees providing canopies of shade for the animals. The scenery brought back a memory. He sat in the cab of the truck.

"I wonder," he said to himself. He remembered the girl he met in college and her mother's plan of starting a riding school in Ocala. It had a simple name. He picked up his smart phone. There it was, 'Big Horse Farm' located a few miles from the project site. He looked up the address and drove the company pickup truck up to the white-fenced driveway. Big Horse Farm was used for anything horse related. A sign next to the barn entrance indicated it had a riding school and was used as a training center for not only dressage, but a variety of equestrian activities. He stopped, got out and looked around, and walked toward the entrance of the barn. He could see a few horses poking their heads out of their stalls. "Well, I'll be," he said to himself and walked down the center of the barn past a few horses and approached the next two.

"Cash?" He paused. "Bob?" At the mention of their names,

the animals simultaneously lifted their heads. Their ears turned directly at Paul. He walked over to them, reached up, and ran both hands down their long snouts and patted their necks. "How are you guys?" Cash snorted and Bob raised his head in recognition.

"I WISH YOU WOULDN'T PET THE HORSES," he heard and stepped away. Two men were walking into the barn from the other end. As they got closer, he noted one was older, wearing a dirty, white Stetson cowboy hat. He had a wrinkled, deeply tanned face and looked to be in his early sixties. He was wearing worn leather flat-heeled riding boots and a denim sweat-stained long-sleeved shirt. He was followed by a younger version of himself, except he was wearing a green John Deere baseball cap covering long, shoulder-length stringy hair and a white dirt-stained tee-shirt with the farm logo of a rearing horse.

"Sorry, there was no one around, and I thought I'd look in here," he replied, peering up and gesturing with his head at the large barn. "I know these horses." He pointed toward them. "That's Cash, and the little guy is Bob." Both men looked at each other.

"Yep, that's them," said the younger of the two.

"Is Liz O'Brien around?" asked Paul. Both men looked at each other and then at Paul.

The older man was a little more intense. "How do you know her?"

Taken aback, Paul asked, "Is there something wrong?" And he added, "Liz and I went to college together at the University of New Hampshire, and I remember her telling me that her mother wanted to start a riding school at the Big Horse Farm in Ocala." And he paused again. "It was an easy name to remember."

"Things aren't good," said the younger man of the two.

"How's that?" questioned Paul.

"Just after we shipped Cash and Bob down from New Hampshire, there was a barn fire at their home in Greenfield. They were supposed to leave a few days after they shipped the horses." He paused to look at Paul. "Liz's mom and Liz got burned pretty good." He stopped to think. "That was a year ago." The older man picked up the narrative.

"Her dad tried to help and died from his burns. When she called after the accident, she said she would be down as soon as she could and asked if we would take care of the horses." He folded his arms, looking down at the ground.

"Oh man, that's terrible. Have you heard from her since?"

"No," said the older man.

Paul retrieved a business card and a pen from his shirt, placed the card on his thigh, and wrote something on the back. He looked up and gave the card to the older gentleman. He looked at the card.

"You're Paul Davis," he said and looked up. "I'll let her know you were asking for her when I see her." He took off his right-hand glove and put out his hand. "Nice to meet you. Name's Rusty Hartwell. I manage the place. And this is my son Tim."

Paul shook his hand as well and added, "I hope she's okay, we were good friends." He looked down for a moment shaking his head. "Boy, you never know, do you?" He looked up at the two men and exhaled a deep breath. "Okay, guys, nice to meet you both," Paul said and thought for an instant. "Mind if I give these two a scratch?" Both horses responded with a gentle snigger and a quick sniff inches from Paul's smile. He got in the pickup, gave the two men a wave, and left wondering.

❖ ❖ ❖

Two years would pass and another hurricane hit Florida with far-reaching damage. Once again, Supreme Roofing would be needed, this time in Clewiston. The major project was a roof repair on a municipal building. They would be there a month or more. "There's some great boar hunting in the area. Maybe I can get away for a few days," said Paul's father, John Davis. The animals were wild or feral pigs, a nuisance to the ranches and farmers, so much so, they could be hunted year-round.

"Shouldn't be a problem, Dad. Just don't shoot your foot off." This was a typical response from Paul. He and his dad had many similar interests but hunting and guns in general was not one of his. He had seen too much in Afghanistan, and most of the bad stuff he saw was the result of a firearm. Golf, softball, and rec-basketball were his recreational activities.

"Yes, John, of course," said Todd Lofton, the owner of 'Old Oaks Ranch.' "There's no one out in the pastures today. We had a bunch over the weekend. It's a wonder no one got shot. Hope they left you some hogs." John was getting permission to hunt the wild pigs. He had been out there a few times in the past on other hunts. The ranch was a favorite place due to its vastness. He and Freddy, a foreman in the company, were hunting buddies. They were taking Wednesday off. "Good luck." And Lofton added, "Keep clear of the Brahmas."

"Thanks, Todd, we will." They headed west on their four-by-fours, with only space and few Black Angus steer in the distance.

In the meantime, a man approached Paul and said, "Is that your truck?"

"Yes."

Paul was having lunch at the Pig House Restaurant and looked suspiciously at the man asking the question. "Is there something wrong?"

"Yes, I need some roofs repaired."

"You may have to wait in line," answered Paul, and not wanting to offend the man with a flip answer, he continued after chewing his grouper sandwich and washing it down with his glass of milk. "Tell you what, here is my card," He reached in his shirt pocket. "What's your name?"

"Gary Johnson, I own Johnson Realty." And he gave Paul his card.

"Call the office, have them put you on our list for this area."

"Thanks, and you are?"

"Paul Davis."

A month later, with the big project completed. John

received a call from Pam, the office manager. "John, before you leave Clewiston, I have a note here about another job."

"Oh?"

"Maybe you should check with Paul."

"Yes, I was having lunch and talking with a realtor. It's out there in cattle country, maybe it's worth a look." And they drove out to investigate a new job possibility.

"I saw this place a few weeks ago when I was hunting with Freddy," said John, as they got out of the truck. The realtor was with them. "I remember thinking it had some nice features," said John. The house was long and low, a classic ranch style design, made of sturdy red brick. The barn's walls were intact, but both structures needed new roofs. Surrounding the house and barn were massive live oaks that had survived the hurricane. But the property had been sitting for a few years and there was other damage. There were gunshot scars in some of the bricks, in the tree trunks, and a few windows were broken, probably shot out. John was disgusted. "There's no need for this. This isn't the Wild West."

Johnson explained he hadn't been out to the property in a while. It was in a trust, and the owner lived in Wisconsin. "It had been part of the Old Oak Ranch, Todd Lofton's place." And he stopped to think. "Let me give you the story, everyone around here knows it," and he continued. "His sister, Sarah Lofton, wanted to start her own business, a riding school. But a family squabble years ago over the water rights to the pond caused a rift." And he paused again. "There are other ponds and tanks kept full by the windmill pumps, but they would dry up occasionally during the winter or a lightning strike would knock out a pump. The one on this property, because it's spring fed, would always have a good amount of water. Sarah wanted it for her horse stock, not for a herd of cattle. I guess she and Todd went back and forth over the situation, and rumor had it that Todd would cut the fence during some dry times."

He had their full attention now. "Well things came to a boil one day when one of her horses, a little colt, was attacked and killed by one of the Brahmas. She sold her stock, and she and her husband moved back to Wisconsin and refused to sell the property back to her brother." He stopped again. "She died of cancer three years ago. I don't think Todd or Sarah had spoken before that." Gary looked at the two men. "That's kinda sad, don't you think?" And he stopped to think. "Anyway, a month before the hurricane, I got a call from a person interested in the property, but the hurricane screwed things up. What's your schedule look like?"

"You know, I'd like to see this place look the way it should," John replied and looked at Johnson. "Why don't we talk?"

Later, the realtor made a call with John and Paul's estimates and suggestions on the work. The new owners agreed to the price. Using the manpower and resources of the company, they would rehab and expand the house, put new roofs on both structures, and put in hurricane-proof windows. The barn was completely gutted, and ten new horse stalls were built. The property was fenced temporarily with barbed wire.

On the final day of the project, John looked at their work and declared, "Now that's what I'm talking about. Doesn't the place look great under those trees?" He shook Johnson's hand, and added, "Nice working with you. I hope the people enjoy it."

"I know one person who's not happy."

"Who's that?"

"Todd Lofton." And he added, "Between you and me, when the property went on the market, he put in the highest bid, and Sarah's husband rejected it."

"Interesting," replied John.

5

"Paul, there's a call on line one for John, do you want to take it?" asked Pam. He was in his office and his father was busy at a job site.

"Yes, this is Paul."

"I'm looking for John Davis," said the voice.

"He's not in the office at the moment, but I can help you."

"My name is Katherine O'Brien, and I've recently purchased the Wildcat Riding Academy."

"Is there a problem?" He had to think. "I'm not sure where that is, ma'am."

"Well, you should, your company fixed the roofs."

"Just a moment, ma'am. Let me check with our office manager."

"That's the place outside of Clewiston. You know, the one your dad was gaga over? It didn't have a name then. That was the name on the payment. We just got it a month ago," said Pam, the office manager.

"Ms. O'Brien, I apologize," he stated as he took the call off hold. "I did not know the name of the property when we were working on it."

"Oh, that's right, we just gave it a name. But still, I'm not happy. We have a leak in the barn roof, and it's Mrs. O'Brien."

"We'll have someone out tomorrow."

"I hope so, I don't like how things are done here in Florida."

"How's that, Mrs. O'Brien?"

"Tomorrow at what time?"

"Early, Mrs. O'Brien."

"I'll be waiting." And she clicked off the phone.

It was 7:30 a.m. when Paul and Freddy pulled in the driveway under the sign that said Wildcat Riding Academy. Before the truck came to a stop, a woman opened the front door of the ranch house, walked out, and strutted purposely toward them. She was wearing a Red Sox baseball cap pulled low, sunglasses, a white long-sleeved shirt, men's jeans, worn riding boots, and she was missing her left hand.

"I have to say, I'm impressed." She introduced herself as Katherine O'Brien as she walked past them and into the barn, waving her good hand in the direction of the barn. The leak was next to the entrance high in the corner. The woman took off her glasses to reveal a mass of scarred skin around her temple and pointing with an equally scarred hand at the spot. "It's right up there, can you see it?" And without skipping a beat, she looked at Paul. "You look familiar."

Behind him, he heard a horse snigger. He turned and had a momentary déjà vu. It was Cash, and next to him, Bob. This took a moment to process.

"Wow, you guys are early. Mom, you must be impressed." And then it all made sense as a petite woman wearing riding pants, boots, and a helmet walked into the barn. She stopped, took off the helmet, revealing her long black hair, and stared.

"Well that was our plan," said Paul and froze. "Hi," was all he could say.

"Hi, Paul." He kept walking toward her. She put the helmet down and stepped forward. They embraced and hung on for a long moment.

"It is you," was all Katherine could say as she put her hand to her mouth in surprise. Liz backed away and looked at him still holding on. "How are you?"

All Paul could do was hold her shoulders at arms' length, stare at her, and say," I am so sorry about your dad." And he looked at Katherine. "And you as well." Katherine put her hand down as Paul turned and gave her a hug. It was an awkward moment.

"You know each other?" said Freddy.

"Sorry, Freddy. Yes, this is Liz O'Brien and her mom, Mrs. O'Brien. Liz and I went to college together in New Hampshire."

"Oh, great," Freddy replied with a questioning look.

"That's up north." They heard another voice and all turned as Rusty and Tim entered the barn. They had noted the truck pull in. "Remember me and Tim?" said Rusty.

"Yes, up in Ocala. How are you guys doing?"

"Great, we just follow Cash and Bob around." They both came over to shake his and Freddie's hands.

"Up in Ocala?" said Liz.

"Oh man, I forgot, Lizzy," said Rusty and reached in his back pocket, taking out his brown leather wallet. He opened it, picked at some worn edges, pulled out a card, and gave the barely readable business card from Supreme Roofing to Liz. She turned the card over and read the note on the back. 'So sorry for your loss, please call me. Paul.' Liz looked down for a long moment.

"Sorry, Lizzy, I messed up. Paul came by one day on a hunch and met up with Cash and Bob. You and Katherine were still in the hospital at the time, and we told him what happened. I put the card in my wallet, and it's been in there ever since."

"No, Rusty, you did nothing of the kind," she replied and looked at Paul.

Katherine intervened. "Tim, could you stay and help Mr. Freddy? Rusty I need help out back, and you two have some catching up to do," she took Rusty's arm and led him away.

"Let's get a coffee, Paul." She turned and led him toward the house. She opened the door, turned, and asked, "Would you like a beer instead?"

"Yes, only if it's cold and Tom is serving it at the Tug Boat," Paul answered, smiling. "Coffee's fine, Liz." She brought him into the kitchen and turned to face him.

"Paul, you don't know how much I've thought about you. I can't believe you're here." There was another awkward moment. "Please sit and tell me what you've been up to... besides fixing roof leaks."

She made the coffee, and they sat across from each other

at the old, ranch-style wooden table. She told him about the fire. The scarring was the result of mostly second-degree burns on her arms and on her left shoulder. She was fortunate to not have to go through any major surgery as her mother had. "My father saved my life and my mother's. There was a bucket of water nearby, and he drenched us with it just before the fire department arrived. Mom lost her left hand when a beam fell and crushed it. She's lucky to be alive, and you can see the scarring, but she is a tough woman." Liz paused again. "This is her dream," she stated as she looked up and around. "We lost a lot, in many ways." She stopped talking and looked down at the floor, shaking her head slowly. "Paul, this must be some kind of miracle."

They talked for over an hour. Then Paul's cell phone buzzed. He answered it quickly. "Yep, be back by two." He put the phone down on the table, keeping his hand on it, and looked at Liz. "I'd like to see you again."

"I'd like that, Paul." The temptation to reach across the table and place her hand over his hand was too much. He got up from his chair. She came around the table, and he pulled her in for another hug. She pulled back, put her hand on his chest, and said, "I think I've missed you for a long time," and kissed him softly on the lips. They walked back to the barn. She couldn't help herself as she held his hand.

Freddy was putting the ladder back on the truck. "All set, Paul. Should be fine."

"That's great, Freddy."

Liz let go of Paul's hand as they stood next to the barn entrance. They looked at each other as she folded her arms across her chest. Tim walked over and extended his hand to shake Paul's and then stepped back.

"Great to see you again. Freddy was filling me in on your business, and you guys are doing well. You're not perfect, but if you were, you wouldn't be here today, right?" he said with an impish smile and a wink.

"You're right there, Tim."

Tim continued. "Well, I'm glad you finally caught up with Liz and her two buddies." He pointed to the two horses looking out of their stall. They all turned and looked at the horses. Paul and Liz walked over to their friends. Both horses were looking for a treat but were content to have two sets of soothing hands pat their necks.

He called her when he got back to the office. They had another long conversation as Pam took all his calls. After working a half day on Friday, he drove out to the Wildcat Riding Academy and drove her back to Fort Myers. He had made dinner reservations at a local steak house. She was wearing a lightweight blue denim vest, a white cotton skirt that stopped at her knees, dress cowboy boots, and her black hair that he remembered so well stopped in the middle of her back.

The hostess took them to a table for two in a quiet section of the well-appointed restaurant. "Almost as nice as the Tug Boat," quipped Paul as he pulled out her chair. Liz looked at him and took off the vest and held it by her side. The dress's shoulder straps were very thin. The discoloration on her shoulder was apparent. She looked down and then up at Paul. He took the vest from her hand and carefully draped it on the back of her chair, stood, and faced her. He gently pulled her in, reached around her shoulders hugged her, then backed away and gently kissed her on the lips, despite the stares from a few nearby tables.

During the meal, the conversations ranged far and wide. They briefly talked about people they had seen after college. She had met a Brit in Germany who wanted to begin a relationship, but in the world of dressage with its constant training and competition, it would make it very difficult, and she wasn't sure if she was ready. Paul had girlfriends but nothing serious. The chemistry was never there. The years after college graduation were forgotten as Paul and Liz re-discovered something that began in left field at the University of New Hampshire.

6

Katherine was tending a small herb garden she had behind the ranch house when she heard a deep-throated bellow near one of the oaks. She walked over to investigate. Contentedly grazing was a very large, brown Brahma bull with its distinctive shoulder hump. She called Rusty and Tim. When they arrived, they took over and investigated the situation. "I don't know, Katherine, he may have busted through on his own, but he would have been cut up," said Rusty. "We'll check things out."

"I think somebody cut the fence," said Tim upon returning from his investigation. "There are a bunch more inside the fence near the pond, and they all have the double circle brand. There's more stuff going on out there. We noticed more trash, beer cans, and bottles around the edges of the pond. It looks like they were using them for target practice."

"I'll look into it, boys," replied Katherine.

Liz was visiting Paul in Fort Myers and called her cell phone. "Yes, Rusty is sure the wire was cut."

"I probably should have talked to the owners before we put up the barbed wire, but that pond is on our land. Before we bought the place, we had to have it surveyed, remember?"

"Yes, I had a feeling this problem wouldn't go away easily." When Rusty and Tim were out there putting up the wire, they noticed there had been a fence before, but it was ripped out and the wire rolled up and tucked away under a tree.

Rusty, Tim, and a couple of cowboys from the Old Oak Ranch began rounding up the wayward cattle, starting with the Brahma who was still in the shade behind the house.

"Hope they're careful with that guy."

"Yeah, they said his name is Bernie. They're giving him his space." It took all day to move the cattle back to their own pasture. Katherine called the main number of Old Oak Ranch three times, and all she got was a recording. She left three messages. As darkness was setting in, she saw the headlights of the four-by-fours appear from the pastures behind the barn.

"What happened?"

When Tim walked into the kitchen, Katherine noticed he had a large welt on his forehead, a cut lip, and blood crusted in his nostrils. Rusty began. "We had all the cattle back and were fixing the fence when a couple of kids, older teenagers, show up on four-by-fours." He looked at his son, shaking his head. "One of them pulls out a pistol from his belt and shoots in the air a couple of times."

Tim added, "What an asshole! Sorry, Katherine."

Rusty continued. "This kid is dangerous. He's about six two, and comes over to Tim and starts waving the gun around. It looked like a .32. He sticks it back in his pants and punches Tim in the face. The other one runs at me and pushed me down. I looked over, and the first kid has Tim on the ground and was punching him some more. The other kid leaves me and grabs the first kid and pulls him off Tim." He stopped to get his emotions together. "He looked a little older. The one that had the gun is yelling about trespassing and getting the sheriff and his uncle and father." He paused. "It happened so fast. They got on their four-by-fours and headed back to where they came from."

Paul took the next day off. He, Liz, Rusty, and Tim went to the sheriff's office and filed a report. Two days later a deputy arrived. He explained the situation. "Both boys, a Donald Spencer and Gunther Lofton, admit to the confrontation. They thought they were trespassing and insisted the pond was on his uncle's property. The Lofton boy admits punching one of the men, and the Spencer boy admitted pushing the other one down but realized he should get the Lofton boy off of Mr. Hartwell, who will be pressing charges against the Lofton boy. At the moment, Gunther Lofton will be spending time in the county jail until his father or uncle bail him out." He looked down at his notes. "Both boys deny that Lofton had fired a handgun. We're still looking into that possibility."

Gunner Lofton's father bailed his son out of jail and proceeded to punch him a number of blows when they got back home, Gunner was put on six months' probation under the supervision of his father.

❖ ❖ ❖

The roof leak repair at Wildcat Riding Academy had taken place two months ago. Paul and Liz were spending more and more time together. He would reacquaint with Cash and Bob by taking slow, leisurely rides around the property with Liz.

The company had completed a large roofing project on Marco Island, and Liz and Paul were having dessert after a celebratory dinner at Flemings, a restaurant in Naples, the city south of Fort Myers. Paul reached inside his Tommy Bahama's shirt pocket and drew out a small black-felt-covered box and handed it to Liz. She opened it revealing the sizable diamond and gold band.

"Will you marry me?"

"Paul, you know I will." He gently reached across the table and took her left hand as she let him slip on the ring. A week later, Liz asked, "Mom, we've been thinking, would you object to us living here?"

The wedding would take place at St. Margaret's Catholic Church in Clewiston, and a reception would be at their new home, 'The Wild Cat Riding Academy.' As a wedding gift, John built a four-rail fence around the property and had it painted white. Paul would no longer commute to Fort Myers.

It was during this time that living accommodations were a large part of their conversations. Paul and Liz were furniture shopping in Clewiston and stopped at 'High End Resales.' A salesman met them at the door and introduced himself as Andy.

That was verified by his name tag, and under the name it said 'owner.' The other thing that Paul noticed was a small, holstered sidearm. They were the only customers in the large barn-like store. "We'd like to wander around and look," said Liz with a smile.

"Great, but just holler if you need help," he said as he moved a little further from them to adjust a price tag. They continued to walk around the crowded and confusing displays of used furniture. "I wish he wouldn't hover like that," said Liz, only loud enough for Paul to hear.

At one point, they passed an open door that led to an office. There was the faint odor of burnt leaves, and inside was a young man wearing camo pants, black boots, and a stained over-used sleeveless undershirt. He had his feet up on a desk and was watching a small TV. As they walked by, he reached over and closed the door. The owner appeared, opened the door, and said something to the boy in a harsh tone and closed the door with a slam. He looked at Paul and Liz. "He's my son. I have to work on his manners."

"Oh," said Paul, and out of curiosity, asked, "Have you been robbed? I noticed your sidearm."

"No, not on my watch, but I'm ready if it happens," said the man, tapping the handgun. "It's a Bobcat Beretta. Ya, it's one of the reasons I moved from New Jersey to Florida. My neighborhood was getting a little too dark, if you catch my drift, and Florida has a great attitude when it comes to guns and self-protection. I live out in cattle country and have a bunch of guns way bigger than this pea shooter." He tapped the holster once more. "Just got an AR-15 the other day. You never know." He paused and refocused. "So how are we doing, anything you need? Like I said I'm here."

"We'll let you know," said Liz. Just then a bell went off as another customer walked through the doors, and the owner left to greet them. "You know I kind of like this piece," said Liz, looking down at an old desk.

"How much is it?" asked Paul, as he looked at the price

tag. "Looks like two hundred, I think?" And he added, "I think a chicken with a pen wrote the price down."

"That's two ninety-nine," said a voice, startling them. It was the owner's son. Another breech of privacy caused Paul's adrenaline level to heat up.

"It looks like two hundred to me," said Paul, turning the price tag in his hand.

"Na, those are two nines."

"I'm sorry, those are zeroes," Paul responded in an annoyed tone.

"Hey, I know what I wrote down, and those are nines."

"Oh, then they must make zeroes different in New Jersey," said Paul.

"I think I want to leave," said Liz.

"Okay by me," responded Paul, now staring at the owner's son. Paul and Liz walked out the front door of the store.

"Wow," said Liz. "I got a chill in there. What were you trying to do, Paul?"

"I'm sorry, Liz. I got carried away. I get tired of ignorant rude people, especially kids like that. He was a punk." Paul paused. "He just pushed my buttons."

7

A week before the wedding, Liz was in the horse barn when she heard a series of gunshots a distance away and, a moment later, a thud on the side of the barn and an instant hole of light and another thud and another beam of light. She then heard the rat-tat of more shots and a ping sound from the roof of the house and what may have been a slug hit the side of the house. Katherine came out of the house as Liz ran toward her mother.

"Get back in the house, Mom, quick." When she got inside, she said, "I'm calling the sheriff's office." The dispatcher assured her there would be a deputy coming, but at the moment, the closest one was twenty-five miles south of them in Montura. She then called Paul.

"I'll be right out, Liz."

The cruiser, with its Hendry County Sheriff's decal spread over the side of the vehicle, pulled into the driveway. The deputy got out. Paul had arrived a few minutes before the cruiser and introduced himself and the others. "Nice to meet you. So what happened, you heard gunshots and slugs hit your property? Could you show me where they hit the barn?" They looked at the barn's dirt floor and located the slugs. The deputy's initial response was that there were many private shooting ranges in the area. He would look into any that were east of them. He took pictures of the damage and collected the slugs. The deputy also determined that the slugs could be Winchester Super Magnum and commented, "Those are big slugs."

On a metal arch over the gated entrance was an elaborate wrought-iron sign in large block letters with the name Old Oak Ranch and the double zero logo above the name. Paul drove up the driveway with the familiar white fencing that brought him to a low, rambling, red-brick home similar to Wildcat Riding Academy's main house, but larger. The front door opened and out stepped an older woman, possibly in her seventies. "Hi, we haven't met. I'm Paul Davis from the Wildcat Riding Academy next door."

"Nice to meet you, Paul. I'm Rita Lofton. How can I help you?"

"Rita, you heard about what happened a few days ago?"

"I can't say I have, Paul," she answered while looking at him, eyes furrowed in concern. "We've been away for the summer visiting our grandkid. What happened?" And she thought for a moment. "I can check with Andy; he lives in the guest house with his son Gunther."

"Andy?"

"Yes, he owns the used furniture store in Clewiston." The woman stopped and thought. "He sells nice pieces, and his son helps out. You should stop in if you need furniture."

"Oh, yes, I know the place. I did stop by, and I've met Andy and his son. Maybe I'll check with him. Thanks."

"Well what happened, Paul?"

"Some stray bullets hit our barn."

"Oh." Just then, two camouflage-painted, mud-splattered, all-terrain vehicles appeared from the back of the ranch house continuing down the driveway. One of the riders was shirtless, and the other wore a sleeveless white undershirt with an AR-15 rifle strapped across his back.

8

The wedding took place in the old Catholic church with its Spanish design. The Hispanic priest with his heavily accented English gave an added warmth to the ceremony. They hired a local rental company to put up a large enclosed tent and dance floor inside the riding corral. Florence Davis, Paul's mother, hired a local four-piece band that had a range of songs they could all dance to. Most of the guests were from Fort Myers, friends of John, Florence, and Paul. A few of his high school friends and their wives made for a good crowd, all making sure Liz and Katherine were comfortable. Todd and Rita Lofton were invited but declined the invitation.

They had been at their new home long enough that Cash and Bob were comfortable with the pastures. The thunderstorms of the summer were over, and the cool, pleasant fall nights were now in the offering. Horses generally did not like loud sounds, and to make Cash and Bob more comfortable during the wedding reception, they opted to let them spend the time in the pasture away from the loud music.

Once the reception was over, Rusty went out and brought the two horses back to the barn. Katherine was there to assist Red. "Something's wrong with Bob," he stated as he handed him off to Katherine. "He's really favoring his right foreleg." Katherine led him into the large stall after Cash was brought in.

"Bob's been running hard," was Katherine's first diagnoses as she ran her hand down the leg and felt the fetlock area just above Bob's hooves. She did the same to his left leg. "I can feel heat on both of them." She stood and patted his side, adding, "You're getting a little too old for that, my friend."

"Cash seems okay, but he looked agitated, don't you think?"

said Rusty.

◆ ◆ ◆

They were at one of the old shooting ranges on the outer edges of the ranch. Gunner was getting bored. They could hear the muffled music from the wedding off in the distance. "That bastard Davis, I hate him. The sheriff was snooping around last week and talked to me and my father. He even came out here to check the backstop in the shooting range."

"Well, if you hadn't put the bump stock on the AR, you wouldn't have had a problem."

"Ya, it kinda got away from me. Those rounds went all over hell. Hey, nothing happened, I put a couple of holes in a f...k'n barn. I'm pissed I shot about fifteen bucks' worth of ammo in, what, five seconds."

"Try not to hold the trigger down so long, and I told you there would be a pretty good kick with those big slugs."

"I know, I know. You're starting to sound like my mother."

"Hey, those must be Davis's horses. I've never seen them out this far," said Gunner, pointing in the direction of the of the new fence. "Let's check'm out." They drove their four-wheelers down to the fence, got off, and leaned on the top rail. Spence gave a soft whistle and clicked his tongue. Cash kept his distance, but Bob was curious and walked over. "I like the looks of that Indian horse," said Gunner.

"He's a Paint, if that's what you mean."

"Spence, Indian, Paint, what the f...k difference does it make?" The reaction by Gunner had both horses' ears up.

"Okay, okay, lighten up," said Spencer.

Gunner then climbed up the fence and sat on the top rail. He calmed himself down and kept looking at Bob. "I just hate it when people keep telling me what I do is wrong."

Spence pulled up some grass and handed it to Gunner. "Here, see if he'll take some grass." He held out the treat toward

Bob who slowly looked up and took a few more tentative steps in Gunner's direction. When he was close enough Bob stretched his neck and took the grass. Gunner climbed down and stood next to the fence. He had been around the cowboy's horses who accepted him being that close, and Bob was acting the same way. "Yes, Indian horse, I like your looks," he said in a quiet voice and stroked Bob's neck. Cash was still skeptical and stayed where he was. "He's really friendly and not that big, I bet I could grab his mane and hop on." And he looked at Spence. "Wouldn't Davis love that?"

"Gunner, I don't think that's a great idea."

"There you go again, Spence." And with that, Gunner took hold of Bob's mane and hoisted himself up. Instinct kicked in, and in Bob's case, it was to run as fast as he could. Surprisingly, Gunner stayed on, squeezing the horse's side with his thighs and feet and holding Bob's mane with both hands. The pain in Bob's joints was too much, and just as quickly as he started, he stopped, much to Gunner's relief.

He jumped off. Spence was howling with laughter as he slapped the fence. When this happened, Cash ran a few yards and stopped, head up and ears alert, pawing the ground in irritation. Bob gingerly walked away, turned, and stared at the man that had been on his back.

"That was awesome, Gunner." And he added, "You are one crazy bastard."

9

Before too long, word spread. Wildcat Riding Academy was in business. The barn was full. All ten stalls had a horse, and some were boarders. Liz and her mother's credentials were enough to bring in clients interested in dressage as well as general riding lessons. Liz was pregnant. Katherine could not have been happier.

But there were still issues around mischief and vandalism. On one occasion, the mailbox near the entrance was smashed, and letters on the sign over the entrance were shot out. An occasional ping could be heard on the clay roof. There was a section of fence along the property line that had bullet holes and cans and bottles on the ground where they had been shot as targets. On these occasions, a phone call would be made to Old Oak Ranch. After a while, the calls would not be answered. Paul remembered what Gary Johnson had said about Todd Lofton's failed bid for the property. Was this payback?

Calls to the sheriff would result in the same answer, an unenthusiastic, "We'll check it out." The incidents would occur randomly, enough to put the family on edge. Frustration over the inaction by the Loftons and the sheriff's office began to set in. When a small bullet hole was discovered in Paul's new office window in the back of the house, the tipping point had been reached.

◆ ◆ ◆

He waited behind the used furniture store. When they walked out into the dimly-lit municipal parking lot, he took a softball bat from behind the front seat and walked toward them."What the f...k do you want," said Gunner as Paul approached them.

"Good, you remember me." Carrying the bat in his left hand, Paul approached him and slapped him hard on the side of his face with his right hand. Gunner staggered back. His father fumbled with his holster, pulling out the Bobcat. Paul swing the bat with two hands, knocking the pistol away.

"Okay, now." He pointed the bat at Gunner and stared at him. "I'm going to say this once. I have seen and done things you do not want to know about. I am no longer in the service of my country in a foreign land. This is my home and you are my neighbors. You do not want to mess with me, my family, or my property any longer." He walked over to the truck, opened the driver's side door, turned, and stared at Gunner, once again pointing the bat. "This is a wake-up call." He paused for emphasis. "Do you understand?" He waited for an answer and repeated, "Do you understand!?"

Gunner nodded his head.

"I want to hear you say it," demanded Paul.

"Yes," replied Gunner while rubbing his face.

"Good." And keeping the bat pointed in Gunner's direction. He looked at Andy. "Your son is a man now. I hope he takes this warning seriously."

The warning worked. Gunner found other venues to occupy his free hours. For months there had been no indications that he was back interrupting their lives. But today, in his chemically altered brain, he decided it was time to catch the big bass. They had been drinking beer and smoking pot most of the afternoon. "Hey, we're not shooting, we're fishing."

"I'm just saying," said Spence. "That Davis guy you don't want to mess with." And he thought for a moment. "How come you didn't sue the bastard for hitting you?"

"Come on, Spence. He slapped me. I just didn't see it coming. Only a pussy sues over a slap, according to my father."

"What about the stand your ground defense thing? He did bust your father's hand."

"Ya, my uncle explained that too." He took another swig of beer and continued. "We would probably lose that argument if it ever went to court. He said because it was a public place and slow-draw Andy pulled the gun. Asshole Davis had the right to defend himself, even if it was with a f...k'n softball bat."

They had climbed over the fence, leaving their four-by-fours on the Old Oak Ranch side, casting their fishing lures and talking. The latest subject was how they beat up the two crackers that worked for the riding academy. "I'd do it again if they showed up now," said Gunner.

"I bet you would," replied his friend, barely able to get the sentence out. The pot was taking over his brain.

"Hey, ain't that the Indian horse over there?" said Gunner, pointing in the direction of the oak tree on the edge of the pond. The sun was setting behind the tree's long, low branches now, and Bob's distinctive white back end was visible. He had just taken a drink of water and looked over at the two men, ears up and alert.

Gunner turned to Spence. "I wonder if he wants to go for a ride?"

"I'm not gonna say it, Gunner." And Spence kept fishing.

"Good." Gunner put down his rod as he smiled and walked unsteadily toward Bob. "Come on, Indian horse."

And out of the shadows appeared Cash. "What the f......" was all Gunner could say. The setting sun was reflecting off the pond and into the black horse's eyes, giving them a red glow like a giant horse from hell. He began pawing the ground. His ears were back, nodding his head and showing his teeth. Gunner stopped in his tracks and tried to walk backward. His heel caught on a root and he fell. As he went down, he yelled and instantly rolled onto his stomach, and just as quickly, got up and ran to the fence, climbing over it.

Spence came out of his fog, looked up at the big, agitated horse, threw down his rod, and headed for the fence. Gunner ran to his four-by-four, stopped, reached behind the seat, and retrieved his .32.

"What are you doing?" yelled Spence as he got on his machine. Gunner raised the pistol, held it in two hands, and aimed.

10

Liz was three months pregnant now, and after a late dinner, she and Paul were walking out to the far pasture to bring Cash and Bob back to the barn before darkness set in. The days were shorter now. "They're probably near the pond," said Liz.

As they approached the pond, they heard a man's yell and could hear the familiar high-pitched sound of an all-terrain vehicle running hard and fast. "Now what," said Paul as he began to run in the direction of the sounds. There was just enough daylight to see Bob emerge from under the oak, followed by Cash. "There you are." And at the same time, he heard another sound off to his right near the fence. He spotted the Brahma looking at him between the rails, snorting.

"What happened…anything?" said Liz, a little out of breath but catching up.

"I don't know," he answered, still looking at the bull. "Maybe Bernie scared someone." He pointed at the Brahman bull. "Let's get these two back to the barn."

Liz had brought two long leather leads and halters to help walk the horses back. When she hooked the lead onto Cash's halter and began to walk, he suddenly did a quick hop, head bob, and loud snort. "Well, what are you so happy about, my handsome boy?" she asked and patted him on the side of his neck. Paul was leading Bob, and suddenly, the horse began some earnest head bobbing.

The next day, a Hendry County Sheriff's car pulled into the driveway, and a deputy got out and knocked on the front door.

Paul greeted him. "How can I help you, Deputy?"

He introduced himself as Deputy Ron Smith, and Paul invited him in. "I just wanted you to be aware of an incident that occurred near your property last evening. I know you've had some complaints about Gunther Loftin in the past." He paused for a moment. "He was killed last night."

Paul looked at Liz and Katherine. They were standing in the kitchen. The deputy continued. "He was gored and crushed by that big Brahma. We found a .32 Special next to his body registered to his father." He shook his head. "Not sure what that was all about. I know we've had a few complaints about Loftin, but between you and me…" And he thought again. "Well I shouldn't say anything," the deputy said and turned and left.

The death of his son under the peculiar circumstances reverberated around the close-knit cattle community. Todd Lofton suggested his nephew should pick-up the pieces and move on. The High End Used Furniture store was closed and Andy returned to the Garden State. Wildcat Riding Academy was no longer plagued by vandalism and dangerous random bullets, and during this tranquil time, a celebrity emerged.

"That's a mean son of a gun," said the cowboy, spitting tobacco juice and talking to his friend and fellow competitor. They were participating in the Bull Riding Championships in Orlando. "Rumor has it he killed a guy in Clewiston. The guy was trying to shoot him." And he added, "Some people call him the Stand Your Ground Bull."

"Great, I just drew him for tonight's go-round." They were discussing Bernie, who had a reputation that was making Five Star Entertainment a lot of money.

◆ ◆ ◆

Paul, Liz, and their new baby were at the Pig House Restaurant when Donald Spencer came over to their booth. He was tending the smoker in the back of the restaurant and had seen the riding academy truck pull into the parking lot.

"Excuse me, I've been meaning to do this for a while." Paul and Liz looked up in mild surprise. The waitress had just taken their order and had delivered their iced teas. Spence waited to get his thoughts together. "May I sit? This shouldn't take but a few minutes."

Paul slid over. "Sure, have a seat."

Spencer looked over. "She's a pretty baby."

"Thank you, Donald, her name is Evelyn Katherine," said a smiling Liz.

Looking down, Spence began. "I never apologized for the things I did with Gunner. I was raised better. I just got caught up in his wildness. I've changed." Looking down at the table, he continued. "I'd like to tell you something about the night he was killed."

This got Liz and Paul's attention, and he began. "We had the day off and had been drinking beer and smoking pot. Gunner came up with this idea that we should go back to your pond and try to catch a bass. He caught it a few years ago and had thrown it back in." And he added for emphasis, "This is how wasted we were. I didn't think it was such a great idea because of your warning," he looked at Paul, "but as usual, I went along with it." And he looked back down at the table, gathering his thoughts. "While we were there, he saw your Paint and decided he wanted to ride it again."

"So it was him," said Liz.

"How did you know?" Spence asked, looking at Liz.

"He came up lame, and it took him a while to recover."

"He was crazy, Mrs. Davis. That's all I can say. Sorry. I told him it wasn't a good idea," And he once again looked down at the table.

"Donald, what happened that night?"

He looked up at Liz and continued. "Gunner stopped fishing and started walking toward your Paint. I heard him yell, and when I turned, he was on the ground. The big black horse came out of nowhere, it was getting dark and all. He walked right up to Gunner with its ears back. Gunner got up, ran to the fence, and jumped over. I did the same and got on my machine." He stopped and looked at both of them. "You know the story going around about how Bernie charged a man before he could shoot him, and we know the man was Gunner." Liz and Paul nodded their heads. "That's not what happened." And he looked at the couple for emphasis.

"When Gunner got to his four-wheel, he pulled out the .32. Your black horse had followed us to the fence. He couldn't have been more than five feet away from Gunner, who had the gun up in two hands aiming at your horse, right here," he explained, pointing at his forehead. Paul and Liz's eyebrows were now raised, staring at him.

"That's when the Bernie charged him. He came out of the dark. It happened so fast. Gunner was standing one minute, and in a blink, he was in air and landed on his back all spread out. He was helpless, just looking up confused like. The bull attacked again, burying his head into Gunner's chest." Spence stopped, closed his eyes, and pinched the bridge of his nose. "I'll never get that sight out of my head. It was awful." He shook his head again and waited a few moments, looked up, and continued. "The bull saw me. He was ready to charge. I don't remember anything after that except pushing my four-wheeler as hard as it would go." Spence looked out the restaurant windows behind Liz and Paul. "He was my friend. When I got home, I called the sheriff and told him where he was."

The waitress arrived with their platter of ribs. Spence slid out of the booth with a vacant look. He turned to leave and stopped as he emerged from his moment. "Your lunch is on me," he said and stood there with a questioning look on his face. "You know a few years ago, before Bernie got as big as he is now, Gunner fired some rounds at a tree near him. I often wonder if animals can remember stuff like that."

Liz and Paul looked at each other. Liz turned and looked up at Spence. "I wouldn't be surprised."

BEACH STONES

1

The Granite State's coast is 13 miles long, beginning three miles north of the mouth of the Merrimack River in Massachusetts and ending at Portsmouth, New Hampshire's, Piscataqua River. The towns of Seabrook, Hampton, North Hampton, and Rye are the picturesque communities that form the eastern border of the state's coastline. They all have one thing in common, wonderful sandy beaches.

New Hampshire's land surface is comprised of a variety of granite rock. Within the granite are other minerals. One of the hardest is quartz. Wave action on the beaches over a millennia have laid the quartz portion of the rock bare, leaving it pure white. This is where our story begins, where the waves meet the sand forming the eternal beach stones.

During the summer months, for thousands of years, the indigenous First Nation Abenaki, Malecite, Passamaquoddy, and Penacook would escape the inland insects and live on the beaches. Later when these populations were decimated by white man's diseases, small fishing villages appeared and became the safe harbors for the dory schooners searching for haddock, cod, mackerel, and all other Atlantic cold-water delicacies. In 1907 Hampton Beach Village was developed but not as a fishing community. Looking for amusements, the beach now served another purpose. It was a summer escape not only for the locals, but for many from surrounding cities and towns and would be referred to as simply Hampton Beach.

The Flanagan brothers, Henry and Patrick, were fishermen, making a living venturing out of Seabrook and Rye Harbors. Their family had been in the trade for generations, but World War One would change all that.

Upon their discharge in 1918, and before returning to the fishing grounds, they spent a weekend in Atlantic City, New Jersey, enjoying the boardwalk and the excitement of the end of the war in Europe.

Tired of fishing, they longed for a change. Their experience in New Jersey triggered a thought for the future. They remembered the fun of playing a game called Skee-Ball. The game was similar to bowling, except there were no pins to knock down. The object was to roll wooden balls, about the size of a baseball, up a short incline with a raised lip at the end, causing the ball to rise in the air and land in one of the concentric cylinder-shaped circles, each with a different point value. The ball would then fall through a hole in the bottom of the cylinder and trigger a score.

The brothers sold their boat, bought a piece of oceanfront property in Hampton Beach, and erected a two-story building. The first floor would be a penny arcade. They would live on the second. The name would be 'Flanagan's Skee-Ball Paradise Arcade.' It would eventually feature other forms of amusements, such as pinball machines, billiards, and shuffle bowl. They also opened a bar that was promptly closed when Prohibition was declared in 1920.

Their next venture would prove to be disastrous. The unpopularity of Prohibition created a new business. The 'speakeasy.' Under the guise of their arcade, they began the illegal business in a newly installed back room. That, too, ended tragically and quickly when, at the age of 25, Patrick died while smuggling Canadian whiskey at the Isle of Shoals, a group of small islands outside of Portsmouth Harbor. Rumor had it that he was drunk and fell into the ocean; his body was never recovered. While investigating Patrick's death, the police discovered the illegal bar. It was quickly dismantled as

Henry watched the United States Revenue Agents break up wooden kegs and bottles of whiskey while members of the Temperance Union supervised the destruction. His life would change dramatically. No arrest was made. The local police chief, Paul Giacobbe had known the Flanagan brothers his whole life. They were boyhood friends.

"Sorry about this, Henry," Paul said, slapping him on the back. "When Patrick was lost, the feds figured out what was going on, and I'm thinking the Union got wind as well." He looked around. "They didn't bust up the other stuff, your Skee-Ball and pool tables and such." Henry could only nod his head.

This was too much. In a matter of a few days, he had lost his brother, who was his best friend, and his business was in peril. He found a case of whiskey that had not been destroyed and began drinking. The arcade was closed, and he retreated to the rooms above.

Chief Giacobbe had not seen Henry for a four days. He banged on the second-floor door, and when it opened, the stench was overwhelming. "Henry, you look like crap and smell like shit," Paul said while holding his hand up to his nose. "You keep this up and you're gonna kill yourself," was the chief's instant observation. Henry had let his beard grow, his eyes were dull and pink, he may have pissed his pants, and there was vomit on his undershirt.

"If you don't stop, you're going to die. Now where in hell are the bottles!?" The chief found the few that were remaining. "Let's start with you going downstairs, taking off those clothes, and dumping six or seven buckets of cold water on your head right now, or I will arrest you and put you in jail for a week."

For reasons only God would know, a guardian angel appeared a week later in the form of Vesta Devlin. She and her sister Madeline carried the temperance crusade in the area. They shared a home in Portland and were the lightning rods of the movement from Portland, Maine, south to Portsmouth and coastal New Hampshire.

Vesta was in Hampton Village visiting the Temperance

Union chapter when she walked by the entrance of the arcade. Henry had taken his friend's advice and was in the process of picking up the pieces of the arcade business. He had not had a drink in a week, his clothes were clean, and he had shaved. He was standing holding a broom.

An attractive woman wearing a wide-brimmed sunhat and an ankle-length summer skirt was walking by. She looked up briefly and nodded a greeting. Henry could not help but stare. In that instant, he was captivated by her blue eyes.

"How's it going today, Henry?" He heard a voice interrupting his stare. It was his friend Chief Giacobbe.

"Good, Paul." They shook hands.

"She is pretty, that one, don't you think?" remarked the chief.

"That she is," replied Henry.

"You don't recognize her, do you?"

"No, why should I?"

"She was here when they broke up the place."

"Oh."

"Yeah, she's a member of the Temperance Union, and my guess is there is a meeting today at the Congregational Church." And he continued, changing the subject. "Place is shaping up, Henry," the chief said as he looked in.

"I may be opening it up tomorrow," said Henry.

"Okay, good luck. I'll come by and see how things are going."

The arcade had been open a week. Chief Giacobbe would come by daily, and they would talk.

"Paul, you know there was no funeral for Patrick. I think I would like to have a service or something. Do people do that?"

"I don't see why not. Why don't you check with Minister Frazier down at the church?"

Henry would have his funeral for his brother and continue to not drink. He also decided to keep going to church. During one sermon, while Minister Frazier was extolling the virtues of temperance and the evils of alcohol, Henry noticed the pretty woman he had seen walking by the arcade a few weeks ago. He would join the Temperance Union and get to know Vesta Devlin. They began seeing each other, at first only at the church meetings, but after a while more socially. They fell in love and were married in 1921.

Vesta was a smart woman. Despite her passion for fighting the evils of alcohol, she was a very level-headed woman and would prove to be a canny business partner for her new husband. She convinced him that the section of the first floor that was intended to be a bar and speakeasy could be expanded to accommodate amusements. The Skee-Ball machines were the most popular and profitable. They bought 10 more machines, and the following summer, 10 more.

When helping to break up bars, Vesta noticed that many of the establishments served food heavily laden with salt. She realized a basic truth about all bars. The thirsty customer would drink more. She convinced Henry to offer, at first, free popcorn, and then she would make fried dough, and they eventually bought a deep fry machine to make French fries. The thirst quencher was Coca-Cola. They made a deal with the local distributor who gave them a cut-rate wholesale price. They guaranteed him two hundred dollars a month selling six-ounce bottles of iced-down Coca-Cola for a nickel. The business flourished.

In January of 1924, Vesta gave birth to their only child, Dorothy. Five years later, a home went up for sale near Rye Harbor, just east of Hampton. The stock market had crashed, and the owner was willing to sell the house at a very reasonable price. The value of hard cash had not changed, and pennies were still considered hard cash. The number of pennies generated by the arcade, particularly Skee-Ball was a considerable amount. Henry and Vesta were frugal and were able to purchase the property with cash, a lot of hard cash.

The small family moved into a large five-bedroom two-story home, a short walk from Jenness Beach on Ocean View Road, on the same coastline as Hampton Beach. Despite the depression, they were wealthy people. Henry soon joined the Abenaqui Country Club golf course, a short walk from his new home, and would become an avid golfer. His days on the fishing boats were a distant memory as he enjoyed a life only few could imagine at that time.

Vesta would soon discover the beauty of Jenness Beach. It became a new part of their lives, with Sunday picnics, a refreshing evening walk, or Henry would bring a long fishing rod in the hopes of landing a striped bass, a local delicacy. Dorothy would collect shells or the bright white beach stones churned up by the waves. Vesta still kept her hand in the temperance movement but confined it to the meetings at the Congregational Church. Prohibition would end in 1933.

At one point, a stray mutt wandered into the arcade and stayed around for a week. It would soon find a home on Ocean View Road. Dorothy was thrilled. She would call it Lucky, and he would prove to be a constant companion of the family, going to the arcade, keeping at Vesta's side, and always enjoying the walks on the beach when Dorothy was home from school.

Then things changed. "C'mon, Lucky, you know you're supposed to do your dog shake outside." And then Dorothy yelled, "Sorry, Mum," as the dog happily walked through the kitchen and into the large living room, followed by Dorothy.

"Dad, why are you home? Where's Mum?"

Vesta had been walking to the First National Bank of Portsmouth delivering counted and wrapped pennies from the day's collection. When crossing Market Square, she was struck down and killed by a drunk driver.

It would take all of Henry's strength to overcome his loss. As it turned out, his 13-year-old daughter would become his new saving angel. She was much like her mother in looks and in temperament, and he would lean on her for help. When not in school, she would take up her mother's responsibilities working in the arcade. Her Aunt Madeline would take the train from Portland whenever she was needed at the house on Ocean View Road and stay as long as was necessary.

The year was 1937.

2

"The trick to Skee-Ball is luck."

This was the advice the boy was imparting on this pretty dark-haired girl with the bright blue eyes and added, "There's no skill here."

"Really?" she responded, looking at the handsome boy with his thick brown hair parted down the middle, but which refused to lay down, and his quiet, welcoming hazel eyes.

"Really."

She rolled the wooden ball as her friends, Joan and Paula, watched. The ball barely made the front half circle. Her friends put their hands to their mouths and laughed. The boy turned to them. "And you're her friends. That wasn't too nice."

He turned, intent on giving more advice. "Okay, don't pay attention to those two," he said, using his thumb to point behind him. The girls kept giggling.

"Here's my suggestion. Besides the luck I told you about, you need more enthusiasm. Roll it harder."

Dorothy was actually very good. She had grown up in the arcade. This was her day off. But today her friends were there, and they had just met some cute boys playing Skee-Ball. They were flirting and having fun. The girls were all juniors at Portsmouth High School and lived near Dorothy. Both of their families had small vegetable and dairy farms.

"Oh, I get it." Dorothy threw a ball, and it landed in the 100-point cylinder, a difficult side target. She looked at the boy again, picked up another ball, and repeated what she had just done to the 100-point target opposite the one she had just landed in. He looked at her.

It was the beginning of summer, 1941, and Hampton Beach was drawing the usual crowds enjoying the amusements and food, despite the occasional sighting of German submarines off the New England coast.

"You've done this before."

"Maybe a couple of times." Dorothy paused. "My father owns the place."

"Mr. Flanagan is your father?"

"Yes."

"He's a great guy. He got me my job at Wentworth Country Club. What's your name?" asked the boy enthusiastically.

"Dorothy."

"Nice to meet you, Dorothy. My name is Odie."

His name was Odba Johnson, but he went by Odie, and was from Jackson, New Hampshire, located in the middle of the White Mountains. He had been an orphan until an older couple, Raymond and Virginia Johnson, adopted him and gave him their name. They owned and ran the Jackson Inn.

Not knowing his parents bothered him, as was the case for many orphans, but he realized at a young age he had to move on. He could not dwell on things he had no control of. The people who adopted him loved him and did all they could to make him feel wanted. Whoever his parents were had created a person with an indomitable spirit that exuded enthusiasm and spunk. He was self-sufficient and looked at life through a lens of positive determination.

As he grew up in the shadow of Mount Washington, Odie became a town treasure. He was an accomplished skier, baseball and basketball player, and quarterbacked the football team, but above all, he was a very good golfer. The local pro, Bud Smith, recognized his talent and took him under his wing at an early age.

Dorothy's father, Henry Flanagan, who never re-married, had become an avid golfer. When he could get away from the arcade, he and friends would visit different golf courses. One of their favorite venues were the courses in Washington Valley.

Henry met Odie at Conway Country Club where Odie was a caddie. He was so impressed with Odie's knowledge of the game, the next day they played a round together. Odie was a scratch golfer, meaning he played to par most of the time.

In 1941, there were three golf tournaments in the seacoast area of New Hampshire. Henry convinced Odie's adoptive parents that he should enter them and stay the summer. They consented, just as long as he worked to earn his keep and was back for the new school year. Henry knew the golf pro at the Wentworth by the Sea resort and secured Odie a place to stay and a job for the summer. As soon as the school year was completed, he took the train to the coast and began caddying at the exclusive resort's golf course, as well as helping the hotel staff with odd jobs.

Today, he and two of his friends and fellow caddies, Phil Olson and Joe Donegan, both from Portsmouth, were hanging out with Odie. The chance meeting at the Skee-Ball games resulted in an afternoon of fun for all going from attraction to attraction. "Odie is hands down the best golfer," Phil announced to the girls. "We have a tournament at Wentworth this week, starting tomorrow. Why don't you come by and watch?"

The tournament would start the next day, Tuesday. Unfortunately, the weather turned against them, but the tournament would go on. Joan and Paula declined the invitation, not wanting to stand in the rain all day.

Dorothy would come and watch. "My dad will probably close the arcade. No one will be at the beach, so I'll tag along with him. He thinks Odie has a chance to win." The second day was truly miserable, with occasional wind squalls blowing off the Atlantic, causing the few people on the course to turn their backs and hold their hats to the onslaught of saltwater-laden wind added to the rain. Moments later, blue skies would appear, teasing the golfers and spectators. Dorothy and her father were dressed in their yellow slickers and yellow rain caps, complete with boots up to their knees. Their attire resembled the lobstermen who were in their boats a few hundred yards offshore.

A bond began as Dorothy sloshed along in the rain, wiping her wet curls from the smiling eyes she had inherited from her mother. They were able to complete the tournament despite the conditions. Odie did well and was the junior division champion, but the overall winner was an older man from Newburyport, Massachusetts.

The friends from their first meeting at the arcade would meet frequently as Odie and Dorothy turned into boyfriend and girlfriend. There were two more tournaments that summer, one at Portsmouth Country Club and the other at the end of the summer at Abenaqui Country Club in Rye.

Three weeks later, Henry and Dorothy were walking along with Odie's group of golfers at the Portsmouth tournament. The weather cooperated, but there was a cloud of another sort hovering over the event. A German submarine had been detected. It had surfaced and was cruising two miles off the coastline. This was unsettling.

There were two power sources that propelled a submarine: when on the surface, diesel engines, and below the surface, batteries. A vital part of a submarine's operation was charging the batteries, normally done at night when they would surface and cruise. On this occasion, possible battery failure forced the sub to surface, leaving them vulnerable for attack. The US Navy sent out two destroyers equipped with depth charges and cannons, but to no avail. The sub disappeared over the continental shelf and hid in its depths. Apparently, the battery issues were solved.

Golf took a back seat to the sub sighting, but Odie was able to concentrate and managed a third place finish out of 35 participants. Later, Odie and Dorothy walked over to the rocky shore next to the golf course to look at the horizon. Possibly there would be another sighting. "I don't know, Dorothy, all I ever hear about is going to war. But right now…" he paused to look at her, "may I have another kiss?" They walked hand in hand along a small sandy beach among the large basalt rock formations. They were out of the wind, and the tide was out. They paused and kissed. They had done this in the past a few times, to solidify being boyfriend and girlfriend, but that was the extent of their intimacy.

The last tournament would take place at Abenaqui Country Club the day before Labor Day, and it did not go well. Having Joan, Paula, and his two caddie friends, Joe and Phil, along did not help. He could not control his drives, and his putting was off, but as usual, his sunny disposition overcame the situation, and he walked away congratulating the winner and wishing him well.

"We'll get it next year, Odie," Henry said to him after the tournament.

"Next year?"

"Sure, unless there are problems with Raymond and Virginia, you are certainly welcome to come back. I know the folks at Wentworth would welcome you, and it looks like you made some nice friends."

Dorothy turned to Odie. "Well I guess we'll see you next summer."

"Yes, you will."

"Come on, guys. I know they have stuff for you to do at the hotel. Let's get going." As Odie passed by Dorothy, he touched her hand briefly, and that's how the summer of 1941 would end for Odba Johnson and Dorothy Flanagan.

Odie would return to Jackson and continue with his work around the Jackson Inn's operation sandwiched between school and athletics. It was their senior year. Dorothy started writing him, but there would be no return letters.

She was perplexed and saddened by this lack of communication from a boy she truly liked and felt the feeling was mutual, but she was able to get over her sadness and move on.

Odie was more than proficient at athletic activities and very social. His senior year in high school was filled with what he had been accustomed to; football, basketball, baseball, social events, and skiing, enjoying all of this in the presence of majestic Mount Washington, the highest peak in the eastern US.

But he had issues. His reading aptitude was at a fourth-grade level. His adopted parents, Raymond and Virginia, knew there was something wrong when he was in early grammar school. They were told by the teachers that this reading and writing problem affects some children, and possibly it was passed on to him by his birth parents. His sunny disposition was challenged many a time over, but he learned to cope and had developed tricks to mask his problem. He was adept at picking up body cues when communicating and would find ways to avoid writing, especially creative writing. He was a very popular student, and at times his friends would write papers for him. He befriended teachers who would pass him along. Odie realized what he was doing was a crutch. He had graduated from high school, but he knew his education was not complete and, in some ways, a sham. He was looking forward to seeing Dorothy again, but he was guilt-ridden. He would have to face her eventually when he went back to the coast for the summer.

It was the 4th of July, 1942. Things in the world had changed dramatically. The previous December, the United States had declared war on Japan. There were no fireworks this year, again, for fear of a U-boat attack around the big harbor in nearby Portsmouth. The Germans would use the light to their advantage, and the government was cautious. There would also be a blackout rule put into effect. All windows facing the Atlantic must be covered at night.

Dorothy had graduated weeks before from Portsmouth High School, and he from Kennet High School in Center Conway, the high school that served many of the local communities in Mount Washington Valley. Odie had taken the train and reported to the hotel at Wentworth by the Sea two weeks earlier and once again kept busy with work around the hotel, caddying and practicing golf. He wanted to see Dorothy but was apprehensive.

The hotel had a fleet of four Chevrolet Coupe Pickups, all

mint green. These were two-door vehicles that had room for four or more people, with a trunk that folded out to carry luggage or other hotel supplies. Despite his issues, he managed to pass the driving test. There was no writing involved.

Odie was delivering beach towels and linens to the Hampton Beach Hotel, a friendly competitor of Wentworth by the Sea. This was his first opportunity to see Dorothy. After making his delivery, he drove to the arcade. She was working, doing her walk-around. This was an integral part of the business, as she went from amusement to amusement, helping if needed or being mindful of troubling customers. Chief Giacobbe or one of his patrol officers was generally on the beat nearby.

As usual, the atmosphere was loud with the mechanical calliope playing circus music in the background. There was loud chatter and an occasional holler of excitement. The smell of popcorn wafted out into the crowded street.

Odie walked up the two steps from the sidewalk to the elaborate entrance of the arcade. He noticed Dorothy immediately. She was wearing a knee-length navy blue skirt, sensible shoes, a white blouse with a bright red vest, and her dark brown hair was now at shoulder length. She was different. She was turning into a woman.

"Odie!" she exclaimed as she turned and noticed him standing at the entrance. She walked toward him a few steps and put her hands on her hips. "I wrote you and you never wrote back."

"I know, I know, I'm sorry. I should have answered you." He paused. "Could we go over there?" he asked, pointing to a quiet spot to the side of the main entrance between the buildings.

"Yes, but I really should be inside," Dorothy replied, now folding her arms in front of her.

"I promise, this won't take but a minute." He led her down the steps and walked to the quiet area.

"Are you okay, Odie?" She was now concerned.

"Yes, I am, but there is something I have to get off my chest."

He paused to think. "I came close to not graduating."

"Oh, why?"

"Because of English. My teacher let me pass because she felt sorry for me. I know it's a lame excuse, but I hate to write. I'm a terrible speller, and most times what I write doesn't make sense. It just frustrates and confuses me."

"I didn't realize that."

"I'm okay, but I did feel bad about not writing you back. I wish I knew how to fix it. I can fix a hook or a slice, but writing and spelling is a mystery to me."

"A hook or a slice?"

"Oh, sorry. That's a golf thing."

"I know that, Odie. You forget who my father is?" she said and smiled. "Well anyway," she looked at him, with her hands by her side, "it's good to see you again."

He stared at her and quietly asked, "Dorothy, do you hate me?"

"No, I could never do that."

"Can I kiss you?"

"Of course."

They would resume the routine they had the previous summer, except now on a few occasions, they would take short drives using the hotel's pickups and at times picnic on one of the quiet beaches, but most days he would be working or practicing. The New Hampshire Amateur Championships were being held the first weekend in August at Abenaqui.

On July 15th he received a letter from the inn in Jackson. "I have to report for my physical in Concord next week."

Odie had been drafted. They were having lunch at Ray's Seaside Restaurant on Rye Beach. "I've been waiting for the letter. I knew it was coming sooner or later." He looked across the table. "Jackson is very small, and all my friends knew we'd be getting the letter soon after graduation."

"When do you report to boot camp?"

Everyone knew the routine by now. If you didn't enlist, you were drafted. If you passed the physical, boot camp was next.

"It can be any time after the physical."

She reached across the rough wooden table and took his hand. He looked up and covered her hand with his other and said, "Hey, hopefully I'll get to play in the championship at Abenaqui," trying to brighten up the atmosphere.

He passed the physical and would wait for his boot camp assignment. It arrived a week later. He was to report to the Concord New Hampshire train station and head to the Atlantic City Training Center in New Jersey on August 17th.

3

On Tuesday, August 15th, the New Hampshire coast was caught in a classic H.H.H. weather pattern: Hazy, Hot, and Humid. And despite the golf course's location near the ocean, there were some golf holes far enough away or tucked in the trees where the sea breeze was not present, causing the conditions to be stiflingly hot and oppressive. Coupled with the heat, the atmosphere was intense.

Bud Smith handed Odie the towel to wipe the sweat from his hands. They were on the eighteenth green. The four-foot putt required all the concentration he could muster. He looked at the imaginary line his ball had to travel and did as Smith, his coach for so many years, had taught him. "Trust the line and keep your head still." It worked. He looked up when the ball fell in the cup and exhaled. He had won the 1942 New Hampshire Amateur at Abenaqui.

After the trophy ceremony, pictures were taken. His parents were on hand to witness the occasion and proudly stood with 'the pride of Jackson,' along with Smith, his coach. Other photos were taken with him and the runners-up, the chairman of the board, and there was one with Dorothy and her dad. There was a dinner after, but truth be told, all Odie wanted to do was to be with Dorothy. The older crowd gathered outside after the dinner for cigarettes, cigars, and drinks. An occasional vesper of a sea breeze mingled with the fans people were waving to keep cool.

"Odie, we'll be heading back," said Virginia. They had driven down from Jackson, along with his old coach, to watch their adopted son play. "We'll see you back home in a few days." Odie would be working one more day at the big hotel and then head home to say goodbye before he left for bootcamp.

"Okay, Mum." And he gave her a hug and got handshakes from Raymond and Bud Smith.

"That was a great putt," said Smith as he patted him on the shoulder while shaking his hand.

"Thanks, Bud," Odie said and nodded his head in appreciation.

Odie had driven one of the hotel pickups to Abenaqui that morning. It was the hotel manager's idea. "Get some extra practice in."

"Let me give you a lift home," said Odie. "I've got to get the car back to Wentworth." It was late afternoon; the tournament had ended hours ago. The air was still hot and thick with humidity. As they drove by Jenness Beach, Odie slowed the car, turned into the gravel parking area, stopped, and turned and looked at Dorothy. "All I thought about while playing today was walking in the water at the beach, it was so hot back there," he said, pointing toward the golf course.

"You have to get the car back, Odie."

"I know, but truth be told, I don't want to leave you." He looked at her. "C'mon, let's take a walk."

He was still wearing his tan cotton golf pants held up with fashionable red suspenders and a white shirt with the sleeves rolled up, but he had removed the tie. As he opened the door, he took off his shoes and socks, put them in the car, and reached in the back seat, grabbing two large white towels that were being returned to the hotel. "Let me grab these, we can wipe off our feet."

Dorothy was wearing a sleeveless, light-blue cotton sundress. She removed her shoes as she walked around the front of the car and reached out for his hand as they walked toward the water's edge.

As soon as they were near enough to feel the moist, packed sand, they felt the cool air radiating from the water. "This is what I've been thinking about all day," as he stepped into a receding wave.

They located a spot to put the towels down. Dorothy removed her wide-brimmed hat with its blue-ribbon band and let her thick hair fall. She had kept it up under the hat. She shook her head and ran her fingers through it and looked at Odie. Her smile got him again. She tossed the hat on the towels, and they began to walk. They talked about the match, friends, family, laughed about their first meeting in the arcade when he instructed her in Skee-Ball, and the future as they walked in the ankle-deep cold water, the product of the Gulf of Maine and its frigid currents. They walked the length of the beach, occasionally stopping to kiss. The need to return the car became less and less pressing.

Stars began to appear in the now darkening eastern sky along with a sliver of a crescent moon filtered by a thin layer of clouds. The sun was beginning to set in the west with a display of purple, orange, and gold. By the time they returned to the hat and the towels, the sun was under the western horizon. Because of the nightly blackout rules, houses facing the sea had their shades drawn, leaving only the light from the forming moon.

When they reached the towels, Dorothy spread them out. She then stood on them facing Odie and began unbuttoning her dress. Odie could only stand and watch this beautiful person with the last glows of sunset illuminating strands of her shoulder-length hair as she concentrated on each button. When she reached the last button at her waist, she stopped, reached up, and held his face in her hands and kissed him with an exploring kiss. While the kiss was in progress, he pulled the suspenders aside and began to unbutton his shirt, shrugging it off, letting it fall to the sand.

As the kiss ended, she then pulled back, reached across with both hands, and pulled the shoulder straps of the dress down and let the dress fall. She stepped out of it and turned her back to Odie, as he pulled his sleeveless undershirt off and tossed it aside. Dorothy looked back over her shoulder. "It's okay, go ahead."

A little muddled, he looked at the simple clasping

arrangement and realized what she was asking him to do. He undid the strap. Dorothy did the rest by pulling the bra off and letting it drop on the discarded dress and turned to face him.

With the gift of the moon's reflection off the Atlantic, he was now looking at perfection as he put his hands gently on her breasts. He looked at her face and those wonderful eyes as they kissed again, this time with more passion as she held him close. He then backed away, reached down, and pulled his golf pants down and kicked them away and proceeded to do the same with his boxer-style shorts and stepped out of them. She backed away and peeled her white cotton undergarment down, stepped out of them, and stood facing him. They embraced and kissed.

The familiar sound of waves was soon replaced by another sense, the sense of touch. They knew they were venturing into unfamiliar territory, exploring a world they had only heard about. They thought they knew what the process involved. It became hectic, confusing and awkward, and they probably did not have enough information, but that was negated by an abundance of enthusiasm and passion.

After, they laid still, enveloped in the wonder of their full body nakedness touching. Odie was the first to speak. "Are you okay?"

She just nodded. They laid where they were a little longer. Odie then stood and held his hand out to help her.

"We need to swim." They walked hand in hand to the surf. She looked at him as the pale light from the moon outlined his strong athletic body. He was a man now. She looked down at her body in the same light. She was a woman.

They walked into the cold water and dove into an oncoming wave. When they emerged, they faced each other and embraced once again as the next wave knocked them over, still clinging to each other, but breathing was more important. They stood up in the waist deep water and laughed.

"We should be getting back."

He looked at her intently and said, "Is this what love is?"

"I think so," responded Dorothy as she pulled him in for

another embrace. This time the hug in the trough of the waves developed into another exploratory adventure as she wrapped her legs around him. They were in water up to their shoulders and were now content to look into each other's eyes and let the ocean and their body's buoyancy dictate.

"I love you, Odie."

"I love you, Dorothy."

They held on, lost in the moment, a moment they would remember forever, but reality interrupted as the stark water temperature reminded them that they were human. "We should be going, Odie."

"I know."

They held hands and walked back as a wave came up behind them to push them along. When they reached the packed sand, they embraced once more and walked hand in hand to the towels. Odie located his clothing and put on his shorts and golf pants. Dorothy picked up a towel, held it in front of her looking at Odie.

"Oh, Odie," she said and began to cry.

He stepped toward her, embraced her, and held her. He could feel her bare shoulders and back in his hands as she shook.

"Is what we did wrong, Odie?" She looked at him.

"I don't think so, Dorothy." He then took the towel from her and wrapped it completely around her and held her.

"No, Odie, it wasn't wrong. I love you," she said after many long minutes, as the sound of the waves returned to her consciousness.

Her question and her answer put feelings back to where they had been before the walk, comfortable and relaxed. Finally, they broke the embrace. Dorothy used the towel to dry herself and did the best she could to dry her hair and began to put her clothes back on.

"Do you need any help with that?" asked Odie as the bra was being replaced.

"No thanks, I think I've got it," said Dorothy. "But I may need some help with this," And she handed him her dress. She stood with her arms extended over her head.

"Oh, I get it," he said as he bunched up the folds and lowered the dress over her head. She slipped her hands through the thin sleeves and let the dress flow down over her body. Odie began to do up the buttons, beginning at her waist and working his way up. She watched him as he carefully put each button in the appropriate hole. When he was done, he stood back, held her at arm's length, and once again he became a captive of her faintly visible Mona Lisa smile. Her lips were all he needed to touch as they hugged and kissed again.

As they were leaving the beach, Dorothy spotted a particularly bright white beach stone in the dim moonlight. She stopped, picked it up, and held it tightly in her hand. The faint light filtering through the light layer of clouds reflected off the pickup's chrome designs, aiding them in locating it. They put on their shoes, and Odie drove her to her house on Ocean View Road.

She and Odie had just completed an embrace at the back door that led to the kitchen, one they did not want to end. When she opened the door, her father appeared immediately. "I fell asleep on the couch. I've been waiting for you. Are you okay?"

"Sorry, Dad. Yes, I'm fine. Please don't be mad at me."

"Well I should be," he answered and paused. "I was really worried, honey." And he stopped, looking at his daughter. Her thick hair was wet. He could never really be angry with his her. She was all he had.

"It was so hot we went for a swim," interjected Dorothy, running her fingers through her hair.

"Oh." And he looked at his daughter with raised eyebrows. He was at a loss for words.

"Mr. Flannigan, it's all my fault, I'm sorry—"

Henry raised his palm and shook his head. "It's okay," Henry said, stopping Odie from further explanation and embarrassment.

And that was how it was left. Henry knew his daughter; she was home and safe. There was no indication that she was any different than she always was. He knew she was in love.

The next day, Dorothy was at the arcade. She was in the office concentrating on counting coins. Odie loved to watch her when she was focused. She had her hair pulled back with what looked like the ribbon that was on her straw hat, emphasizing the impossible blue in her eyes. He stood and leaned on the doorjamb. He had promised his mother and father he would be home later that day.

Dorothy looked up, sensing someone was staring at her.

"Oh, hi." She got up and walked toward him. Nothing was said as they easily embraced and kissed. The kiss felt different. There was a melancholy they could both feel. She broke the embrace, held his arms, stared at him, and then put her head on his shoulder. They stayed that way for a long time. They both knew they would not see each other for over three months.

"I just came by to say…" And he paused. "I don't know what to say, Dorothy, but, I'll be back." She walked him out to the street where the green hotel pickup was waiting. He turned and kissed her again, but this time it was a gentle, long, slow kiss. He hugged her gently and turned as her eyes teared. When he got to the driver's side door, he looked up and said, "Follow your line and keep your head still, I love you." That's all he could think of.

"I will, Odie. I love you too.

"Are you okay, Dorothy?" asked her father an hour later when he stopped to look in on her. She nodded her head and wiped her eyes with the back of her hand. She had been crying. He came over and sat on the desk, looking down at her. He put his hand on her shoulder. "He'll be back, hon." And he gave her his handkerchief.

Odie would spend sixteen weeks in basic training. One of the first things that Odie noticed when arriving in Atlantic City was a sign over a penny arcade on the boardwalk that said, 'Where Skee-Ball was invented.' He couldn't help but smile.

The Army insisted that recruits write home every week, and Odie did his best. His letters home to Virginia and Raymond were read over and over and placed in a special drawer in the kitchen of the inn. The excitement was also felt when a letter arrived at Ocean View Street. She knew he was doing his best.

Odie slogged through the misery of bootcamp. He was now a buck private in the US Army. After the 16th week, he was given a 10-day pass. He would be home for Christmas. After reuniting with Raymond and Virginia and spending Christmas at the inn, he borrowed their car and drove to the coast of New Hampshire, where he would spend the last few days of his pass. He was welcomed back by the staff at Wentworth by the Sea.

"Odie, I didn't recognize you. You're a man now," quipped Phyllis, one of the few waitstaff in the restaurant. This time of year the hotel operated with a skeleton crew. The war didn't help the business, but everyone realized fighting the Japanese and looking to the East and the German threat was what was important now.

All the rooms, except for a few, were closed and shades were drawn at night. "If I promise to keep the lights off, could I have the big room in the middle tower?" asked Odie. The four-story hotel had over 160 rooms. The one Odie was asking about was on the 4th floor and had a grand view of the coastal area. The heat in the hotel was kept at a minimal temperature. Steam pipes and the water system were operating but at minimal efficiency for fear they may freeze. Many rooms had fireplaces. This would be his room for the remainder of his pass.

He stopped by Dorothy's house early. Henry was home, and they sat and had a light breakfast and coffee. The day was clear with the temperatures in the low teens with only a few clear-weather clouds.

They were wearing heavy winter clothing, Odie with a long, Army-issued overcoat, but hatless, and Dorothy wore an ankle-length brown wool coat, a red scarf, white wool mittens, matching white fur earmuffs, and stylish but comfortable brown fur-lined boots. They were walking along empty Jenness

Beach with only the flocks of shore birds as their companions. The day was exhilaratingly bright with a light breeze off the ocean. The waves were marching in perfectly formed size and spacing, as they, too, were subdued by the cold. The sun in its low winter travel caused the white caps to appear brighter. The tide was out as Odie noticed a group of islands off the beach.

"That's the Isle of Shoals," explained Dorothy.

"I never noticed them before."

She pulled his arm in and looked up at him. "That's because the only time you were here was at night." And she reached up and kissed him on the cheek.

"Oh yeah, I remember," he said and squeezed her arm.

They slowly walked the mile and a half beach, both understanding this could be the last time they would see each other. It never occurred to Dorothy to look for a beach stone.

"Let's go for a ride," suggested Odie, as they got in his parents' car.

She was fine with that, she just wanted to be with him. They rode up the coast to Ogunquit, had lunch, and were riding back when Odie surprised her by stopping at the Wentworth by the Sea hotel.

"Dorothy, if you don't want to do this, I understand."

"What?"

He opened the door and walked around to her side and opened hers.

"I have a room," and he pointed up to the large 4th-floor window, "up there."

She looked up at him as he extended his hand. She took it and got out of the car. They walked up the snow-lined path to the hotel's entrance. He opened the door and stepped aside as Dorothy walked into a large elaborate lobby decorated with mirrors, pictures of New Hampshire, sailing vessels, and of famous people she did not know.

"Hi, champ," a well-dressed black man greeted them, appearing from a side door next to the reception deck.

"Hi, Alfonse. How are you doing today?"

"I'm mighty fine, thank you, and glad to be inside today."

"Alfonse Franklin, I'd like you to meet my friend, Dorothy Flanagan."

"Nice to meet you, Dorothy," Alfonse said and nodded his pure white kinky-curled head toward her.

"Nice to meet you, Mr. Franklin." Dorothy did an old-fashioned curtsy and extended her hand, which Alfonse took gently and shook.

"I'm taking Dorothy up to the 4th floor to show her the view."

"There surely is a wonderful view up there," replied Alfonse.

They got in the elevator. Both had stomach butterflies. When the elevator stopped and the doors opened, it revealed exactly what Alfonse had been so excited about. They stayed at the large window and held hands. The view was spectacular as they scanned east to the horizon and south where Odie noticed the Isle of Shoals once again and smiled. There were also military ships plying their way in and out of Portsmouth Harbor, his smile diminished slightly. She turned and kissed him, a prolonged kiss.

He took her hand one more time and led her down the hall to a door that said 4A. It was unlocked. He opened it, and the first thing they noticed was the temperature in the room. It was warm. The other thing was the view from another large window, once again revealing another angle of the vast coast.

A fire was slowly burning in the large fireplace. He closed the door. Dorothy walked to the window. She could see forever.

"Let me take your coat."

She undid the buttons and slipped it off as he hung it on a nearby coat rack.

"You and Alfonse conspired to do this," she guessed, pointing at the fireplace.

"Yes, sorry, I was hoping you would agree."

"Yes, I think I do."

Unlike on the beach 16 weeks ago, this adventure in

lovemaking was less frantic. It was more casual and relaxed, simply touching and holding each other, seemed more profound than the act itself. Much of the time was spent talking about the future or what they hoped would be the future. Their time together they knew would be minimal, but nothing was rushed; it was savored.

One of the room amenities was a shower, which was surprisingly hot and luxurious. Wearing the soft white bathrobes after was an extra added pleasure. They were lost in each other, but not lost to time as daylight diminished and the curtains were closed to the ocean. The robes fell to the floor one more time.

He would drive her back to Ocean View Road and the familiar back door where they held each other once again. It was the embrace they both dreaded.

Dorothy was first to face their reality. "Odie Johnson, what did you say back in August?" And she stopped to think. "Something like 'follow your line and keep your head still'? she asked as she held him at arm's length.

"Yes." He smiled at her for remembering the advice imparted to him by Bud Smith so long ago.

"Well, here's what I think. I think that's good advice for both of us." She pulled him in for a final hug, speaking into his ear quietly, "I love you, Odie."

He responded in the same manner; "I love you, Dorothy."

She then took his face in her two hands and gently kissed him on the lips, looking at him intently, and said, "It's time, Odie." She turned, opened the door to the warm kitchen, closed it behind her, and leaned against it, taking a deep breath. He turned and walked toward the car.

Odie began the long drive back to Mount Washington Valley but stopped abruptly when he noticed the parking lot at Abenaqui Country Club had been plowed. He drove in and pointed the car and its headlights at the snow-covered 18th hole and stayed there thinking for a long time.

4

"That must have been hard for both of you, Odie." It was 6 a.m. and dawn was an hour away. He was sitting at the end of the long dinner table. A couple from Massachusetts were staying at the inn but would not be at breakfast till later. Virginia had heard Odie when he walked in the inn at 1 a.m. She would have trouble sleeping the remainder of the night.

Odie's duffel bag was on the floor next to a chair with his long Army-issued winter coat draped over it.

"Yes it was, Mum," he replied as she began to clear the dishes.

"You think a lot of her, don't you?" As she faced the sink, she could see her image in the window.

"Yes I do, Mum. I love her."

When Raymond and Virginia Johnson adopted Odie, he was three years old. That was 15 years ago, when Raymond was 59 and Virginia was 49 at the time. It was time to say goodbye at the Jackson Inn. They knew he could have received a deferment from the draft based on their age and his role in the family, but Raymond would have none of it. Odie had a more important duty, and they all agreed.

"Well, it's time," said Raymond. He would drive Odie to the Concord train station.

Odie had given Virginia a long hug. And while wiping her eyes with her apron, she tearfully said, "I love you, Odie. Please be careful. Try to write when you can."

"I will, Mum."

And later at the Concord train station, "Good luck, Son. Do your best." As Odie shook his stoic adoptive father's hand.

"I will, Dad."

The imposing black train engine blew its whistle, and the porter yelled, "All board."

He was soon back in Atlantic City, where he was given his assignment. The war was on, and like the millions of young men and women at that time, it swallowed him up. The 13-mile shoreline of New Hampshire would take on a new role. No longer was it used for entertainment. It was now a lookout post, and keeping watch and preparing for the worst was now the order of the day. Germany was becoming more aggressive, and U-boat sightings were very common.

The arcade, however, unlike many businesses, kept up with a steady clientele during the day. The need to escape the worry for a while and try their hand at Skee-Ball was a thankful diversion. It still only cost a penny for nine balls. The copper pennies, however, were no longer made from copper but from steel-covered zinc. The copper was needed for munitions.

Like most Americans, Dorothy wanted to help with the war effort, and soon after Odie's departure, she came across a notice in the Hampton Beach Times newspaper asking for volunteers to become nurses at Portland General Hospital. She discussed it with her father, and he assured her he would be fine operating the arcade without her.

Portland, Maine, was a 45-minute train ride up the coast. So on January 5th, 1943, Dorothy began her training to be a nurse. Her home now was a hotel. The rooms in the old building were shared by older and younger women. Some had experience in nursing, and many, like Dorothy, did not. She was befriended by one of the older volunteers. Her name was Beverly, an experienced nurse. Her skills and Dorothy's eagerness to learn brought them together. By the time March rolled around, she was given more and more responsibility and loved the work.

She also began to think something was not right. She had always been fairly regular, most months, but it had been close to three since her last period. On some occasions, certain odors in the hospital that had never bothered her before caused her to feel nauseous. On one unusually warm day, she put on her light blue sundress and realized the bottom button at her waist was very tight.

Soon after, while helping Beverly at the nurse's station, Beverly said, "You don't look good," which caused Dorothy to walk quickly to the bathroom. When she returned, Beverly took her into one of the nearby empty patient rooms and closed the door.

"Dorothy, are you pregnant?"

She sat on the empty bed and looked up at her friend. "I don't know."

"I think you are, honey. When did you have your last period?"

"It's been a few months, I think, but sometimes I don't have one."

"I've been watching you; I think you are. Who's the guy?"

"Oh, Bev, what should I do?"

Beverly asked one of the nurses to watch the front desk. It was a mild day for March in New England, a good day for a walk. The sun was bright, reflecting off of the harbor. As they walked, the older woman listened intently, smiling at times as her young friend told her about the young man she loved.

Two weeks would go by before Dorothy gave her father the news. He could never be angry with his daughter but wanted to protect her. They met with Madeline who was surprisingly very sympathetic to her niece. Dorothy would stay with her in Portland until the baby was born. She would continue with her nursing program on a limited basis and confine herself to her aunt's home.

❖ ❖ ❖

Today there was only fog, unlike the day before, when the rain-filled wind gusts were near hurricane proportions. His foxhole in the craggy rocks still had a good amount of water in the bottom. Despite the conditions, the Japanese continued the fight, they did not care, there would be no surrender, they would die first.

The US government underestimated the tenacity of the enemy, presuming the operation would only take a month. The troops were ill prepared for the weather conditions, while the Japanese were dug in and accustomed to the cold, hostile climate.

"You okay, Private?" whispered Sergeant May.

"Doing okay, Sarge," replied Odie in the same soft voice. The wind and rain had dissipated overnight and so did the Japanese, but Sergeant May knew they would not be gone long; the fog would be the ally of this relentless enemy.

Private Odba Johnson from Jackson, New Hampshire, was in a foxhole on the island of Komandorski in the Bering Sea. He was a member of US Army's 7th Infantry Division.

The Japanese had captured a string of islands that were US territories, creating a possible jumping off point for an attack on the US mainland. Odie was part of a force of 11,000 sent to reclaim the islands. Although heavily outnumbered, the Japanese would not relinquish the islands and swore death before dishonor.

He was in the midst of one of many small skirmishes that took place daily. The conditions were brutal: rain, strong winds, some reaching 100 miles per hour, and snow were the real enemies. They had been on the island a month. The campaign had been going on for three months.

One of the byproducts of the conditions and lack of preparedness was foot rot and, in some cases, frostbite and possibly toe amputations. The leather combat boots had long lost any type of water resistance or insulation.

"How are your feet?" whispered the sergeant.

"Last time I checked they were still on, Sarge."

"Okay, kid, hang in there," was all he could say. He had the same problems. They could tell a new day was dawning; the fog surrounding them was brighter. Sergeant May loved this kid from New Hampshire. He was tough, with a disposition always leaning to the positive side.

Odie was laying on his side looking past his sergeant when he suddenly felt the hair on the back of his neck raise. As he peered into the thick fog, a face began to form. It had a red bandana tied around the forehead. "SARGE!" yelled Odie. In an instant, the figure raised his bayonetted rifle and aimed at Odie. He heard a click; the weapon had jammed. Odie had his carbine laying at his side and, without attempting to raise up, put the gun to his shoulder and looked down the barrel's sight calmly, aimed at the bandana, and pulled the trigger. He was familiar with the carbine's kick as the Japanese soldier fell forward, his face falling against volcanic rock with a thud at the edge of the foxhole. An instant later, Sergeant May had his Browning on automatic, sweeping the area with hundreds of rounds of fire. There was no response.

"You okay, Private?" asked the sergeant when he stopped firing.

Odie was stunned, looking at the face and the mass of blood that was once the back of the soldier's skull laying a few feet away.

"I think so, Sarge," he answered and promptly threw up. This was Odie's first close encounter with the enemy.

"It's what we signed up for, Private," and added as he patted Odie on the shoulder, "It's us or them. Thanks, you just saved my life." Odie kept retching.

Foot by grudging foot, the Japanese made the American and Canadian forces fight to retain possession of the island chain. This was a typical attack.

Eventually, the Allies would capture Kiska. This was the last Japanese stronghold. They uncharacteristically abandoned the island in the middle of the night. By August of 1943, the Japanese were no longer present on American soil.

"I hope you've been writing home, Odie," said May, reminding the young private occasionally.

"I have," replied Odie, feeling guilty. The truth was when

he had an opportunity to write, he would face the same issues. He managed to write two letters while on the Aleutian Islands informing his parents and Dorothy of his whereabouts. Both made it to New Hampshire, but the letter to Dorothy was sent to the wrong address. He had spelled the street name wrong. The word View looked like Vine.

Their communication was plagued with mishaps. Dorothy knew his unit and brigade and mailed her letters to that address. At one point there were twenty, but because of the weather conditions on the foreboding islands, mail delivery was intermittent at best, and unbeknownst to either one of them, her letters were lost when a mail bag fell into the Bering Sea on a transfer to another ship during rough weather.

Odie was next sent to Hawaii for more training, but it was short-lived. They would be housed at what was left of the Schofield Barracks, which had been partially destroyed after the Japanese attack. It was also where the letter writing would stall once again.

He had one letter written and had left it on his bunk. A second lieutenant happened by and spotted the letter. "I can't believe you are sending this piece of shit home. They must have a different language in New Hampshire," he mocked and threw it at Odie, shaking his head as he walked out the back door of the barracks. His name was Adam Richardson from Old Saybrook, Connecticut, a community of old money and wealth.

"What the f...k was that all about?" asked Sergeant May who was standing nearby, and added, "That was none of his f... king business. What an asshole," and continued with his rant. "He's another 90-day wonder, goes to college, jumps into officer's candidate school, and thinks his shit smells better than ours." The next day they received their orders. They would be heading into the South Pacific.

Using the knowledge gained from the battles in the Aleutians, the 7th and other combat units would begin what characterized the war in the Pacific, the tenacious and dogged capture of the islands, one by deadly one, leading to the Empire of Japan. Odie's unit would be going to the Marshal Islands, a group of many islands. They would make an amphibious landing at the island of Kwajalein in February of 1944 and quickly disperse the enemy, which was followed by the capture of the Eniwetok Atoll. At the beginning of October in 1944, they were involved in heavy fighting on the island of Leyte that would progress through February of 1945.

In the two and a half years he had been in the war, Odie had become a hardened combat veteran. He understood what it meant be a warrior, much of it gained from observing the Japanese. He did not hate them, but he understood what it meant to be focused. Not the focus he used in the game of golf he loved but focused to survive and keep your wits about you. The 7th was able to finally take the island of Leyte.

Odie was in one of the medical tents near the beachhead behind the battle lines. He had received his share of injuries in the time he had been fighting; a toe lost to frostbite in the Aleutians, a possible cracked rib, and a jammed shoulder suffered in a fall in the attack on Eniwetok Atoll. His latest was kidney pain from a hand-to-hand encounter a few days ago. He had been struck in the lower back with the butt of a rifle. It was diagnosed as a bruised kidney. He was peeing blood.

"What happened to the nip?" asked the corpsman as he wrapped a large roll of gauze bandaging around Odie's lower back.

"Well we were going at it pretty good, and I went down but was able to roll away when Sergeant May shot him before he could bayonet me."

"Is that you, Johnson?"

"Yes, sir," Odie answered as he looked over to the sound of a familiar voice. It was Second Lieutenant Richardson. He was laying on one of the stained canvas-covered cots with a large bandage over his eyes.

Despite their initial encounter over Odie's letter in Hawaii, the lieutenant had proven himself to be a good leader. He also realized what a solid person and tough soldier Odie was.

"You okay, Private?"

"Yeah, just a little banged up, Lieutenant."

"What do you think, Doc? Is he out of action for a while?" he asked, directing his question to the corpsman.

"It's up to the real doc, Lieutenant."

Lieutenant Richardson had received a head wound that required many stitches, but it was not life threatening. Odie was told he had to stay out of the fight for a few weeks, and as it turned out, so did the lieutenant. During this time there would be an interesting bonding between the two soldiers.

They were outside one of the tents and sitting at a small camp table. Most of the guys he knew smoked. The government was always pushing the free cigarettes on the troops, but Odie never took up the habit. The lieutenant was inhaling his ever-present cigarette. "When this is over, I'm going to quit these things."

Through the previous battles, Richardson's platoon held their own and had jelled into a dependable fighting unit. The chain of command in the small group was respected, but on this occasion, the non-com and the officer barrier was lowered as free conversation took place. This had happened before. That was the trust that had built up in the platoon. He and private Johnson had much in common.

Richardson had graduated from Dartmouth College in New Hampshire and was an avid skier. One of his favorite ski areas was Cranmore Mountain in North Conway, in Odie's backyard. This was the topic of their conversation today: skiing.

"Because the ski slopes face the west, there is nothing better, Odie. That mountain on a sunny day with the temperatures in the 20s is the best." And then out of the blue, the letter issue cropped up.

"Hey, I'm sorry about what I said about your letter back in Hawaii." And Richardson paused to take another drag on his Lucky Strike. "Sarge told me I really should mind my own business." And he continued with, "Odie, it didn't take me long to realize why we have sergeants." He thought for a moment. "I learned to listen to his advice." Then he added, "I'm, no — we are lucky to have him in this platoon."

"I know. I'd follow him anywhere, Lieutenant."

Richardson nodded his head. "Hey, we have some time. Feel like writing a letter home?"

Odie looked at him. "Lieutenant, sometimes I'd rather do KP than write. It's embarrassing."

"Look, you talk and I'll write."

"That may be even more embarrassing," said Odie, looking at him.

The lieutenant got up and went into the First Aid tent and returned with a pad of paper and a pencil, put the pad on the table, and sat across from Odie. "I owe you at least this. Now start." And he looked across the table. "That's an order."

◆ ◆ ◆

"My God, Odie, I just wrote what you said, and it was well said," commented Richardson, looking at Odie. He had another layer of respect for this private. "She sounds like a sweet girl. I wasn't embarrassed to put down your thoughts, I think I love her too." He smiled. "Let me grab an envelope and we'll get this right out tomorrow." He picked up the pad of paper with the three-page letter. "I'll put this with my stuff."

"Thanks, Lieutenant. I'd appreciate that." And Odie added, "Lieutenant, any idea where we'll be going next?"

"Just another rumor, but probably Okinawa. The Marines, the 7th, and as many troops as the brass can round up will be going." He took a drag on the last of his cigarette, blew out the smoke, tossed it on the ground, stepped on it, and looked at Odie. "Something big is in the works."

He was right. The 7th was going to Okinawa, but Odie

would not be taking part. They were worried about the blood in his urine and kept him out of the fight. The war was over for him. He was put on a hospital ship.

The letter was never mailed. Odie found out a week later that the ship his platoon was on was hit by three Japanese planes in a kamikaze attack, sinking the ship immediately, with very few survivors. The sadness continued. His comrades were all gone.

◆ ◆ ◆

On September 15th, 1943, Dorothy gave birth to a daughter at Portland General Hospital. The baby would be called Rosemary Johanna Flanagan, but would go by Rosey. Dorothy and her daughter would stay with Aunt Madeline in Portland while resuming her nursing duties and begin a life of motherhood.

There were still no letters from Odie, but she settled into a routine at the hospital, at times working 60-hour weeks, but made time to care for Rosemary and get some sleep at her aunt's home. Madeline was more than capable of taking care of the new baby. She never had children and thought of this as a blessing.

In the fall of 1944, Dorothy was attending to patients recently flown in from England. One of the many casualties of the D-Day invasion was Thomas Cassidy, who was in critical condition. He had bullet and shrapnel wounds. It would be a long convalescence but would prove to have a major benefit. He could not help but notice the lovely blue-eyed nurse that was part of the team attending to him.

By the spring of 1945, he was recovering nicely from 95% of his wounds and was discharged from the hospital that summer, but not before he let Dorothy know he was in love with her. They had taken long walks around the hospital grounds during his convalescence, and the subject of her having a daughter and no husband was brought up frequently at the beginning of the budding relationship. She knew he was interested in her, and this issue would have to be faced and settled before anything else could take place. The knowledge soon became a normal part of their talks, and eventually, as sad as it made her feel, she had to let go. Odie was no longer in her life, but she needed some form of closure.

She and Tom drove to Jackson and the White Mountains on a spring day in 1947. Dorothy had met Odie's parents five years ago, the day he won the Amateur in 1942, and knew they operated the Jackson Inn. The war had been over for two years. She had not heard from him.

"Yes, Mr. and Mrs. Johnson sold the inn last year." Dorothy and Tom were at the reception desk talking to a young woman. "They moved to California."

"Did you know their son?" asked Dorothy.

"Gosh, everyone knew Odie," And she continued, "He sold the inn to me."

"Oh," said Dorothy, looking at Tom.

"Yes, he came by after the war. He said the weather was warmer in California for his parents and they would settle there. He was still in the Army at the time."

The information left Dorothy numb. On the trip south heading to the coast, after a prolonged silence and staring out of the passenger side window, she said, "So he's alive." The long drive back was in an atmosphere of angst, sadness, and confusion on Dorothy's part. Tom could only look ahead and drive. He knew she was at a crossroads in her life. Which road would she take?

In the spring of 1948, Tom and Dorothy were married Rosemary would grow upn in the house on Ocean View Road. Dorothy stopped nursing and to return to do the books and count the coins at the arcade. She brought Tim began working at the arcade and as time moved along, the arrangement would morph into a partnership, and Tom Cassidy would eventually take over the business.

Life would take on a new normal, complete with new discoveries, new wars, new politics, all the things the spectrum of life could offer through the 1950s, '60s, and into the '70s, but the beach would stay the same.

Tom and Dorothy would not have children. Tom's injuries may have affected that, but Dorothy truly loved Tom. The marriage was a success. The memory of the father of Rosemary grew dimmer and dimmer, but every once in a while Dorothy would wounder.

5

Rosemary was 22 now and a senior nursing student at Colby-Sawyer College in Lebanon, New Hampshire. When it was time to do her internship to become a registered nurse, because of its proximity to her home in Rye Beach, she chose Wentworth Douglass Hospital in Dover, New Hampshire. She had a deep attachment to the area. She loved the outdoors, was an avid skier, had run cross-country for four years while in college, and was a better than average golfer, taught by her grandfather, Henry Flanagan.

She had a few boyfriends, but that's all they were, just friends. She was immersed in nursing. If she needed to socialize, Portsmouth was just a few miles away, and many of her girl-hood friends were still in the area. Hampton Beach was down the coast road from her house, and the University of New Hampshire, with all its student and cultural activities, was just a few miles away.

For the last month, she had been assigned to the emergency room, and at the moment, two EMTs were wheeling in a young man on a collapsible gurney. He was laying back, looking up with a perplexed look on his face. The head nurse, Alice Semple, knew the driver. He had called ahead to let the hospital know they would be bringing in a skiing accident from Gunstock Mountain, the preliminary diagnosis: a broken leg.

"Hey, Brennon, this is the fourth one this weekend," she said as she took the paperwork.

"Conditions have really iced up on the mountain, and this poor guy hit a tree sideways." He looked over at the casualty. "How are you doing, Will?"

"Just great," was the reply from the man without looking

up.

Alice looked at his name on the report. "We'll take good care of you, William." And she patted his arm for reassurance. They wheeled the gurney into the emergency room just as three men in their 20s appeared at the hospital entrance.

"Hey, Will, how you doing?" said one who smelled of alcohol. "We were in the bar. We didn't think it was you they were hauling off the mountain."

"You guys are gonna haft a wait in the lobby," said Brennon the EMT. "I'm afraid your buddy is on the DL for the rest of the season."

"Okay, sorry," said another.

"I'll call mom and dad and let them know," said the third.

The EMTs continued pushing the gurney into the hospital and helped lower William Lincoln from Andover, Massachusetts, onto one of the emergency room's beds.

"My name is Rosemary, and I'll be helping Alice take care of you. How are you feeling?" asked the young nurse.

"I think I'm more embarrassed than anything," he revealed and immediately felt a shock of pain shoot up his leg. He winced as he turned to look at the pretty nurse, noting her name tag.

He was still wearing a thick turtleneck sweater over an insulated undershirt and heavy ski pants.

"Can you scooch up a little?" said Alice as she raised the back of the bed. He did as he was asked and suffered another shock from the afflicted leg, and this time there was an audible "Ouch shit, that hurts!"

"As soon as we can get the sweater off ,we'll take your blood pressure, but now take this for your pain." Alice handed him a small cup with a large pill and Dixie cup of water. He downed the pill and drank the water. Rosemary took the cup when he was finished. He looked up and then at her name tag once again. The closeness of this exchange, inches from her chest, caused her to blush as she looked at him and smiled. Rosemary had a nice figure.

He had sustained a compound fracture; the tibia and fibula,

the two bones in his lower leg, were broken. He was lucky. X-rays showed they were broken but non-displaced, meaning they were still in position and should heal quickly. The procedure would take a few days. Once put under anesthesia, the leg would be casted, then they would hold him for a day to make sure things went as planned and released.

His room was along the corridor that led to the emergency room. Rosemary was walking by the day after the accident and peeked in just to say hello and see how he was doing. Will was in bed with his hands behind his head, watching TV. His newly casted leg was raised on two pillows.

"So how did you manage this?" she asked, startling him.

He looked at her, shut off the TV with the remote control, and sat up, folding his arms and pausing to think.

"I should have listened to my brother." And he stopped again. "Which I don't want to admit." He continued. "The ice was thick but had a good snow cover. We had been skiing all day. My brother and the other guys were ready to quit and head for the lodge. I wanted to make one more run." He shook his head. "When I got off the lift at the top, I knew I was in trouble. It was colder and windier than it had been. Most of the snow was blown or skied away. It was all ice now. I managed to ski halfway down 'Trigger' when I lost my edge and skied into a tree."

"You were lucky," said Rosemary.

"Yes, I was." And he thought for a moment. "And stupid. My brother always said 'if you're going to get hurt skiing, it will happen when you force the last run,' and I did," he finished, looking up at her.

"That's what was drilled into me," said Rosemary.

"You ski?" he asked, looking up.

She nodded her head. "I know 'Trigger' very well. That's the trail we all skied when we thought we were good enough to do double diamonds. 'Trigger' to 'Shotgun' was our favorite run."

"That's where I met the tree, right around the beginning of 'Shotgun.'

"I know that stretch. There's a steep drop at the turn."

"Let's go, Rosemary," she heard as Alice walked by her.

"Ooh, have to go." She looked over her shoulder as her mentor was hurriedly walking by. She quickly turned to leave but stopped to look back. "Nice talking to you, Will."

"Same here, Rosemary."

The next day, he was standing next to his bed with the help of his new crutches. Rosemary walked by and was secretly hoping he was still in his room. She looked in.

"How's it going, Will?" she asked, folding her arms, smiling and observing. She had to admit she liked his looks. He was close to six feet with thick brown hair and an athletic body. He spoke well and didn't take his situation too seriously. He knew he screwed up and would move on.

"How are you doing with the crutches?"

"Hi, Rosemary." As he looked up, he stated, "Well I just took them for another test run. They showed me how to do stairs this morning. I guess I'm good to go."

"Well, good luck. Nice meeting you, Will."

"Same here." And he paused. "Rosemary, do you live around here?"

"Yes, I live in Rye."

"I know this is a little weird, but would you give me your telephone number," and added, "just in case I have some questions about using these crutches or skiing?"

She smiled and thought for a moment. "Okay, Alice warned me about this, but I'm not a real nurse yet, and you look like you may need help." She took out a small pad and pen she had in her uniform's pocket, wrote her number on the small page, and gave it to him and said, "My friends call me Rosy."

"Thanks, Rosy."

He was in the 'TV room' sitting in his father's recliner with his leg up in his parents' house in Andover, Massachusetts, and had been there two days. "You okay, Will?" asked his mother. "Can I get you more soup?"

"I'm good, Mum."

"Dad and I are going over to Bernie and Barbara's to play

cards."

"Okay."

He couldn't wait to call the nurse he had met in the hospital. As soon as his parents left, he picked up the phone and punched in the numbers. She answered. Once the preliminary questions about his condition were out of the way, the important ones had to be asked and answered.

"Yes, I'd like to get together," was her answer.

Will's older brother, Mike, had graduated the from Northeastern University and was working in nearby Lowell, Massachusetts.

A few days later, Will called Rosy and suggested a double date. Northeastern was playing hockey against the University of New Hampshire at UNH. Mike would drive. Rosy would bring her friend, Ann, and they would go into Portsmouth after the game.

It was late. The brothers and their dates had 'bar-hopped' around the old city.

Mike looked in the rear-view mirror. "Despite me having to drag you around all night, that was a good time, Brother," said Mike as they drove back to Andover. "I'm not sure about Ann, I think she just put up with me."

"Maybe your lame jokes about nurses had something to do with that," replied his brother. Will was sitting across the back seat with his leg up.

"How's your leg?"

"Man, it's pounding."

"Probably wasn't the best idea to try and dance."

"Right again, Brother, but she is cute."

"She is that. And besides, I think she likes you." He paused. "I don't know why," said Mike looking straight ahead.

"Just keep driving," replied Will.

❖ ❖ ❖

"I met the cutest guy, Mum."

"Oh, tell me…but I think Mickey needs to chase a Frisbee first."

Rosemary loved Jenness Beach, where she would walk with her mother, Dorothy, and their latest rescue dog, Mickey, a mix who loved nothing better than chasing down a thrown Frisbee. Despite the winter conditions, gray, overcast, with a possibility of snow, Jenness Beach was still an inviting place to be. The tide was out, which left a vast expanse of open flat-packed sand for the mixed shepherd/husky dog to run. Rosemary was a skilled Frisbee thrower and knew, no matter how high or far she threw it, Mickey would catch it and proudly strut back with it.

"Okay, Mickey, get ready." And the dog crouched in front of her.

"No cheating, wait for me to throw it."

Dorothy couldn't help but smile. Of all the dogs who had walked the beach with her, he was one of her favorites.

"Good one, Rosy," said her mother as the disk caught the wind and did a steady glide, challenging the dog. "So tell me please," she said later as she took her daughter's arm and pulled her into her body.

"Well his name is William Lincoln, but he likes to be called Will. He lives in Andover Massachusetts, and goes to Merrimack. He's a senior and is majoring in economics. I met him at the hospital."

"That sounds like me and dad."

"Yes, I guess so. Yes, you're right." She looked at her mother smiling and continued but not before squeezing her mother's arm.

"He was in a skiing accident up at Gunstock and broke his leg. I was there when he was admitted. We just got talking and hit it off. I gave him my number, which I'm not supposed to do, and he called me a few days after he left the hospital."

"Is that who you've been talking to?"

"Yes, we went to a hockey game at UNH with his brother

and Ann, and The Dolphin Striker Restaurant after. He's still on crutches, but we managed. He even tried to dance.

"He called me three times this week. Mom, he's so cute. He keeps asking things like, 'I need some professional advice on how to use these crutches,' and his leg itches, 'how do you scratch a leg in a cast?'"

"Oh, he's back and he's soaking wet. The Frisbee must have sailed into the water," said Rosemary as they were interrupted.

"You know that wasn't going to stop him," said Dorothy as Mickey dropped the Frisbee at Rosemary's feet and proceeded to do the traditional dog shake, starting with his nose and moving through his body. Rosemary picked up the plastic disk and held it.

"Okay, let's give Mr. Frisbee and you a break," she announced as she looked down at the pet. She tucked it under her arm, which meant Frisbee time was over, and said quietly to him, 'sit.' The dog did as he was told. This was followed by the command 'heel.' This meant they were going to walk, and he would stay on Dorothy's left side. "Good boy." The weather began to deteriorate as large snow snowflakes gently began to fall. They continued their conversation about Rosy's new friend and headed back to Ocean View Road. Mickey was content to sniff anything that looked unusual, but not for long. He knew that to heel meant he had to stay close. "You're doing a good job, Mickey," said Dorothy, reassuring his good behavior. While petting him, she spotted a bright beach stone in the sand, reached down, and put it into her coat pocket.

Rosemary and Will began seeing each other. After a month, the cast was removed for a boot. He could now negotiate the stairs at some of the restaurants in Portsmouth. The relationship was blossoming. By the time graduation rolled around, his leg had healed. He also landed a job working for an investment firm in Portsmouth. Rosy would become a registered nurse and continue to work with Alice at Wentworth-Douglass Hospital.

She would become Mrs. William Lincoln in the spring of

1966 and move into a small ranch house in Somersworth, New Hampshire, not too far from Dorothy and Tom. A year later Randy would be born, and Martha would appear two years later.

The arcade, under Tom's guidance, continued to be a successful piece of Hampton Beach's amusements. Henry would pitch in on occasions, as well as Dorothy. Skee-Ball was still one of the primary attractions. Over the years, the circus music had been the baseline of the background sound, but the new electronic pinball games were part of the din flowing out of the elaborate entrance.

When Henry was working, he would find quiet in the glass-enclosed inner office. Coin counting was no longer part of the routine. Customers would purchase tokens using paper currency, ones, fives, tens, and every once in a while, a fifty or a one-hundred-dollar bill would be part of the day's transactions.

It was early spring, 1975, and the crowds seemed different this year. The country was in turmoil. The political atmosphere following the Chicago riots, the ending of war in Vietnam, the Watergate scandal, and Nixon's resignation may have been factors. There was a different element creeping into the crowds ascending on Hampton Beach. They were louder, with more motorcycles. Exotic dancers were now part of the attractions, and police presence had to be ramped up due to the number of drunks and fights. The lowered drinking age to 18 did not help matters.

On this day, the arcade was overcrowded and seemed louder with an air of hyperactivity. Henry had been working along with Tom and Dorothy during the 12-hour day. He took the opportunity to escape the noise and go in the office, as was his habit. He was tired. He folded his arms and put his head down on the old wooden desk for a brief rest and fell asleep. He never woke up. He was 75.

The year would produce other life-changing events. Tom was still haunted by war injuries from World War Two. There was shrapnel in his body that could not be removed. The doctors did not want to operate. It was considered too dangerous, and they elected to 'just watch it.' Over the years, scar tissue had built up around it. The infection that was feared never occurred, and the decision was made to leave it. Every year he would have an X-ray, always negative, which produced the same comment from the young X-ray technicians about the toughness of the soldiers from his generation.

Tom was working one Sunday afternoon in early August, five months after Henry died, when an argument broke out in the Skee-Ball section. He went over to investigate. Two heavily tattooed boys in their late teens were chest to chest, and as Tom approached, one backed away, picked up a Skee-Ball and threw it at the other. They were both intoxicated. The ball missed its intended target and hit Tom.

Tom knew he was in trouble. He stumbled backward, held his hands to his chest, sat on the low edge of the Skee-Ball token deposit assembly, turned ashen white, and toppled forward onto the old wooden floor. By the time Dorothy arrived on the scene, he was gone. The two teenagers could only stare. The cause of Tom's sudden death was shrapnel from a German bomb that had entered his body 32 years ago. It dislodged from the force of the Skee-Ball hitting his chest, penetrating his aorta. He was 52.

They would close the arcade and put 'Flanagan's Skee-Ball Paradise Arcade' up for sale. The Lincoln family; Will, Rosemary, Randy, and Martha would move in with Dorothy on Ocean View Road in Rye, New Hampshire. Rosy would be back in the house she and her mother grew up in, a short walk from Jenness Beach.

6

During the summer months, it was not unusual to have extended days of overcast skies and rain along the coasts of Maine, New Hampshire, and Massachusetts, but this was day four and enough was enough.

"Boy, there are a lot of these," said 11-year-old Martha, directing her comments to her 13-year-old brother, Randy. Boredom was setting in. What had their attention was a large five-gallon clay Crock-Pot. At one time used for storing large quantities of eggs or for pickling garden vegetables, its purpose now was to hold a collection of white beach stones, suitable for writing on.

Their grandmother, Dorothy, and great grandmother, Vesta, loved to walk on Jenness Beach. Dorothy remembered her job was to find the white stones to commemorate each walk. Using her fountain pen, Vesta would print the date and the initials of the participants and put the beach stone in a container. Over the years, the containers changed in size to accommodate the mementos. After her mother died, Dorothy continued the tradition.

"Gram, how many stones are in this thing?" asked Martha.

"I have no idea," replied their grandmother, looking up from her book.

"When did people start collecting the stones?" asked Randy.

"Well, your great grandmother Vesta and I started collecting them when I was around five or six, about the time we moved into this house.

"Wow, our family has taken a lot of walks on the beach," quipped Martha.

"Well, I'd say more than the number of stones in that old crock," answered her grandmother.

"Do you know all the people that initialed them?" continued Martha.

"I guess most of them, but we've collected the stones for a long time, and I'm sure there were times when a stone may not have been added, and I may have forgotten some of the names." And she paused. "You know it's just an initial, it was kind of hit or miss."

"But still, Gram." Randy dug down deep into the stones. "Our family and friends did a lot of walking." Randy was the inquisitive one in the family and also the math person. "Hey, I have an idea."

Martha turned to her grandmother and stared at her momentarily, and in a dry tone said, "Gram, he's thinking again."

"What else do we have to do?" said her brother, looking at his sister and continuing. "So, the beach is a mile and a half long. Down and back would be three miles, not counting the walk to the beach, so every stone here is a little over three miles."

"So you are thinking of counting all the stones?"

"Yep."

Martha paused and looked at her grandmother sitting next to her. "I think I have to wash my hair."

"No problem," he answered, recognizing the sarcasm in his sister's tone. "I'm on a mission," said Randy without looking up and took a handful of beach stones.

Dorothy just smiled and tapped her granddaughter on the back of her hand. Martha rolled her eyes as Dorothy winked at her. Martha repeated, "Yes, I have to wash my hair," and left for the upstairs bathroom.

The room was now filled with small stones clicking. Dorothy would look up occasionally at the serious look in her grandson's welcoming light-blue eyes as he counted. She was a contented woman, enjoying her grandchildren, the solitude of her beautiful home, and a life with all its foibles that had been good to her.

When Martha returned, her thick dark-brown hair wrapped in a towel, there were neat stacks of stones near the crock. "Each pile is ten stones," said Randy without looking up. The crock was half empty.

"I'm back," said their mother, Rosemary, just as the family dog, Penny, the ever affectionate and curious dog, bounded into the quiet of the large family room.

"No, Penny," said a startled Randy, as the over-exuberant, still puppyish mutt of many breeds stepped on a few of the piles, scattering some stones, and attempted to smell every one of them. Rosemary walked in behind the dog.

"Oh my," was her first reaction, followed by, "PENNY, COME!" Having a member of her pack on the floor, which Penny considered to be her territory, could mean time for rough play. This was too much for the young forty-pound all-legs dog. The neat piles of stones were now scattered in all directions. It was a short interlude of chaos, and Rosemary soon had the dog's attention with a chew toy, and the friendly mutt was content to go in her kennel off to the side of the room and gnaw away. "What are you doing, Randy?"

"Mum, can you believe—"

Rosemary could see the devil was creeping in her daughter's eyes and cut her off.

"I asked Randy, Martha." She gave her daughter 'the look' and glanced over at her mother, who had taken off her reading glasses and put the book down.

"Well Randy was wondering how many stones were in the old crock and was interested in determining how many miles, give or take a few, our family and friends have walked over the years." She paused. "Is that about right, Randy?"

Randy was sitting in the midst of the scattered white stones. "You got it, Gram, but I think I've lost my enthusiasm for it now, thanks to Penny." The dog looked up, cocked her head, and continued her chewing.

"Sorry, Randy. Let me go change and I'll help you pick them up."

"That's okay, Mum. I'll help him," said Martha.

"So how was your walk in the rain?" asked Dorothy.

"It was good. I think it's letting up. It looks like its clearing off to the west. Oh, here's another stone." Rosemary dug into her jacket pocket "Let me date it." She took the old fountain pen from the nearby kitchen counter and put down the information P+R 6/15/80. "Here you go, Randy, one more."

"Just toss it in the crock, who knows when I'll be motivated again." Rosemary did as her son requested. The stone landed among the others with a quiet 'chink.'

"Are you and Will playing in the tournament this weekend?" asked her mother.

"I hope so. The course should be dried out by then," she replied as she headed to the stairs to the second floor. "I'm going up to change, be down in a sec." She looked at the contented dog chewing in her kennel. "I don't know what I'm going to do with you, Penny. After chasing all the seagulls off the beach and playing Frisbee, you should be exhausted." The dog kept chewing.

Gathering the beach stones turned out to be a fun activity. "Gram, here is one that says D and JM, 6-13-33. Who could that be?" asked Martha.

"Hmm, I believe it would be my friend Joan Miller. You may find lots of those. She was one of my best friends. She lived on her family's farm not too far from here. It's no longer there, and you may see a bunch with the letter 'P.' That was Paula. We were constantly together."

"Here's one, D and TC, 11-12-46. That's Gramp and you. Right, Gram?" said Martha.

"Yes it is, and I'm sure you will see plenty of those."

"How about this one, M and D and R and B, it says, 11-12-57." Martha had scooped up a handful and pulled one out.

A smile came over Dorothy's face. "Well the M would be me, Mum. The D would be for dad, your grandfather, Tom. The R is for Rosemary, and we had Butch the boxer. He was such a sweet dog." And she added, "You may find some with great Grammy

Vesta and me with an 'L.' That would be for Lucky, my first dog."

Rosemary came down the stairs, which prompted Penny to emerge from her kennel to greet her favorite person with a gentle bite and lick to Rosemary's hand. "Okay, Penny, I was only gone a few minutes, go bother someone else." Dorothy clicked her tongue to get the dog's attention. The dog was intelligent enough to know this member of the pack should be respected and came to Dorothy for what would be a good ear scratch and possibly a kiss on her head. She sat obediently next to the couch and laid her head on Dorothy's lap.

"Here's one from the forties," said Randy. "It says 'D' and 'O', 8-15-42. I'm guessing D is you, Gram. Who is O?"

Dorothy's expression changed. "May I see that one, Randy?"

He handed the beach stone up to his grandmother as she continued to scratch the dog's ear. Dorothy took the stone and reached for her glasses with her ear scratching hand and held it in the thumb and index finger of both hands. Penny attempted to sniff the stone and in doing so knocked it from Dorothy's fingers. It fell and landed among the other stones scattered on the floor.

"Okay, kids, let's get the stones back in the crock," directed Rosemary.

"Randy, do you think you could find the one you just gave me? I dropped it."

He stopped and picked through the ones near her feet.

"The O one, Gram? Sorry, I don't see it."

Penny, as usual, was on high alert for things different and interesting. She was pawing at something under the couch. She retrieved it and began chewing it. "PENNY, GIVE." The dog dropped the stone on the carpet. "Good dog," said Randy, knowing the dog needed affirmation when she did something correctly. His grandmother had taught him that.

"I think she found it, Gram. Yes, 1942, you and O." As he handed her the white stone he asked, "Who is O, Gram?"

"Just someone from the old days, Randy."

7

Randy, now 25, and Martha 23, were in a dust-covered storage room at Abenaqui Country Club. Jerry, the head pro, had asked for volunteers to help prepare for the new season. They were charged with straightening out the storage room. Their job was to take inventory of anything of value and get rid of the rest. There was a hodgepodge of old golf clubs, bags, spiked leather shoes, and an assortment of clothing as well as old pictures. They were engaged in the friendly banter that marked their relationship.

"I thought you had some pull around here. How'd we get this job?" said his sister. "Is that a dead mouse?"

"Hey, it's dead."

"I don't care. Dead or alive, I freak when I see a mouse." Martha was married, had a one-year-old daughter, and was pregnant and expecting a son. She and her husband, Carl, lived in Dover. Randy was engaged to Tanisha, a woman he met at work, and they were living together in a condo in Portsmouth.

"Shouldn't the new secretary of the board have someone under him do the closet cleaning?"

"Yes, that's why I brought you along."

"Ahh, I think I volunteered."

She had picked up a stack of dust-covered framed pictures from a shelf. "What do you want to do with these?" There was no answer. He had his back turned to her, separating a stack of old clubs. She found a towel and wiped the dust from the top picture. It was a photo of a group of golfers from the 1950s. "We can't throw these out."

This got both their attention. "Maybe we should put these

back up on the walls," suggested Martha. "Let me set them aside and clean them up a little."

They spent another hour making decisions about what stayed and what would go. The dust in the room was getting to Martha. She took the stack of pictures into an adjacent office and set them down on a desk.

Her curiosity got to her as she revisited each picture. At the bottom of the stack was a group of black-and-white pictures. The first was an older gentleman presenting a young man a trophy. The caption said 'Chairman of the Board Ben Forrester presenting the 1942 New England Amateur Champion trophy to Odie Johnson of Jackson, New Hampshire.' The next picture in the stack featured three people. "Oh my," Martha said to herself.

"Hi, Penny, mind if I sit here?" Rosemary had just walked into her mother's bedroom. Dorothy was 72 now and was battling cancer. This was her bad week. She'd had a chemo treatment three days earlier and was tired. Her head was wrapped in a light blue turban wrap, emphasizing her still bright blue eyes and wonderful smile. Eleven-year-old Penny was her constant companion. Her puppy days were well behind her. No longer able to jump up on the bed, she was content to sit and lean against it, looking at one of her favorite pack members and getting her nose scratched once in a while.

"How are you doing, Mum?"

"Feel a little better today, hon." And she paused to look at the faithful dog. "I've got nurse Penny here to watch over things." The dog gave her hand a quick lick.

"What have you got?" she asked, looking at her daughter's hand.

"A picture," and she explained. "I was over at Martha's the other day. She and Randy were cleaning out the storage room up at the club and came across some old pictures. She found this one of you, Gramp, and a boy named Odie Johnson." She looked at the picture. "He was in another picture receiving the 1942 New Hampshire Amateur Championship trophy. Martha wanted to know if you and he were boyfriend and girlfriend." And she paused. "So do I," she said with a smile and gave the picture to her mother.

Dorothy took the picture in two hands. "May I have my reading glassed, hon?" Rosemary retrieved them from the bedside table and handed them to her mother.

"That was quite a day," she said as she held the picture. "We were all so happy, especially Grampy Henry." There was a long pause as she stared at the images, and then, holding the picture in her left hand, she touched the face of the boy with the tip of her right index finger. "Yes, we were boyfriend and girlfriend," she confessed and laid the picture face down on her lap and closed her eyes.

"Are you okay, Mum? I'm sorry if I brought up a bad time."

Dorothy, without looking, slid her hand over to her daughter. Rosemary covered it with hers. "Yes, he was my first love, hon, and we were truly in love." Dorothy then opened her eyes and looked at her daughter. "Rosy, would you open the drawer to the bedside table?" It was next to where Rosy was sitting. She looked at her mother.

"Reach in, and in the back there is a letter."

Rosemary did as requested, pulling out the envelope with the familiar Ocean View Road address, and once again looked at her mother. "It's okay, Rosy, open it. I received it soon after Tom died." Rosemary looked at the postmark. It was dated August 15, 1975.

The letter was neatly typed from what may have been an older computer and printed on what felt like thinner, more fragile paper.

July 10, 1975
Dear Dorothy,
I have instructed my daughter Abbie to send this letter upon

my passing. I am writing to explain and help you understand what happened. This letter, in many ways, represents a miracle. It is the only letter you will have received from me since my few feeble attempts over 30 years ago.

Coming to grips with losing you was one of the lowest points in my life, but I have to say before I go any further, I would not change my life. I came into this world unwanted and, by the grace of God, have ventured through it as a child, young man, and adult, reaping the goodness that life can bestow on few people.

Presently, I have internal injuries from the war that eventually caught up with me and recently have shown to be incurable. That is the purpose of this letter.

In 1941 and '42, we were at the very beginning of what it means to be human, 17 and 18 years old. What an exciting time. We were so in love. The thoughts of you kept me alive during the war. There was nothing else. Death was all around. I could only fall asleep when you were in my thoughts. Thank you for keeping me sane. One of my greatest regrets was not having your words in my mind during the war. I know you wrote letters, you had to, that's who you were. I can only speculate that, like the war itself, much would go wrong, and in this case, I'm sure things did go wrong and your letters were lost. I was in some awful places and moved quite a bit. Regardless, I cannot be bitter. What I was in the middle of was incomprehensible.

I didn't help with our communication. I would put off writing. Having a pen or pencil in my hand caused me to freeze. The words were a jumble, I loved you and didn't know how to make my thoughts reach you. When I finally had a letter written, with the help of Lieutenant Richardson, it was lost. He promised he would put it in the ship's mail when he was on his way to Okinawa. His ship was attacked and sunk. I should have been on the same boat, but instead I was placed on a hospital ship. My wounds brought me away from hell.

I stayed in the Army. Someone recognized my 'people skills' and placed me in a position helping veterans. My mother and father decided to sell the Jackson Inn when they realized I would be working in California. We returned to New Hampshire briefly to complete the sale. Unfortunately, Dad passed not too long after in 1947, and Mom died five years later in 1952.

My life changed when I met my secretary. She helped me with my reports. As it turned out, Christine, I call her Missie, became my wife. We were married in 1948. She is a love and very smart. She was the one who cured me. I have dyslexia; a condition that affects my reading, writing, and spelling. In my case, it was severe. She learned about this while she was in secretarial school and helped me understand and deal with it, a frustrating and slow process, but in the end, a new world of understanding opened up, and then later, when Apple Computers came along with word processing and spell check! The result is this letter.

In 1955 Abigale was born. The years had been good to Missie and I, but California did not have the appeal that Washington Valley has. I convinced Missie and Abbie that we should move east. I retired from the army in 1965. What was my scourge is now a blessing. I am a writer now and have a few books under the pen name of Odba Jackson, mostly stories about the White Mountains.

I could go on about many things, things I wish I could have expressed to you, but did not, so, I'm closing with this.

I made a promise to myself when the war was over. I would get back to you. The war ended in September of 1945. On October 3rd I began a trip across the United States and eventually got off the train in Portsmouth, New Hampshire. I walked to Rye along the coast road past Jenness Beach and to your home. I knocked on the door, heard a dog bark, no one was home. I continued walking, heading toward Hampton Beach. I have to say I smiled when I saw the Isle of Shoals off in the distance.

When I got to the arcade. I wasn't sure what to expect. I just know I was so excited. I walked in and could see you through the office windows. Your head was down, possibly counting coins. A little girl was with you, it looked like she was busy with a coloring book, and then a good looking man appeared. You stood and kiss him. He then kissed the little girl and then hugged you again. You were all smiling. To say it pained me to watch will not be sufficient to how that sight impacted me at that moment. All I could do was turn and *walk back to Portsmouth. On the long journey back to California, I realized it was too late. I had to let go. You had a family, and I could not interfere. You were happy. That's all that mattered.*

I have come to this conclusion: we have no control over our lives, God does. He allowed me to be adopted by two wonderful people. I met you and discovered love. He allowed me to survive the war, allowed you to find a husband and have a family. He found a purpose for our lives.

I'm not sure when you will receive this letter. Abbie does not know its contents, but I'm sure she will comply with my final wish. I hope the family I saw that day in 1945 continued to smile and life was good to them. My place in your life was short, but my love lasted a lifetime.

Odie

"Oh, Mum."

Rosemary put her hand to her mouth, looked up, and brushed a tear away as she gently folded the letter and put it back in the envelope and put it in the drawer.

"Rosy, he's your father." But before Rosemary could respond, Dorothy squeezed her daughter's hand. "Your dad knew." And she paused. "Tom was very good about what happened. He wasn't a jealous man. He knew I had a daughter and what the circumstances were." She picked up the picture again. "I've been fortunate to have two wonderful men love me."

Rosemary leaned over and hugged her mother and held on for a long time until they heard a whimper from Penny. She sat back, gave the dog an ear scratch, and looked at her mother. "Wow, Mum, that's a lot," Rosy said, wiping tears from both eyes and reflecting for a moment. "So you were more than boyfriend and girlfriend," she said in a quiet, thoughtful voice.

"Yes, I guess you could say that, hon." And she added, "We were so in love," while, again, staring at the picture.

"You know what? I'm glad I know this, Mum," said Rosemary. "Thank you for telling me." She stood. "Let me get Penny out of here and you get more rest. I have to think about this." She turned again at the door before closing it. "Was he nice, Mum? Was my father nice?"

"Yes, he was, Rosy, like you."

After Rosemary left, Dorothy opened the drawer to the bed stand. Tucked in the corner she found what she was looking for, the beach stone with D and O, 8-15-42. She closed her hand around the stone, laid the picture on her chest and fell asleep.

Dorothy would pass a year later.

8

Rosemary was sitting at the kitchen table reading the letter again. In the past year, she had done this a few times. She was looking at the postmark on the envelope. It was the one year anniversary of her mother's passing.

"Hmm, I wonder," she said to herself. She looked up for a moment and then carried out the impulse.

"Jackson Inn, this is Cindy, how may I help you?"

"Hi," said Rosemary. "I was hoping you could help me."

"I'll try."

"I'm trying to locate a person who may still live in Jackson by the name of Abigale Johnson."

"I know Abbie." And there was a pause. "I'm not sure she would want me to be giving out information about her to a stranger."

"No, no, please, I'm sorry." And she continued quickly so as not to lose the connection. "My name is Rosemary Lincoln. I don't mean to pry," and added, "my maiden name was Cassidy, and I live in Rye Beach."

There was another pause. "Johnson was Abbie's maiden name, and she's a good friend of mine. I don't know about this."

"Okay, it's a long story, but a very nice story about her late father." And she paused. "I'll tell you what, if you see her, here's my phone number. Tell her to call me at any time."

Rosemary and Abbie were having a glass of wine, sitting at the large kitchen table. The picture and beach stone from 1942

were in front of them. They had just returned from Jenness Beach with Penny. Abbie was printing letters and numbers on a new stone, A-R-P, 8/15/95. She dropped it in the old crock with the others.

"It was a sad time. I was in my early twenties, and Dad was very sick, but he was never sad. He would spend his days going over to the driving range in Center Conway giving tips on putting, driving, chipping, and all things golf, or he would sit at the computer writing or go for long walks in the valley, until his strength gave out, but he was a happy man." She paused. "My mom, Missie, didn't know. I guess he thought she wouldn't be interested in a girlfriend when he was younger. But I have to say, your mom, Dorothy, was the one who had to be strong. In one year she lost her father, husband." She paused to look at the picture and said quietly, "Odie." She looked up. "They were so young, and I have to say, she was beautiful, like you."

"Thanks, Abbie, and I can see him in you," said Rosy, smiling, and she stopped to think. "The day she first showed me the letter was very emotional. When I asked her if they were boyfriend and girlfriend, I could tell it was more than that." Once again there was silence and an excuse to have a sip of wine and think. Abbie broke the moment.

"I remember the day he asked me when the letter should be mailed. Gosh, that was close to twenty years ago. His kidneys had given out, and cancer had set in. His war injuries had caught up with him. He was dying." And she thought for a moment. "He said, 'This is my final wish, please mail this letter after I pass,'" she said, looking up at Rosemary "I just remember being so sad and completely forgot about the letter, until our phone conversation." She paused again for another sip, and they sat once again with their own thoughts.

Abbie then stood and came around the table with her arms extended. It was time to go. Rosemary stood facing her. "Thank you for this day, Rosy. It was special. I'll expect you and the whole family to be coming up to Cranmore this winter." She was the general manager of the ski area. "I know Dad would have loved it."

"We'll be there," replied Rosemary as they hugged again.

When she came back in the house after walking her sister to her car, she took the beach stone from the kitchen table, squeezed it, and gently dropped it in the old crock. She then picked up the picture and put it back in its place on the wall next to the kitchen's back door, where her mother and father last held each other in 1942.

Acknowledgement

I would like to thank my beta readers friends and golf buddies Ken Berquist and Paul Giacobbe, a special thanks to Amy Kittrick my horse expert, my family, and especially my wife Pam for helping with these random thoughts that turned into stories. And finally, a shout out to Tony Paolicelli. Without him the cottonmouth would not have a story.

ABOUT THE AUTHOR

J R Madore

Is a retired public school teacher, coach and administrator now living in Florida with his wife Pam of 56 years. He enjoys, writing, playing golf and guitar.

BOOKS BY THIS AUTHOR

The Stick: A Family's Journey

An historical fiction novel that follows a family's immigration path through five generations beginning in Irvine, Scotland in the mid 19th century, to Nova Scotia, Northern Maine and ends in the North Shore of Massachusetts in the 21st century.

It is a story of grit, determination, and family strength as each generation builds on the strengths of the previous generation as leaders emerge to face the challenges of their time and the stick, a family artfact passed along serves as the symbol to keep moving forward.

Made in United States
North Haven, CT
19 July 2023

39241340R00147